FIRE AND FORGET

FIRE AND FORGET

SHORT STORIES FROM THE LONG WAR

EDITED BY

ROY SCRANTON AND MATT GALLAGHER

FOREWORD BY

COLUM MCCANN

DA CAPO PRESS

A Member of the Perseus Books Group

"Big Two-Hearted Hunting Creek" first appeared in
The Southern Review 45:3 (Summer 2009);
"Redeployment" first appeared in *Granta* 116 (September 2011);
"Tips for a Smooth Transition" first appeared in *Salamander* (June 2012).

Editorial production by Lori Hobkirk at the Book Factory.
Book design by Cynthia Young at Sagecraft.
Set in 11.5 point Adobe Garamond Pro

A CIP catalog record for this book is
available from the Library of Congress.
ISBN: 978-0-306-82176-9 (paperback)
ISBN: 978-0-306-82117-6 (e-book)

Published by Da Capo Press
A Member of the Perseus Books Group
www.dacapopress.com

Da Capo Press books are available at special discounts for bulk purchases in
the U.S. by corporations, institutions, and other organizations. For more
information, please contact the Special Markets Department at the Perseus Books
Group, 2300 Chestnut Street, Suite 200, Philadelphia, PA 19103, or call (800) 810-
4145, ext. 5000, or e-mail special.markets@perseusbooks.com.

10 9 8 7 6 5 4 3 2 1

CONTENTS

FOREWORD

Eclipsing War

Colum McCann

All stories are war stories somehow. Every one of us has stepped from one war or another. Our grandfathers were there when the stench of Dresden hung over the world, and our fathers were there when Vietnam sent its children running napalmed down the dirt road. Our grandmothers were there when Belfast fell into rubble, and our mothers were there when Cambodia became a crucible of bones. Our sisters in South Africa, our brothers in Gaza. And, God forbid, our sons and daughters will have stories to tell too. We are scripted by war.

It is the job of literature to confront the terrible truths of what war has done and continues to do to us. It is also the job of literature to make sense of whatever small beauty we can rescue from the maelstrom.

Writing fiction is necessarily a political act. And writing war fiction, during a time of war, by veterans of the conflicts we are still fighting, is a fervent, and occasionally anguished, political act.

The stories of the wars that defined the first decade of the twenty-first century are only just beginning to be told. Television programs, newspaper columns, Internet blogs. We've even had a couple of average Hollywood movies, but we don't yet have all the stories, the kind of reinterpretive truth-telling that fiction and poetry can offer.

It is the dream of writers to get at the pulse of the moment. To inhabit the depth of the wound. E. L. Doctorow gave us the Civil War in *The March*. Jennifer Johnston gave us the First World War in *How Many Miles to Babylon?* Tim O'Brien gave us Vietnam in *The Things They Carried*. Norman Mailer gave us World War II in *The Naked and the Dead*. Edna O'Brien gave us Ireland in *House of Splendid Isolation*. Chimamanda Ngozi Adichie gave us the Biafran War in *Half of a Yellow Sun*.

We are drawn to war because we are, in the words of William Faulkner, drawn to "the human heart in conflict with itself." We all know that happiness throws white ink against a white page. What we need is darkness for the meaning to come clear. We discover ourselves through our battles—our awful revelations, our highest dreams, our basest instincts are all on display.

For the fifteen writers of this anthology, the war is not simply a sequence of unpleasant images or unremitting woes. By entering into the lives of their characters, they allow the reader access to the viscerally intense but morally ambiguous realities of war. The consequences echo back to the American culture that our soldiers have emerged from. This, in turn, kicks forward into a global culture. Each bullet is inevitably followed by another. One story becomes all stories. And we have to keep on telling them. It is our duty to continue spinning the kaleidoscope.

I have a special and abiding relationship to this anthology. Along with several other writers and teachers, I was also honored to be a guest at New York University. It was ambassador Jean Kennedy Smith—one of the great humanitarians of our time—

who called me up and asked me if I would attend. It was my privilege—and indeed my education.

The group was intended to be non-ideological, focused purely on the craft of writing and free to all veterans. Six of the writers in this anthology (Matt Gallagher, Gavin Kovite, Phil Klay, Perry O'Brien, Roy Scranton, and Jake Siegel) met at the program where the veterans discussed fiction, read each other's work, and had an opportunity to share their ideas about representations of the wars. The group began reaching out beyond New York, and connections were established between veterans across the country committed to writing serious, literary fiction.

The war went literary. And the literature broke our tired hearts. The fact of the matter is that we get our voices from the voices of others. Most prominently we get our voices from those who are on the front line. This anthology is a testament to that. It is something to be taught down through the years. There are stories by infantrymen, staff officers, public affairs Marines, a military lawyer, an artilleryman, a military spouse, a medic, an Army Ranger, and a Green Beret. This is not simply the first fiction anthology by veterans of those wars, it is also a harbinger of the novels and short story collections we will be seeing in the future, as those who served continue to try to make sense of our wars for us in the most rigorous way possible, through fiction.

As a teacher at Hunter College, New York, I am always looking for new writers who are prepared to wake me up from my stupor. I will never forget the day, four years ago now, when I opened up the file by a young Phil Klay. The first line stunned me. "We shot dogs." I knew from that very moment that I was in the hands of a masterful young writer. The story, published here as "Redeployment," puts you in the boots of a Marine returning home but still besieged by memories of the Second Battle of Fallujah. It unflinchingly explores the effects of battle and the bizarre challenges of returning home. The truth of the matter is that you can't go back to the country that doesn't exist anymore.

More recently I stumbled upon the fiction of Mariette Kalinowski. She is the sort of writer who is prepared to step off cliffs and develop her wings on the way down. In this anthology, her story, "The Train," puts us in the head of a female veteran who obsessively rides the New York City subway back and forth, back and forth. Her combat trauma forces her underground, farther from her time in Iraq and from the friend that she lost there.

Here it is, the cyclorama of war.

In Roman Skaskiw's "Television," a lieutenant handles the aftermath of an engagement where, "No one was hurt, just a local kid they shot," and has to deal with the murky realities of a war where enemies are hard to spot, and some soldiers are overeager to pull the trigger.

In "Roll Call," by twenty-year career Army non-commissioned officer David Abrams, a memorial ceremony held in the country becomes an occasion to reflect on all the dead, and on the individual soldier's chances of survival.

Renowned poet Brian Turner, in "The Wave That Takes Us Under," turns a lost patrol into a meditation on death and the dying.

"For us, there had been no fields of battle to frame the enemy," writes Jake Siegel. "Our shocks of battle came on the road, brief, dark, and anonymous." But in Siegel's story the terrors of the road seem almost simple when compared with the narrator's difficulties in truly coming home from his war. Unable to talk about his time in Iraq, he opens up only when two buddies from overseas meet him for a night of drinking in New York. What he finds, though, is that even that camaraderie he cherished is nothing but a memory.

Other authors give us different homecomings, intersecting the memories of war with an American culture far removed from the worlds of poverty, violence, and pain the veterans have experienced. Siobhan Fallon, author of the short story collection *You Know When the Men Are Gone*, tells the other side of the story, from the perspective of an army wife. Though her character's guidebook offers helpful suggestions, ("Typically, a 'honeymoon' period follows in which couples reunite physically, but not necessarily emotionally. . . . Be patient and communicate"), she finds the actual experience of putting that advice into action challenging and terrifying.

In this anthology, the authors deal not just with the raw reportage of war, but with its aftermath too.

Brian Van Reet, awarded the Bronze Star for valor, writes of the soldiers receiving medical care for horrific burns. These men, some without faces or, in one case, without genitals, go on a fishing trip that is meant to boost their morale but which turns into a potentially violent encounter with a pair of civilian girls. Colby Buzzell's "Play the Game" details the limited options for an infantry veteran who doesn't want to stay in the Army but can't find a job in an America wracked by recession. Former Green Beret Andrew Slater, in "New Me," puts the reader into the mind of a soldier with a traumatic brain injury, whose past enters his dreams and overshadows his new life. Matt Gallagher, author of the memoir *Kaboom*, dramatizes the strange difficulties in adjusting to life back home with "And Bugs Don't Bleed," a story where a soldier's increasing alienation ends in a small act of perversely cruel violence that seems directed at himself as much as it is against the complacent and happy civilian world.

These are wars that America is so determined not to see that we banned images of soldiers' coffins from our nightly broadcasts, as if the clean lines of a flag-draped coffin would somehow convey the disturbing ugliness of the exercise of military power. The writers in this anthology don't just show you the dead, they put you in the minds and hearts of the men and women who fought on the ground.

Gavin Ford Kovite's "When Engaging Targets, Remember," is written as a Choose-Your-Own-Adventure story, albeit one where the reader is confronted with the restricted options of an American soldier in a convoy and the horrific, moral seriousness of decisions that have to be made in a split second. Ted Janis's "Raid" chronicles the special operations life, where the most proficient—and most lethal—of America's military forces raid targets every night in a haze of shadows and night-vision green. Roy Scranton's Beckettian "Red Steel India" reduces the scope of the war to what is seen through a gate guard post, where routine and boredom rule and bizarre acts of childish defiance punctuate the days more than the deaths that are happening all around.

There is humor too. Perry O'Brien's hilarious "Poughkeepsie" tells of an alienated, AWOL soldier and his fantasies about training the rabbits at his ex-girlfriend's college to take over the school. The absurd premise and wild imagery keep the story feeling lightly comic, even as it slips into an increasingly dark satire of American military ambitions and their effects on the psychologies of American soldiers.

That these stories are important to the national conversation (or the lack of a national conversation) on our use of violent military force goes without saying, but this anthology did not come about simply because of the efforts of these veterans to transmute their experience into fiction. It has its origin in the necessity of truth telling. Facts are mercenary things. Deep truths know their correct battlefields.

As a civilian, I salute these writers. As a protestor, I salute them. As one who was protected by them, I salute them yet again. These men and women have gone away and come home. They speak of those who haven't. Their words eclipse war, and bring back the very humanity we have always desired.

PREFACE

On War Stories

One thing a vet will always tell you is that it's never like it is in the stories. Then he'll tell you his.

We convened at the White Horse Tavern, under the glum and bleary eyes of Dylan Thomas, Norman Mailer, and Jack Kerouac. It was a warm March day, not spring yet but with winter fading, eight years and change since we'd invaded Iraq. Afghanistan loomed shadowy behind that, then 9/11, then the Cold War, Vietnam, Korea, World War II, Pickett's Charge, the Battle of Austerlitz, the conquest of New Spain, Agincourt, Thermopylae, and the rage of Achilles—stories upon stories—stories of war.

We had our own stories to tell, and in each other had found just the right audience to test the telling. There'd be no bullshit, yet we shared among us a subtle understanding that the real truth might never make it on the page. We each knew the problem we altogether struggled with, which was how to say something true about an experience unreal, to a people fed and wadded about with lies. As Conrad's Marlowe put it, somewhere in another "war on terror": "Do you see the story? Do you see anything? It seems to me I am trying to tell you a dream—making a vain attempt, because no relation of a dream can convey the dream-sensation, that commingling of absurdity, surprise, and bewilderment in a tremor of struggling revolt, that notion of being captured by the incredible which is of the very essence of dreams. . . . "

There's always that wobble in war between romance and vision, between reality and imagination, between propaganda and what you lean on to survive. Each story has one ending, the same ending, and it can come sudden, silent, unseen: the street blows up under your feet or a sniper gets lucky. Who knows? Meanwhile, home is a place you lived once, a different person, a different life, and all the people you loved somehow alien. You come to depend on the hard matter of things, because what's "real" so quickly goes up in smoke.

How do you put that on a page? How do we tell you? How do we capture the totality of the thing in a handful of words? How do you make something whole from just fragments?

We'd met, the five of us, through the NYU Veterans Writing Workshop and other vet events in New York City. There was Jake Siegel, Brooklyn-born, still serving in the National Guard; Perry O'Brien, Airborne medic turned peace and labor activist; Phil Klay, Dartmouth grad and smooth-talking Marine public affairs officer, earning his MFA at Hunter; Matt Gallagher, a rangy westerner, once a cavalry officer in a big blue Stetson and now fighting for vets' rights with the nonprofit Iraq and Afghanistan Veterans of America; and myself, college dropout and one-time hitchhiker made good, now at Princeton earning a PhD in English. We came from different places and had different wars, but we shared a common set of concerns: good whiskey, great writing, the challenges and possibilities of making art out of war, and the funny gray zone we found ourselves in, where you shape truths out of fiction pulled out of truth—which might only be the illusion of truth in the first place.

We made a date for the White Horse, where this anthology took root. Over the next year, we collected stories, soliciting, nurturing, pruning, trying to put together something we could feel proud of, something if not representative, at least vivid enough to inscribe on the wars our mark—our signature.

Truth, *truthiness*, in this mass media cacophony we live in, comes up something for grabs. Well, here's some. Grab it. We were there. This is what we saw. This is *how it felt*. And we're here to say, it's not like you heard in the stories.

*   *   *

We the editors owe a tremendous debt of gratitude, first, to all the writers who trusted us with their work. We were lucky to attract talented, hard-working craftspeople, who thought highly enough of us and our project to throw their chips in with ours. We thank our fellow writers for their work, faith, and steadfastness.

We owe as much of a debt to the people who fostered and aided us along the way, who made the collection happen. The NYU Veterans Writing Workshop was a place to come together and meet other vets, men and women who had different stories, but the same interest in bridging that gap between here and there. A free workshop with open enrollment to anyone with military service overseas, it helped establish the community of literary-minded vets now thriving in New York. Thanks to everyone involved, most especially Ambassador Jean Kennedy Smith, Laren McClung, Deborah Landau, Zachary Sussman, Sativa January, Brian Trimboli, Emily Brandt, Craig Moreau, and the Disabled American Veterans Charitable Service Trust. Thanks also to the many mentors and role models who came through and gave so generously of their time and advice: Kevin Buckley, Bruce Weigl, our own Brian Turner, Yusef Komunyakaa, E. L. Doctorow, David Lipsky, Joseph McElroy, Megan O'Rourke, Breten Breytenbach, and of course, Colum McCann. We've been honored and privileged to share in their wisdom and craft.

Our thanks to our tireless agent, E. J. McCarthy, and to our editor at Da Capo, Robert Pigeon, will be never-ending, and even so we'll never do justice to the great boon and opportunity they've given us. Thanks to them both for believing in the work. Thanks also to Lori Hobkirk at the Book Factory, who saw this book through production.

We all have our personal thanks as well—to those who brought us home, to those who helped us along—and our personal remembrances—to those who didn't come back—or to those who did, but found themselves so weighed down by what happened that they couldn't make the transition. In a sense, this entire volume is dedicated to every soldier and Marine who found coming back to the Mall of America stranger, even, than their first time under fire. We thank our fellow veterans, the ones we leaned on, the ones who carried us.

Finally, a word about the title. We tossed around several ideas, including *Did You Kill Anybody?* and *I Waged a War on Terror and All I Got Was This Lousy T-Shirt*, but stuck with *Fire and Forget* because it seemed to touch so aptly on the double-edged problem we face in figuring out what to do with our experience. On the one hand, we want to remind you, dear reader, of what happened. Some new danger is already arcing the horizon, but we tug at your sleeve to hold you fast, make you pause, and insist you recollect those men and women who fought, bled, and died in dangerous and far-away places. On the other hand, there's nothing most of us would rather do than leave these wars behind.

No matter what we do next, the soft tension of the trigger pull is something we'll carry with us forever. We've assembled *Fire and Forget* to tell you, because we had to—*remember*.

THE EDITORS:

Roy Scranton

Matt Gallagher

Jacob Siegel

Phil Klay

Perry O'Brien

1

SMILE, THERE ARE IEDS EVERYWHERE

Jacob Siegel

I GOT OFF THE SUBWAY AT THE PORT AUTHORITY and waited outside for the buses to arrive. The after-work rush still echoed in the half-empty streets but the city almost looked peaceful in the faded light of this in-between hour. You could stand still without feigning purpose.

When I saw Cole, he just laughed. We had a long embrace, squeezing and clapping each other hard on the back. I was still thinking about the last time I'd seen him when it hit me that he was here, in front of me now.

"What time's Jimmy getting in?" he asked.

"We've got a while," I said.

After the Army released us, we rushed to find those we hoped had been waiting. All of us but Cole. He cut the other way, turning back in the airport with a plan he carried through the long hours in Iraq, and went rogue, all over the world.

We had talked since he got back. He was applying to law schools and I asked how the applications were going.

"I might end up here," he said. "I'll live with you and Annie. You got a couch, right, and plenty of time to loaf around? We could grow beards and walk around in our DCUs. Go to parties and stand next to girls and talk about the horror of it all."

"I sold my DCUs to a protester, or maybe it was an art student," I said. "Anyway, I got more than I paid for them, and then I saw them on the news when those kids burned that effigy."

This was the rhythm we knew from overseas. With just the right amount of disinterested aggression you could talk about almost anything.

I remembered that he used to talk about finding a government job when we got back. "Law school sounds exciting. That helping-the-troops racket couldn't compete huh?" I was looking for a rise, but his eyes were hard and steady.

"You know," his head turned toward the line of taxis at the curb, "I just want something new." He smiled and looked back at me. "After I got back from Tokyo, I actually thought about reenlisting to catch another deployment. Things were fine at first, leaving right after we came home was good, I pretty much got everyone happy to see me without too many long looks and worried questions about how things were *over there*. But after I'd been home a couple weeks, I just felt the whole world slowing to a crawl. I had a couple of long nights where I thought, what the hell, you know? Like if I do it one more time then I'll be able to work things out, and when I get back then I'll be back for good. I figured that whatever I wanted to do would be here but the war could end and it still needed me."

"The war needed you?"

"Or I needed it, but what's the difference. It went away."

"The war's still there."

"The feeling went away."

"So it's all about your feelings."

I was joking but it felt good to goad him. Cole was the last one I would have picked to go back into uniform, I thought he had figured out how make a clean break. Besides, he had things going for him when we left, the reliable kind, not the sort that could leave in the middle of the night. He had the kind where if you devoted yourself, it wasn't insane to expect some kind of return.

I couldn't remember what I had going before we left. There must have been plenty, a whole life probably, but it wasn't what I thought of when we were overseas. It shamed me to think now of what I had imagined over there. I didn't have any real plans or ambitions for when we got back. I only had fantasies of other lives, like the fevered dreams of a sick man growing bolder and more intense the closer he gets to death.

I dreamed of whole cities in heat. Ribald boulevards flushed with women. Greatness around every corner, New York at my feet, the buildings bowed, the whole city supine.

We could see up 42nd Street. Movie theaters, marquees, and theme restaurants lined both sides. Crowds began to gather. Cole looked nothing like he had overseas, nothing like a soldier or veteran. It wasn't hard to imagine him in a suit, laughing with coworkers.

"Where does that energy go?" I wanted to know. "I thought when we got back I was going to step off the plane and pounce."

"Well, what did you want to do before we left?" Cole asked. It was the same question he'd asked from the front seat of our Humvee, only the tense had changed.

My thoughts came out half-finished but Cole understood, if not what I was saying, at least that it had to be said. I was trying to say something about being back, that it was hard, that it almost made me nostalgic. I was talking about *over there*, how it felt when you got everything right. You could make the guns talk. Your words hardened into instruments controlling the machine, everything moving like you told it to. When you got it right there was a pure flow, thoughtless and unfeeling, unlike anything else. That was all it took, I said, " . . . and I could hear the world blow my horn."

Even the tedium felt fraught with anxious purpose, the restless hours waiting for time to pass, watching the hourglass spill sand and thinking, "Now I know, now I know, get me home, get me home."

"Over there things were clear," I said, "and they were always on the line. How could anything compare to that?"

People were close enough to hear; I lowered my voice and looked at Cole for a sign to stop, but he gave none.

"And after the bomb goes off and you make it out okay, what about the silence after that when it's still ringing in your ears like a bell from somewhere else? How are you going to hear your old self through that, whatever you thought you wanted? All that fear and heat, satisfaction and lust, that's what your dreams are made of. Look around you, man, this is not what I was coming back to. This is just dirt and steel and other people."

"Jesus," Cole waved his hand dismissively, and I laughed to make it easier and egg him on. "I bet you still got a working bull-shit detector somewhere in there, but I'm sure that speech gets more convincing every time. Is that what you want to be good at? Making speeches about the war? Look what kind of company that puts you in. Try another line of work, man. Even if you're a failure, which I'm not ruling out, it's gotta beat this crooning about the war racket."

When I told him Jimmy's bus was due any minute, he gave me a serious look. "Don't mention any of that reenlisting and going back over stuff," he said. "Last thing I want to do is put ideas in the kid's head."

Jimmy worked as a security guard at some college in Michigan. He moved from Indiana to be closer to the Detroit music scene and closer to his wife's family. He got her pregnant before we left, married her on his two weeks of leave, and came home a father.

We saw him as soon as he stepped outside, scanning excitedly. He beamed when he saw us. "Hey fellas!"

"Jimmy boy!"

"C'mere." Cole grabbed him around the waist, bent back, and lifted him into the air.

Jimmy was taller than either of us, but he always seemed like the frailest of the bunch. Over there, he'd seen more than most, blood from both sides and some of his own, but he never lost his little-brother manner. You could see it in his stooped shoulders and shuffling walk and hear it in his voice, always hungry for attention, never sure what to do when he got it but ask for more. He seemed somehow still naïve. He'd act out his pain without masking it as rage or contempt. It felt needy, sometimes, even weak, but it was more honest than the subterfuge I went through with Annie. Being angry with her in just the right way never seemed to make her understand.

* * *

I was somewhere else when she came in from work and saw me looking through old photos on my laptop, Jimmy's tracks playing quiet through its tiny speakers. It wasn't the first time, and it didn't take long after she kissed me hello. We collected our silence, poised to resume the scene we'd been playing out for months.

"It doesn't help," was all she said at first, as one hand clenched the other and they went bright with white and red spots where the blood stopped and started. "Yesterday you barely spoke to me, and when you did your teeth were clenched. It wasn't fair."

She waited, but I didn't say anything. She went on. "You reminding yourself of better times? Or what it was like to be there?

What's it gonna be like when Jimmy and Cole get here? You gonna tell them everything you won't tell me and pretend one year is all there is to you? Then you'll come home, this, here, your home, and be mad at me for not knowing what they know."

She held in a breath and her eyes flickered. For a moment I thought she was going to laugh and I wanted to laugh with her, but her mouth never moved and I realized that she was somewhere else, caught in the middle register between a memory of happiness and the feeling of its loss.

When she spoke again, it was gone. "What about Petersburg and the Neva River? We were gonna be Vadim and Ludmilla. You could go there with Cole, but would he know why? What do they know about that? What do they know about *you*?"

Her voice was still soft and she dipped her head to catch my eye, but I stared down at her feet and pressed my tongue to the back of my teeth.

"You don't even try to talk to me about it," she said.

How many times had I tried. While I was there, I imagined telling her everything, and now that I was back we couldn't pass a word between us that sounded the same on both sides. "It only makes it worse," I said.

She moved toward me, shaking her still-clenched hands. "No, you don't talk to me, you lecture. You spend an hour telling me how many frequencies your different radios can hold and which one's better in your car and which one's better on foot. And if I ask one wrong question, if I stray the tiniest bit outside these rules I don't even know, that you won't tell me, then you shut down again and punish me for not understanding."

"We didn't have cars."

"Hummers, whatever."

I spoke deliberately, forcefully enunciating like I was talking to a child. "High-mobility multipurpose wheeled vehicle. H.M.M.W.V. Humvee."

"Hummer, Humvee, whatever. Is that what I don't understand, that it's not a Hummer? Is that what you're holding against me?" She reeled back and imitated my voice, "H.M.M.W.V. Humvee."

*　*　*

Then we were out on the street, the three of us. I took them through Times Square and waited until Jimmy noticed.

"Woah, wait a minute, man. This is Times Square."

"Yeah," I said, "this is Times Square. Come on, I'll show you the world's most famous recruiting station. Unless you like corporate-sponsored seizure lights, there's not much else to see around here."

"Too cool," Jimmy said, mocking me.

"Way too cool," added Cole. "Maybe we should just hang out at the bus station."

"I'm not too cool, I just don't need any daiquiris or T-shirts. Come on, it'll be fun. We can go mess with the recruiters and see if any of them have combat patches, the non-deployable bastards."

Cole shook his head and snorted. "We're here for one day and that's how you want to spend it? They're over there working and you want to give them a hard time." He turned from me to Jimmy. "All of a sudden he's a subversive. This guy who probably threw himself at the first recruiter he found: *Hey Sarn't, please won't you make a man out of me?*"

We stood in front of the small recruiting building as Broadway traffic surged around us and people found their way to livelier attractions. Cole and I watched a father assemble his family for a photograph, their heads crowned by "U.S. Armed Forces" etched in glass on the façade, while Jimmy craned to look up at the buildings, making little comments to himself about what he should buy for his daughter. A recruiter stepped outside to smoke, ignoring all of us. I couldn't see his right shoulder to check for a combat patch. We grabbed Jimmy and headed southwest, out of the lights, looking for a drink.

We found a bar on 39th Street. The room smelled of peanuts, sweat, and spilled beer. Aside from the old man serving drinks, there were only two other people in the place. They stayed by the TV.

The first few rounds were easy. Cole talked about the beauty of Tibetan women, the bad manners of New Zealanders, and his plan to volunteer for some vets group while he got his law degree. With a little prodding, Jimmy gave us a few bars of a song he was working on.

He sang, "Headlights hold one space of breath, the last one till the next, / we clear the road, we hold the road but all it holds is death / or rest, maybe rest / and I got MySpace and my guitar and my own games to play, / I'll walk to chow and wash my truck, cross off another day. / If I was waiting for the next one then I might start to scare, but I just wash my socks, have a smoke, and wait to grow my hair. / It's cool, be cool, and smile, there's IEDs everywhere. / There's mine, there's yours, so smile, there are IEDs everywhere."

Jimmy spent his year in the turret, up on the gun. He manned the 240B from the lead vehicle—the most exposed man in the platoon. Once, as we mounted up to head outside the wire, he tossed me his camera and asked for a picture. Jumping on the roof of his Humvee he cranked his turret till the glass shield faced me. He'd written in the dust: "Smile, there are IEDs everywhere."

The high pitch of his voice strained to the point of breaking, then sunk low and finished easy. When he was done we told him how great it was and how we couldn't wait till he cut a CD. Bashfully, he soaked up our praise. Cole asked if he had an agent or what, but he said he was mainly just playing at bars now, worried about his wife making more money than him and what kind of father he'd be and whether he could afford to keep playing or if he had to get a real job.

But he brightened up when he talked about the college kids where he worked security, how they came to see him play and always came around when he was done to tell him how moving his songs were and how it was like when he sang about it they finally understood the war.

I imagined what else the college kids asked him. What did he think of the president? Was it right for us to be over there? Had he lost any friends—or been forced to do any horrible, unimaginable, unforgivable things that he didn't have to talk about if he didn't want to?

Jimmy might have answered their questions, but he wasn't a barroom boast or some vainglorious artist trading on his story. He just needed people to hear him and was willing to talk frankly, if sometimes mawkishly, about his troubles. We tried not to hold it against him.

* * *

It was well past midnight and a dozen rounds in when I started telling them about my writing.

"What are you writing about?" Jimmy asked.

"You gonna tell our story?" asked Cole, dryly, so I wasn't sure if he was serious.

"Never!" I shouted, slamming the bar. My hand came up ringing and the bartender looked over. "I'd rather write blasphemies and technical manuals."

Another round of short browns showed up and I swallowed mine while they waited.

"I'd rather write on a chalkboard with a steak knife." I stabbed my hand at the air between us. "I'd rather write lullabies for pedophiles. I will not pimp myself out. I will never, by everything that's holy, never feed a hungry mob the red meat off my brother's bones."

I caught myself when the words came out, felt them clearing my throat, and looked up at Jimmy and Cole. Their expressions hadn't changed, but I was drunk now and things were hard to register. Suddenly ashamed, I changed tack. "The hell with the war, anyway, you think anybody's actually interested in that bullshit? It's old news. It was all ash before the bombs dropped."

I had not finished so much as a story since I'd gotten home. Usually when someone asked what I was working on, I gave them the line about my epic detective novel set inside a pulp detective novel. I called it *Lucifer's Nightgown*.

It wasn't for lack of trying. I got up every day after Annie went to work and tried to make sense of what happened over there, how it all fit together, why it counted for so much if I wasn't even sure how to add it up. I sat at my computer staring at the same words—the plain words, the gruesome words, the sentimental words, words that belonged only here, had no claim to that, no purchase on the ground over there. I couldn't write the things that haunted me for fear of dishonesty and cheap manipulation, which I blamed on not being haunted enough. How much blood did I need to justify spilling it on the page? I felt this incredible urge, heat on every inch of skin. I needed something cold to press to my face. There was something I had to say, something I had to tell them, but Jimmy was frowning at me with narrow eyes.

"I write about the war. Am I pimping myself out?"

Both of them stared.

"Aw Jimmy, no man. No, no, no, that's not what I meant. Your songs are a million times more truthful and powerful than anything I could ever come up with. I'm not good enough to write about that stuff. Either I'd tell people what they wanted to hear or just give them what I wanted them to think."

I went on, but I could see I didn't have to. I could tell from his face he believed me.

* * *

We went past drunk and slid like water finding its level to the stories we knew best. We traded a few funny ones then started reminiscing about who was a scumbag and who was a coward, who was squared away, who you could count on but was a prick, and who was an alright guy but no kind of soldier.

For us, there had been no fields of battle to frame the enemy. There was no chance to throw yourself against another man and fight for life. Our shocks of battle came on the road, brief, dark, and anonymous. We were always on the road and it could always explode. There was no enemy: we had only each other to hate.

Whenever we got together certain names came up again and again. It was hard to imagine, even years from now, a conversation about that time that didn't revolve around these men, these fuckers we'd never forget. They were anyone who'd made things harder than they had to be, or hurt our chances of coming home, or almost got us killed by some mistake. They were the shitbags, martinets, and weaklings who fucked us with their petty tyranny, corrupt leadership, selfishness, cowardice, incompetence, or even just that lack some men had—that thing that left them passive in the face of danger.

War stories are almost never about *war* unless they're told by someone who was never there. Every now and then maybe you talk about something or listen to someone who needs to get it off their chest, but those aren't the stories you come back to, not for telling.

* * *

"H.M.M.W.V.," she said. "Humvee."

She repeated the word almost playfully, half-smiling and looking for some recognition of the absurdity. When I stared back blankly, she started to lose it.

"Do I pretend you can never understand me because you had a nice family and I had to watch my mom die and my brother get sent off? Should I hold that over you like it's some precious toy you don't get to play with? Should I pretend you won't ever get it, 'cause you didn't see her flatline? Huh? Who would I be to you if you didn't know? Who would I be if I never talked about it to you?"

She was shouting now. I'd told her as much myself, but I didn't want to hear it, not again, and I felt just then that she had no right. I shouted back. "You think I need to relive it? Just 'cause I'm not crying all the time and having flashbacks, you think I've forgotten! You don't even want me to forget. Without it, I'd be just another schmuck with his hands in his pockets. I'm no captain of industry if you haven't noticed."

I realized I wasn't making any sense, but I couldn't stop until I pushed it too far, until I'd have to ask forgiveness.

"Where were you when I was over there? Some bar? Some party? And God help you if you say you were thinking of me— you forgot me before I even left."

She flinched. I went on.

"You can't admit it but your heart would have sung if I got killed over there. A dead soldier's so much more romantic, just a framed photo and a story you can tell in that broken voice that comes so easy. Wouldn't that be easier to deal with? Fucking say something!"

Her eyes, wet, broke contact. She sat slowly, perfectly still at first, on the old crimson couch that her mother gave us years ago. Above her on the wall was a picture of us as teenagers, before there was any Army, long before I left. Standing on a downtown corner in those late twilight hours when we felt our fevers peak and converge. Facing each other under the humid glow of street-lights, our faces mad with secrets, our arms raised like two conductors in private concert. It was an ambition of mine in those days to look like I deserved her in every photograph, and this was as close as I ever got.

Annie started sobbing, to herself, into her hands. I went to her, absently comforting, without looking away from the picture.

Later, while she slept beside me, I finished looking through the photos: Cole and Jimmy, Vargas and Finney, the desert, our truck, the sun. Annie lay on her back, her body along my arm, her hands folded across her stomach, her face turned and lit by the screen's ochre glow. Slowly her head listed until it brushed my arm and she startled. Small sounds murmured up from her sleep as she shifted and turned away. She seemed in that stillness unbearably beautiful, unbearably remote. Outside the pictures there was only the darkness around us, closing in, and the dimly lit pleading arch of her neck. I shut down my computer and tried to sleep.

* * *

Finally the bartender said, "Alright boys, last call." We couldn't complain, that last one was on the house, and it was an hour past the city's curfew. He'd earned the weathered "We support the troops!" sticker pasted to the wall, puckering up at one corner below a framed photo of the '86 Giants.

Outside, the shops were closed and the moon hidden. I stopped in the middle of the street and turned to grab Cole and Jimmy, pulling the three of us into a huddle.

"Fellas, where you been? I've missed you."

Jimmy leaned in close. "Well I'm here now," he said.

Cole chortled and pushed us together. We both turned and Jimmy caught the top of my head with his eye, staggering back and cursing.

At the next corner we stopped for a minute and when we felt a breeze carry strong from the west, we turned and sought its source toward the water. We passed the auto shops that had taken over the old longshoreman district. I was staring up at an old car mounted on a pole, relying on it as the fixed point to pull me weaving down the block, when Cole asked, "What the hell is that?" I thought he saw it too, that it looked just like the old hulk we used for test fires, right outside the wire on the shoulder between the desert and the road.

He was trying to point, but was too drunk to keep his arm steady. Finally he braced the pointer with his other arm, and the rest of his body began to sway. He hadn't seen the car, was pointing at something else.

"That used to be an elevated train line. South of here they turned it into a park, but the construction hasn't made it this far." It took effort to speak and make sense at the same time. The words dropped from my head into the back of my throat and sounded strange as I pushed them out, like the bleats of a muted horn.

The platform Cole was asking about looked like a short bridge that ran north-south, cutting through the middle of the streets.

"Let's go," said Cole, his eyes focusing and unfocusing.

"No, the park is south, south, and it closes at twelve."

Jimmy turned to me, his face waxen under the lights, arms hanging limply at his sides, his eyes glazed over, but his mouth grinning like a fool. "Leh's go, hero."

"Listen." I looked from one to the other and felt my balance tip precipitously. "It's a no-go, let's just walk along the water."

"You walk on water," Cole said. He started forward with Jimmy, and I followed. When we got closer we saw construction scaffold running up to the platform. There was no lock on the door and we climbed the metal stairs meant for the work crew and out onto the High Line.

We were level with the third or fourth story of the buildings around us, close enough to jump in through some of the windows if we wanted. Rebar spanned the width, twenty feet or so, stretching out in a checkerboard pattern. We walked over to the western ledge and looked down the broad crosstown street to the river and the winking lights across the water. To our south we saw gates and security trailers, east the streets we'd just come from, and north more rebar, an abandoned bridge aloft in the city's night mind. We went that way, where the High Line stretched, brightened here and there by streetlights and the odd apartment, past what we could see.

I felt our footfalls through the grid as we walked above the street, a corridor with darkened buildings on either side. Among the offices shut down for the night and the residential towers where people slept were half-built shells, skeletons of steel you could see clean through, menacing us with their cranes and lifts hanging like gargoyles in the shadows. For a moment I thought I heard voices from one of the apartments but it was only someone's radio, some alarm-clock sports talk. Then it was silent again, as quiet as the city gets, when the river, the distant traffic, and the electric hum come together and whisper through the streets.

We reached a bend where the platform turned toward the water. At the crook the rebar stopped and gave way to weeds and stacks of construction materials. We took seats on a pile of I-beams and Cole made himself comfortable.

"I love places like this," he said. "Everywhere has them, the deep pockets that other people never bother to find. This I could have come back to. See," pointing at me in the dark, "not ideas or principles or weird-fevered fantasies. You go back to *people* and *things*. This place would have missed me."

"You think things miss you."

"Of course they do. My car needed a ton of work when I got back, who else was going to do it? Pianos need piano tuners. And other sorts of things, more idea-type things."

"I thought you don't come back to ideas."

"Solid ideas that don't twist around every time you look at them from a different angle. Law school was an idea, but a solid, thing idea."

"You weren't even sure about law school, how is that solid?"
Cole sat up.

"How does anything get solid? You make it that way." He
stressed every word, angry from repeating himself so many times,
over so many months, over so many missions.

Jimmy cut through our weird jangle. "You should join a cult,
one of those where they worship things."

"I'm a cult of one," Cole came back. "I'm an army of Cole."

"Army strong." I pounded my chest.

"Jimmy strong," mumbled Jimmy, his voice trailing off.

I walked over to look at the water again. The night was starting to lift off the sky. My eyes went to the dim light in one of the
buildings nearest us, and I watched two silhouettes on a curtain.
The shadows moved closer, merging, pulling away and then re-
joining. There was no rhythm to the movement as they went back
and forth, cutting off the light and then breaking apart so it
glowed between them again.

When I came back Jimmy was sleeping. Spindly Jimmy so
small against the I-beams. Another couple of steps back and he
was tiny against the city, barely there at all. I noticed Cole looking
at him too.

"He's doing pretty well," I said. "Taking care of his kid, still
playing music."

"He barely covers costs playing those bars. How far you think
that security guard money's gonna stretch? Why didn't he take
that job Vargas tried to set him up with?"

"Said he didn't want to move, and the unpaid training was
too much. He'll figure something out."

"We've been back a year, and a year from now his kid will be
eating more and needing new things, plus he's got that wife to
keep happy." He paused for a moment. "I didn't forget that letter
she wrote him."

"I didn't forget it either but what's the point in bringing it up now?"

"What's the point?" Cole turned and grabbed me under the shoulder, gripping my armpit.

"They got a kid now," I said, pulling away. "He made his peace. I think they're getting along alright these days."

"You can make peace with anything. Doesn't mean it won't blow up on you."

Lights were coming on in the apartment windows. I felt the late effects of a heavy drunk and knew Cole couldn't be much better. "Let's get out of here," I said.

"Alright, how about a balloon wake up?"

I smirked and nodded.

Cole kneeled with his mouth an inch from Jimmy's ear. I stood on the other side with a steel rod raised and ready to come down against the stack of I-beams. I put my hand up for Cole to see and silently started counting down from three fingers. Two. One. I swung the rod hard and struck only inches from Jimmy's head. A loud clang boomed from the metal and shattered the silence, then Cole screamed, "IED! IED!"

First the white from Jimmy's eyes and a split second later he jerked up like he'd been resting on a spring. I kept swinging the rod. My balance was gone and I thought I might fall over if I stopped too abruptly. I could feel the ringing in my ears. Cole put a hand on my back and I stopped. I looked at a mask of wide eyes and grimace as Jimmy stared straight ahead, past us. Nobody laughed, none of us moved. Jimmy's face came back and he looked placid, then in one sharp move he grabbed the rod and yanked hard, pulling me down onto the I-beams.

Jimmy was on my back holding me down. The impact forced the air out and now he was pushing out the rest as I struggled for breath. Just as I was about to gulp in—"IED! IED!" Jimmy's voice, manic and angry. Cole at the other ear "IED! You better get a SITREP and move the hell out of the kill zone!" I felt myself squeezed between the weight on my back and the steel beneath me. I still couldn't breathe or speak, only hear and look out at the weeds and the rebar and the bridge spanning the city that was leaking light as it stirred. Then the weight was gone.

I turned over and saw them standing a few feet away in the middle of the platform, silent and staring off in opposite directions. I walked over and stood between them.

Light came through the canyons from the east in a wash of color overhead. Commuters were out and cops were off the skell beat back patrolling. Soon the guys who were supposed to be working here would show up.

"Let's take off," I said.

We started back toward the scaffold. When the weeds returned to rebar, quietly, plaintively, Jimmy said, "You know, this reminds me of over there. It's kind of like the road up here. Like this is the road. And it's always dark and there's all this around us but it's only us and we can't see any of it and as soon as it's light we're gone. Back where we started."

"There was a whole country around us." I said. "I don't know what goes on here. I have no idea what these people are thinking. They sure as hell don't know anything about me."

The city was fully awake now, the sun up and every light on. Figures moved in the windows, some of them looking out at us.

"Hold up," Jimmy said. "Let's just stay here for a while. I can catch a later bus. It'll be alright."

Cole spun around. "Like the road?" His voice clear and contemptuous, he lunged at Jimmy. "How the hell is this like the road? There aren't any fucking IEDs here. Nobody telling you what to do. You can leave any time you want." Then he turned on me. "And you. You should know better." He moved closer and my hands coiled in my pockets. "Nobody knows you?

They're not trying to kill you, that's all. But you're afraid of ending up like them."

Jimmy looked down and Cole rounded on him again. "Look at me," he barked. Jimmy's eyes went sideways. "Look at me!" Cole said again, but his voice carried the evenness and authority of an old note, and I heard it as "look at me, Specialist."

Jimmy looked up.

"You can't stay here. There's nothing for you here."

Cole took a deep breath and cupped his hand over his mouth as if about to throw up. Then he shook himself and said, "For starters, I'm hungry, my head hurts, I'm sweating booze, and there's no eggs up here. Let's go get chow."

My eyes, squinting, adjusted to the light. I was about to say something to Cole when he cut me off. "You, both of you, whatever's out there, I'm taking it. You don't want it, that's your business, but don't lie to yourselves and pretend it's not there for the taking."

On my face I felt the crispness of the morning air as it rolled chill across the water. I smacked Cole on the ass and pointed an elbow at him, smiling at Jimmy. "The conquering hero returns. What village next, good sir? The world is yours to plunder."

"Wherever there are eggs. Let's go get fed."

And with that we started again to the scaffold. On our way down the stairs we passed some of the workers heading up. They carried cups of coffee and tools and had too much day ahead to worry about three guys who weren't carrying anything out. When we passed the last of them, Jimmy turned back and shouted, "Gentlemen, hell of a view."

And then we were out on the street, the three of us. We stretched and started toward the Port Authority, my head getting heavier with every step. I remembered Annie, remembered I wanted to talk to them about Annie, and felt a sudden urgency now. The early light was shining on everything at once with a ghostly pallor. I saw the blank open spaces between everything that stood or moved. Ordering those spaces is most of a soldier's job, but now, back here, that's all there is, and I don't know if I can do it anymore without the other part.

"What do I say to her?" I asked, but they were already gone.

2

TIPS FOR A SMOOTH TRANSITION

Siobhan Fallon

When your soldier returns, take it easy, take it slow. Your own backyard might be paradise enough for a soldier who hasn't seen grass in a year. Let him just sit in a hammock and relax.

BUT THE HAMMOCK EVIE INSTALLED in the backyard isn't enough for Colin. A week after his return from Afghanistan, they are already on a plane to Hawaii. This trip is a surprise anniversary gift, and Evie is a girl who hates surprises.

Colin and Evie have spent the week awkwardly trying to get used to each other after a year apart. Awkward because Colin has been working long hours at the base dealing with the accountability of the men, weapons, and vehicles that returned with him.

Evie tried to adapt to his uneven schedule, mostly by taking time off from Florence's Home Cooking Catering, sitting around the house waiting for Colin to get back while thinking about the money she should be making, and then smiling too much when he finally came through the door.

Awkward yet again because each time Colin returns from a deployment, and this is his third, there are more classes for Evie to attend: Redeployment Briefs, Family Readiness Group Meetings led by the chaplain, lectures by the "military life consultants." There are glossy pamphlets, charts on the wall, checklists printed out from the Internet. When Colin got back from his first tour four years ago, he came home to a wife in a thong and high heels, frying up pork chops, and that was all the "healing" he needed. Now the worry doesn't end when the deployment does. Now there is talk of soldiers who seem whole at first but are actually damaged: brain injuries, nightmares, prescription drug abuse, attempted suicides.

Colin did not use the hammock once.

But he seems fine. Especially now, curled up in his North Face jacket, his head jammed into the oval eye of the window, sleeping peacefully as the plane hurries them through time zones.

So Evie puts away her *Battle Spouses' Tips for a Smooth Transition* and pages through the *Lonely Planet Guide to Oahu*. The more she reads, the more she underlines, the better she feels. The guide offers a highlighted route to the restaurants with stars, the hotels with the plushest pillows, the shops with the best-priced souvenirs. She is lulled into believing the illusion of the word "vacation": that the ordinary unpleasantness of life—traffic jams, bed bugs, salmonella—will somehow be avoided if only they follow the author's map. Evie rests her cheek against Colin's sleeping shoulder, trying to peer out as the merged blue of sea and sky are severed by a sudden cresting green.

A stewardess bangs down the aisle, collecting the last bits of pre-landing trash, telling everyone to put their seats forward and stow their tray tables. Colin lurches upright, his shoulder hitting Evie's chin, and she bites her tongue hard. It takes him a moment to realize where he is. He turns and looks at her. Fiercely. It's a face Evie has never seen before: his blue eyes narrow, his teeth so clenched a pulse beats in his cheek. In that moment, Evie thinks that he must know about the man in Austin, and she leans away from her husband, her hand over her mouth.

Colin blinks. He uses his palm to push back whatever thoughts are there. Evie's fingers are still on her lips, her tongue feeling around her teeth to see if she is bleeding (she is not), and he turns back to his window, not even noticing she is hurt.

Some things may have changed while you were gone, including your spouse. You both may have refigured your outlook and priorities. Try to share expectations, especially for the first weeks of being together again. Discuss topics such as social activities and household routines. Go slowly—don't try to make up for lost time. Be flexible.

As they land and wait to disembark, Evie wonders if some acquaintance, a witness at the party four months ago, had seen the man press his mouth against hers, if anyone had told Colin all about it. Which is a conundrum, of course. If Colin has been waiting for an explanation, each day she hasn't mentioned it must be weighing on him, the moment looming and illicit. But if Colin doesn't know and she blurts out the story, it will seem like a confession, and he will wonder if she is hiding more.

"Well, what are we going to do?" Colin asks and Evie glances up. He is holding her *Lonely Planet*, flipping it open to a picture of the blasted volcano, Diamond Head.

Evie grins, flushed with relief, ready with an answer.

This is what she wants to do: traipse around the island, snorkeling in the warm water of Hanauma Bay while striped fish nibble at their fingers. Walk the reef-sheltered lagoon of Kaneohe, dine at the Moroccan restaurant, Casablanca, with its silk pillows and hookahs gem-like in the center of each table, eating with their hands, wrapping spicy chickpeas and spinach in flatbread and laughing as it drips down their arms. Visit the red-lacquered Japanese temple of Byodo-In, tossing crumbs to the peacocks ambling across the lawn. Drive through the tree-canopied

Nuuanu Pali Drive, stopping at the lookout to see the Pacific below, so serene as it laps the site where King Kamehameha's warriors threw his enemies down the twelve-hundred-foot cliff.
Watch the surfers at Pipeline Beach and swallow sweet mounds of
"shave" ice, kissing with syrup-dyed lips.

Colin nods, an eyebrow lifted in amusement, seemingly
amazed at the detail behind his wife's desires.

"What about you?" Evie asks.

This is what Colin wants to do: paddle a kayak out to
Chinaman's Hat and kayak-surf the big waves back. Take a scuba
recertification course at Kaneohe Bay. Eat fat burgers at Jameson's
in Haleiwa while drinking Jameson whiskey—she admits this has
an irresistible symmetry. Then go to a luau and devour as much
of a pit-roasted pig as possible (yes, *devour*) while slugging back
the fruity rainbow drinks a soldier can only drink in a place like
Hawaii. Cliff jump into Waimea Bay. Rock climb at Dillingham
Airfield, followed up with a six-mile hike out to the tip of Kaena
Point. Do a shark encounter he found online.

There is nothing called "shark encounter" in Evie's guidebook.

She looks out the window at the runway as her husband talks.
He thinks he will convince her to do a shark encounter? She hates
sharks. Evie hates everything on Colin's list. She does not kayak
or hike or rock climb or scuba. She knows her husband is a man
full of energy, his body an animal that must be tended, fed,
groomed, and put out to run. And yet she assumed this trip, like
other vacations they've taken, would be a compromise between
her love of museums and good food and his love of sweat and activity. But all of Colin's options seem like adventures he ought to
do alone or with a soldier buddy. With a bitterness that surprises
her, she suddenly wishes she never agreed to this trip.

She turns to the people in the aisle, everyone hunched and
stalled, trying to get off the plane, and she moves from foot to
foot, wanting out.

Typically, a "honeymoon" period follows in which couples re-unite, but not necessarily emotionally. Sexual intimacy may take time. Be patient and communicate—you and your spouse may have expectations that are not met right away. Talk about each other's emotional and physical needs without assuming what the other wants. Needs and wants may change over the course of a year.

Colin had booked the hotel. Evie was hoping for something in Waikiki or Honolulu, close to the high-end shopping and placid beaches where Japanese tourists stayed. Instead, they drive their rental car out to the sun-bleached world of the North Shore, passing beach after beach, surfers tiny spots of color delicately clinging to the tremendous winter waves.

Colin valet-parks at a hotel that seems to be constructed out of sun and marble. As Colin checks in, Evie inspects the garden in the lobby, trying to figure out how the orchids grow from the black lava rock. Evie thinks the flowers look like impaled heads with lolling purple tongues, and she makes sure they do not brush her arm as she and Colin head to the elevators.

Their room is the most extravagant Evie has ever seen: a buffed, gleaming floor; a king-size bed that looks like a confection of meringue and marshmallow; a balcony facing the ocean. She turns to ask Colin how much the room will cost. What was he thinking while they drove past plenty of perfectly decent budget hotels?

Before she can get the words out, before she can even put her purse on that monstrosity of a bed, Colin's hand is on her back, pulling her into his grip, and his lips shut hers to speech. Her body stiffens. She's weary from the flight. She wants a long shower or a longer bath. She wants room service and a nap. This is how it's been since he's been back, a sudden mauling as if Colin is a teenager with no control over his urges. Their bags are piled by the door, her purse strap weighing on her shoulder, her hair heavy on her neck, sweat sticky along the trail of her spine. She is intensely aware of not having brushed her teeth for hours. But there is no doubt on his part, just the certainty they will have sex *now*, this moment, without any communication other than his body pressing into hers. In response, her shoulders relent. Her purse slides down and crashes on the marble and her lipstick rolls out and hits her foot. Colin releases her long enough to tug his T-shirt over his head. One glimpse of his chest and something shifts inside of her; she stops thinking about her unbrushed teeth, just kicks off her shoes and reaches for his belt buckle.

This is one thing army wives do not complain about: the return of the deployed husband to his marriage bed. After all those months apart, eager hands on timid flesh, exciting and yet familiar, the true return boiled down to two bodies snapping together like puzzle pieces, still fitting, new and familiar at once.

*   *   *

Colin collapses beside her, careful not to crush her with his muscled weight, both of them breathing hard. The air conditioning cools the edges of Evie's exposed skin. There's a ceiling fan, too. She watches it twirl above and waits for an ache in her chest to go away. Then she gets up on an elbow. Now that they are naked, whether she wants to or not, she can tell him everything, get it over with. Maybe her revelation will nudge him into telling her how he is *really* doing, maybe the post-coital intimacy will allow him to reveal the things he couldn't tell her when he was so far away, communicating by satellite phone or e-mail.

But he is already asleep.

It is important for both of you to share your deployment stories. You both may have made significant self-discoveries and participated in events that should be communicated when you are ready. Be patient. Wait for your soldier to share his/her experiences.

A few hours later, Colin rouses her from the bed. He is wearing pressed khakis and a buttoned shirt. Evie rubs her sanded eyes. "You *ironed?*"

"Went to the gym, made dinner reservations, showered, ironed, and hung up all of our clothes. Chop-chop, lady friend."

Twenty minutes later, Evie yawning, Colin leads the way to the hotel restaurant. Evie is impressed: candlelight, etched-glass candleholders, each table draped with white linen, Hawaiian music from speakers hidden in the greenery. Volcano photographs adorn every wall, glowing with tumult, bleeding lava.

The hostess seats them on the highest tier, overlooking an ocean streaked with setting sun.

"I told her it was our anniversary," Colin whispers proudly, and Evie feels a spark of hope.

She orders the Wilted Escarole with Macadamia Nuts and Pomegranate; Colin gets a steak, medium rare. They order a bottle of Big Island white.

"To five great years," Colin toasts. "May we have at least fifty more."

She hesitates with her wine glass midair; the tiny light inside extinguished. Five years is past the honeymoon but before the seven-year itch, five years ought to be a time of sweatpants, leaving the bathroom door open, no more breakfast in bed. A time to be comfortable. But Colin was deployed for three of those five years, and when Evie looks back, she sees all the white squares on her calendar, squares she crossed out each day as she waited for Colin to come home. This time, halfway through his tour, she gave up crossing out those squares. She cannot imagine fifty more calendars, all those blank days, a long future ahead with a husband home one year, gone the next, more a perverse punishment devised by King Kamehameha than any kind of triumph.

So she drinks too quickly. The wine is overly sweet and not chilled enough, but it is doing its job, blurring the edges of the room.

"That's all you ordered?" Colin says when their entrées arrive, looking down at her salad as if he feels sorry for her. "Have a bit of this." He nudges his steak in Evie's direction. She shakes her head.

"We had steak and crab legs once a week. Fridays," he says, putting a piece on her plate anyway. "But it was only a memory of the real thing. Every bite of that overcooked hide made you realize how far you were from home. At first the crab was good, just the novelty of eating something so decadent. But every goddamn week? Really? I never want a crab leg again."

She keeps a mouthful of wine on her tongue while Colin speaks, as if afraid the sound of her swallowing will stop him. She wants her husband to keep talking; she wants to know about the entire life he lived without her. But he takes another bite in silence.

Evie cautiously asks, "Remember that trip we took to Hunter Mountain? How we stayed locked up in the cabin, eating omelets and drinking cheap wine—all those secrets we told each other?" It was early in their courtship, their first trip anywhere, to a ski resort though they never went skiing. That's when Evie told him about a waitress trick of hers, how she'd lick the desserts of the rude customers before serving them, leaving the groove of her tongue in scoops of ice cream like guilty fingerprints. And Colin told her how he had pissed in an ex-girlfriend's open convertible, costing him a baseball scholarship. Young enough to think sharing their flaws was an act of love in itself, they tried to cram the story of their whole lives into that weekend.

"Colin, you know you can tell me anything—"

He watches her for a moment. "Don't make me go back to Afghanistan," he says, tapping his knife against a smear of cooling grease on his plate. "It's a shithole full of goats, dirt, and men with matted beards." He puts the knife down and takes her hand. "I'm here with you. I made it back. That ought to be enough."

"Is there anything you want to ask *me* about?" she asks.

Colin lets go of her, picks up his knife, begins to cut again. "No," he answers. "Unless there is something you need to tell me?"

"No, nothing," Evie murmurs, sticking a fork in her pretty, pomegranate-jeweled salad. She thinks about the word *need*. A necessity, an obligation. Is there anything she *needs* to tell her husband? She thinks about the things she kept from him while he was away, things that would worry him, because of what she knew: *A worried soldier is a soldier who is not focused on his mission; a worried soldier is a danger to himself and his fellow soldiers.* She does not *need* to tell him about Lana, the major's wife who packed up her house and four-year-old and went home to New Jersey two months ago, without returning any of Evie's calls or her two Pyrex casserole dishes. She doesn't *need* to tell him about the rodent problem in their housing development, how one night Evie came home to a full-grown rat licking its paws on her front stoop.

Nor does she *need* to tell Colin about the kiss. She was doing a catering job with Florence and her son, setting up and breaking down for a sergeant major's retirement party at the Fort Hood Club. She was tidying up the kitchen when a man brought her a tequila sunrise. He said he was the sergeant major's cousin, that his name was John, from Austin, and that he hated disco, which happened to be the only thing the DJ was playing. Was there anything he could do to help her? So she gave him some baking sheets to dry, told him about the rat, admitted the tartlets he kept praising were her contribution to Florence's spread, and let him keep her sweet drink filled to the brim. They talked through the disco; they talked as most of the revelers went home; they talked as the styros and tea lights sputtered out and tablecloths were folded into boxes. They talked until he suddenly leaned in and put his lips against hers. After a dazed moment, Evie pushed him away. He followed her out to the parking lot, trying to give her his business card, but she refused.

She did all the things a good wife should. Of course she did. And yet, for a fluttering split second, with that strange mouth on hers, she had closed her eyes. Closed them and considered leaning into whatever he was offering. She tasted adultery, a smudge of Florence's signature peach-and-pepper barbeque sauce on his lips. That is what she needs to tell Colin, can't tell Colin, won't ever tell Colin: the moment when she didn't know what she would do, when she waited for John to secure her in his embrace rather than letting her pull away so easily.

If your spouse experiences vivid waking nightmares or flashbacks, set up a security plan. Your spouse can be dangerous to himself and everyone around him; he might be reliving an experience and might not know what's real. Do not touch your soldier when he is having nightmares—get out of bed, turn on the lights, call his name from across the room until he is reoriented. Make sure to have a wireless phone nearby in case you need help, and keep dangerous objects like knives and guns in places easily accessible only to you. Practice a quick exit that you can safely execute in the dark.

Evie starts awake, feeling the bed quake. She realizes it is Colin. He gasps, a thick and struggling sound as if he can't get enough air.

"Shhh, Colin. You're alright." Evie slips out of the bed. "Everything is OK." She walks across the dark room and turns on one of the lamps. "Wake up, Colin."

Her husband groans and Evie wonders what images wrack him: cars that won't stop at checkpoints, the hiss of a mortar too close, smoke and gunfire.

She tiptoes around the room, turning on each lamp. Colin's legs are twitching, on the verge of kicking. He moans again.

"Colin!" Evie says loudly, feeling cruel. "Wake up!" She flicks on the main light. She also puts her hand on the doorknob, ready to run down the hotel hallway.

Colin sits, an elbow over his eyes, shielding himself from the brightness.

"What the fuck?" he says. He sees her hand on the door handle, and then his eyes move up her flimsy nightgown, stopping with confusion at her face, as if she is the one who might be crazy, as if she might be a danger to herself.

Be aware that many soldiers return home with a feeling of post-combat invincibility. One consequence of combat exposure may be an increased propensity for risk-taking and unsafe behavior. Specific combat experiences, including greater exposure to violent combat and contact with high levels of human trauma, are predictive of greater risk-taking after homecoming, as well as more frequent alcohol use and increased verbal and physical aggression toward others.

The next morning, Evie listens to the too-nice-wife voice in her head. She agrees to go with Colin to the Haleiwa Marina and onto the boat with the Hawaiian word for shark, *Mano*, emblazoned on the side. The captain is a middle-aged Hawaiian with a dark geometry of tribal tattoos up and down both arms. His second mate is a teenage boy with a lip piercing. They seem calm while the white mainland tourists, in their tropical print sarongs and board shorts, whisper with excitement and fear, the word *shark* looming unspoken in the air. Evie has no idea what to expect, but the boat has the feel of a haunted house, of pampered people paying good money to feel a rush of adrenaline.

"Call me Ishmael," the captain says without smiling. "And you gonna see some Moby-Dick-sized sharks today. You better be good and scared."

Evie glances at Colin, who shakes his head. The motor roars and she motions to her husband with a tube of sunblock. Colin relaxes, pulls his shirt off and offers her his back. He is sunburned across his shoulders, and Evie feels a wave of guilt about not reminding him to apply sunblock before his early morning run. There are so few ways she can keep him safe and yet she couldn't even protect him for one day against the Hawaiian sun.

About four miles from shore, far enough out that they can no longer see land, the boat slows. Ishmael's lackey drags buckets from the stern and starts chumming the water, fish blood pooling on the surface like oil. The passengers watch the fins rise up as if summoned.

There are suddenly so many sharks, long slabs of shadow under the boat, the gash of white rubbery mouths occasionally breaching the surface. Evie recoils from the edge while Colin eagerly takes photos, chatting with the pierced boy who keeps pouring fish chunks overboard.

"Galapagos," says the boy. "They recognize the sound of our motor." He grins with crooked teeth and Evie wonders if he pierced his lip to distract from the mess inside his mouth. "They range from six to twelve feet."

Ishmael cranks down the large steel cage suspended off the side of the boat. The cage is for humans. Evie supposes there are windows of Plexiglas within the bars to make for clearer underwater viewing, but from where she stands, it just looks like a lot of big holes.

"Who's going first?" the boy asks.

Of course Colin raises a hand, putting the other on Evie's elbow. "We will."

Evie takes off her T-shirt and sarong, then slowly slips on flippers and snorkel gear. She follows Colin down the ladder into the cage. The water is ice cold and she treads frantically, as if about to drown. She is too afraid to put her face into the water. The fins circle the cage and her breath comes in hissing gasps; she gags on the salty mouthpiece. Colin emerges next to her. He points down but she shies away. He pulls the mouthpiece from his lips and offers her his hand.

"Trust me," he says.

She hesitates, and they stare at each other for a moment, their view distorted by the slowly fogging plastic of the masks. He reaches for her and she pulls her hand loose. He reaches for her again, both hands this time clutching hers, and she fights an impulse to kick him. She takes a deep breath, tells herself the hands gripping hers belong to the man she loves, but she looks back at the boat, looks frantically at the people watching, and wants them to save her. She can feel the sharks underneath, feel their snouts and serrated teeth brushing along the side of the cage.

The cage shakes with a bump and she rips her hands free, grabs the boat's ladder, and pulls herself up. For a moment Colin treads water alone in the cage, watching her. Then he too climbs up into the boat.

Evie looks down at her flippers. "I'm sorry, Colin. I just can't."

He stands there in his mask, the mouthpiece flapping against the side of his face. "It's safe, Evie. It'd be safe if we weren't even in the cage. Galapagos sharks are harmless." He takes off his mask and looks to the pierced boy for backup, but the kid is sneering, as if pleased Evie is such a coward, as if the whole purpose of his job is to terrify at least one tourist a day. Then Colin's eyes lock on her, and calm suffuses his face. "I'll prove it," he says softly.

His eyes still on Evie's, never hesitating, he climbs up on the boat railing and, before anyone can even think to stop him, he steps off, right into open water, sinking into the center of the feeding animals.

Evie screams, rushes to the edge, feels Ishmael wrench her arm as if he thinks she will follow her husband.

Colin surfaces, still facing the boat. He keeps his eyes on his wife as he reaches out to pet a shark, his palm running easily along its shiny back.

Both of you may need to discuss any issues you've had involving trust or jealousy, even if infidelity was not a problem. It takes time to re-establish or develop a trusting relationship. Be appreciative of each other, and make time for each other. Marriage requires continuing commitment.

John from Austin called her once a few weeks after they met, still long before Colin's return. He left a message: "I finally convinced Florence to give me your number. Said I couldn't live without the recipe for your tartlets." Then the easy chuckle of a man who does not often go to such lengths to track a woman down. "Meet me for a cup of coffee. A harmless little cup, at this place I know that serves the best damn brunch you ever tasted. Then maybe we'll hit the new Goya exhibit at the Blanton. C'mon. Call me."

Evie didn't call but a few days later she went to the Blanton Art Museum, wearing a blue dress and a pair of heels, glancing too often over her shoulder. She kept his message, replaying it now and then, not deleting it until the eve of Colin's return. She waited for him to call again, knowing the next time she'd answer.

Emotional changes occur for all family members during and after deployments. A spouse's expectations about a soldier's emotional involvement upon return may not be met. It can be a challenge for a soldier to turn emotions back on after controlling them for a year. The soldier may initially show only anger or detachment. It may take time for the soldier to feel comfortable enough to establish a full emotional range.

Colin and Evie sit by themselves on the ride back to shore. Evie feels sick. The boat had erupted in shouts, one of the newlyweds had fainted, and the captain had muttered a string of obscenities when Colin hefted himself back onboard. There was even more chaos after that: passengers yelling at the captain, at each other, the captain threatening to turn back to shore unless "you crazy *haoles* calm the hell down." Then the tentative peace as the other couples went into the shark cage and came back quickly, while Evie shivered in her towel and refused to let Colin put his arm around her.

"Did you take a picture?" he asks, unable to stop grinning.

"*Take a picture*? I thought you were going to die." Her chest hurts, her heart still thrashing against its walls as if it will never beat calmly again. "If one of your soldiers did that, you wouldn't be smiling." Her throat fills as if she is back in the ocean, her eyes haze over, and she is crying so convulsively she can barely speak. "Dammnit, Colin." She rubs her towel across the mess of her face, not caring if anyone on the boat can hear her. "I was scared enough when you were deployed. I shouldn't have to be scared when I'm right next to you, watching you do something reckless and stupid."

Colin puts his hand on her knee, his grin gone. "OK," he says simply. "Roger that."

But a few moments later, when her shuddering slows, when they can see land and the flags of the marina in the distance, he is defensive. "It was bullshit, Evie," he says. "Can't you see that? I had to prove these jackasses wrong." He struggles to find the right words, lowering his voice. "I've seen kid toys loaded with explosives, snipers hiding in an elementary school. I've been in a Humvee with soldiers singing 'Brown Eyed Girl' and a second later it was upside down, full of fire and screams." He motions his thumb over his shoulder. "That, back there? That wasn't anything to be afraid of. That was nothing but a bunch of fat fish having lunch."

During the deployment, both of you may have needed reassurance that your spouse was committed to the relationship; these reassurances are still important post-deployment. Most marriages survive deployments but the issue of loyalty and commitment must be mutual for your relationship to remain resilient.

They stop for a bag of burgers and a six-pack then head to the hotel. Evie opens the curtains wide so they can see the sunset. Colin takes his damp clothes off, slips into a pair of boxers, and climbs on top of the bed. He plumps the pillows behind his head, rests a burger on his stomach, and scrolls through the television channels with the remote control. Evie cracks open a beer and hands it to him. "You want to sit out on the lanai with me? We can watch the sunset while we eat."

"I'm great here," he says, tuning in to a football game.

She touches the balcony's door handle, about to go outside alone.

"This feels good," Colin says, and she looks at him, mystified. The beer bottle and remote? The burger on his belly? The football game on a TV smaller than the flat-screen they have at home?

"What?" she asks. "What feels good?"

His eyes meet hers. "I almost forgot what it's like. . . . " He hesitates, as if realizing whatever he is about to say is as much an insult as a compliment.

"What? To be married?" she finishes.

Colin nods. His eyes go back to the game. Evie continues to watch him, waiting for more. But she notices something. He is sitting still. He has not moved the remote or the burger or the beer. If she squints, the man almost looks like he is in a hammock.

Evie glances out the window, watching the waves come in or out, high tide or low tide, she's not sure. She imagines sharks, always moving through that dark unknown, searching and hungry. She lets go of the door handle and goes to the bed, slides in next to Colin. He hands her his beer and she takes a sip.

Not taking his eyes off the television, he says, "Guys would hear a lot of shit, a lot of stories about their wives back home." Evie pauses, the bottle midair, too much beer filling her mouth. "But I never doubted you, Evie. Never."

"Good," she replies, wiping her mouth with the back of her hand. She can't tell if she is relieved or horrified at the implication of rumors, at the thought that Colin might have heard something after all. It is the moment she has been waiting for. But she is suddenly so tired she can barely hold the bottle out to him.

He takes the beer and she curls deep into the bed, watching his profile, hearing the sportscasters murmur and the air conditioner hum. She needs to stop thinking, she tells herself, she needs to stop wondering where she'd be right now if John from Austin had called again and thoroughly changed the events of her life, changed them in such a way that she would never have heard how much her husband trusted her.

All soldiers are affected by combat. It is normal for soldiers to experience symptoms due to their deployment experiences. Some may need help for their reactions. You, too, may experience mental health issues after your soldier's deployment. A family member with a mental health concern may affect the rest of the family. Make your family's mental health a priority!

Evie wakes with a start. Colin's hands are sliding along the sides of his body, searching his ribs, his hips, his thighs.

"Shhh, Colin, you're alright. Wake up, baby," she whispers, sitting up and swinging her legs off the bed, her toes on the cool floor, ready to run. "It's me, it's Evie." She can see the glitter of sweat and feel the heat coming off his body; she watches him roll over, his elbow hitting her now empty pillow. She stands, takes a step toward the bedside lamp, then hesitates. The balcony curtains are wide open and the moon, peeled and pale, hangs loosely over the night. It illuminates Colin so clearly she can see his reedy, powerful muscles working under the wrapper of sunburned skin.

She thinks of the shark cage, how she pulled her hand out of his, how she left him alone and surrounded, watching from the safety of the boat. She thinks of John from Austin and his kiss. For these reasons, for so many others that might be flashing across Colin's brain, jerking his unconscious body, she knows she ought to put as much distance as possible between herself and her husband.

But Evie gets back into the bed. She touches him, her hand on his shoulder, daring the military life consultants, the chaplains, the psychiatrists, to be right, daring the sleeping man to strike.

Her palm on his skin has the opposite effect. His breathing slows, his body stills, his sleep is quiet again.

"You're OK. I'm here," she says over and over like a lullaby. She's not quite sure when the refrain changes to, "I'm OK. You're here." She does not think of all the years she found herself in a big bed, pillows piled up in poor imitation of her husband, and she does not think about the years ahead, when she will be alone again. Colin is here now and Evie is content. At last she is certain of what she needs: her arm around her husband's chest, his warm breath on her wrist.

3

REDEPLOYMENT

Phil Klay

WE SHOT DOGS. Not by accident. We did it on purpose, and we called it "Operation Scooby." I'm a dog person, so I thought about that a lot.

First time was instinct. I hear O'Leary go, "Jesus," and there's a skinny brown dog lapping up blood the same way he'd lap up water from a bowl. It wasn't American blood, but still, there's that dog, lapping it up. And that's the last straw, I guess, and then it's open season on dogs.

At the time you don't think about it. You're thinking about who's in that house, what's he armed with, how's he gonna kill you, your buddies. You're going block by block, fighting with rifles good to 550 meters, and you're killing people at five in a concrete box.

The thinking comes later, when they give you the time. See, it's not a straight shot back, from war to the Jacksonville mall. When our deployment was up, they put us on TQ, this logistics base out in the desert, let us decompress a bit. I'm not sure what they meant by that. Decompress. We took it to mean jerk off a lot in the showers. Smoke a lot of cigarettes and play a lot of cards.

And then they took us to Kuwait and put us on a commercial airliner to go home.

So there you are. You've been in a no-shit war zone and then you're sitting in a plush chair looking up at a little nozzle shooting air conditioning, thinking, what the fuck? You've got a rifle between your knees, and so does everyone else. Some Marines got M9 pistols, but they take away your bayonets because you aren't allowed to have knives on an airplane. Even though you've showered, you all look grimy and lean. Everybody's hollow-eyed and their cammies are beat to shit. And you sit there, and close your eyes, and think.

The problem is, your thoughts don't come out in any kind of straight order. You don't think, oh, I did A, then B, then C, then D. You try to think about home, then you're in the torture house. You see the body parts in the locker and the retarded guy in the cage. He squawked like a chicken. His head was shrunk down to a coconut. It takes you a while to remember Doc saying they'd shot mercury into his skull, and then it still doesn't make any sense.

You see the things you saw the times you nearly died. The broken television and the hajji corpse. Eicholtz covered in blood. The lieutenant on the radio.

You see the little girl, the photographs Curtis found in a desk. First had a beautiful Iraqi kid, maybe seven or eight years old, in bare feet and a pretty white dress like it's First Communion. Next she's in a red dress, high heels, heavy make-up. Next photo, same dress, but her face is smudged and she's holding a gun to her head.

I tried to think of other things, like my wife Cheryl. She's got pale skin and fine dark hairs on her arms. She's ashamed of them but they're soft. Delicate.

But thinking of Cheryl made me feel guilty, and I'd think about Lance Corporal Hernandez, Corporal Smith, and Eicholtz. We were like brothers, Eicholtz and me. The two of us saved this Marine's life one time. A few weeks later Eicholtz is climbing over a wall. Insurgent pops out a window, shoots him in the back when he's halfway over.

So I'm thinking about that. And I'm seeing the retard, and the girl, and the wall Eicholtz died on. But here's the thing. I'm thinking a lot, and I mean a lot, about those fucking dogs.

And I'm thinking about my dog. Vicar. About the shelter we'd got him from, where Cheryl said we had to get an older dog because nobody takes older dogs. How we could never teach him anything. How he'd throw up shit he shouldn't have eaten in the first place. How he'd slink away all guilty, tail down and head low and back legs crouched. How his fur started turning grey two years after we got him, and he had so many white hairs on his face it looked like a moustache.

So there it was. Vicar and Operation Scooby, all the way home.

Maybe, I don't know, you're prepared to kill people. You practice on man-shaped targets so you're ready. Of course, we got targets they call "dog targets." Target shape Delta. But they don't look like fucking dogs.

And it's not easy to kill people, either. Out of boot camp, Marines act like they're gonna play Rambo, but it's fucking serious, it's professional. Usually. We found this one insurgent doing the death rattle, foaming and shaking, fucked up, you know? He's hit with a 7.62 in the chest and pelvic girdle; he'll be gone in a second, but the company XO walks up, pulls out his KA-BAR, and slits his throat. Says, "It's good to kill a man with a knife." All the Marines look at each other like, "What the fuck?" Didn't expect that from the XO. That's some PFC bullshit.

On the flight, I thought about that too.

It's so funny. You're sitting there with your rifle in your hands but no ammo in sight. And then you touch down in Ireland to refuel. And it's so foggy you can't see shit but, you know, this is Ireland, there's got to be beer. And the plane's captain, a fucking civilian, reads off some message about how general orders stay in effect until you reach the States, and you're still considered on duty. So no alcohol.

Well, our CO jumped up and said, "That makes about as much sense as a goddamn football bat. Alright, Marines, you've got three hours. I hear they serve Guinness." Ooh-fucking-rah. Corporal Weissert ordered five beers at once and had them laid out in front of him. He didn't even drink for a while, just sat there looking at 'em all, happy. O'Leary said, "Look at you, smiling like a faggot in a dick tree," which is a DI expression Curtis loves. So Curtis laughs and says, "What a horrible fucking tree," and we all start cracking up, happy just knowing we can get fucked up, let our guard down.

We got crazy quick. Most of us had lost about twenty pounds and it'd been seven months since we'd had a drop of alcohol. MacManigan, Second Award PFC, was rolling around the bar with his nuts hanging out of his cammies telling Marines, "Stop looking at my balls, faggot." Lance Corporal Slaughter was there all of a half hour before he puked in the bathroom, with Corporal Craig, the sober Mormon, helping him out, and Lance Corporal Greeley, the drunk Mormon, puking in the stall next to him. Even the Company Guns got wrecked.

It was good. We got back on the plane and passed the fuck out. Woke up in America.

Except, when we touched down in Cherry Point there was nobody there. It was zero dark and cold and half of us were rocking the first hangover we'd had in months, which at that point was a kind of shitty that felt pretty fucking good. And we got off the plane and there's a big empty landing strip, maybe a half-dozen red patchers and a bunch of seven tons lined up. No families.

The Company Guns said that they were waiting for us at Lejeune. The sooner we get the gear loaded on the trucks, the sooner we see 'em.

Roger that. We set up working parties, tossed our rucks and seabags into the seven tons. Heavy work and it got the blood flowing in the cold. Sweat a little of the alcohol out too.

Then they pulled up a bunch of buses and we all got on, packed in, M16s sticking everywhere, muzzle awareness gone to shit but it didn't matter.

Cherry Point to Lejeune's an hour. First bit's through trees. You don't see much in the dark. Not much when you get on 24 either. Stores that haven't opened yet. Neon lights off at the gas stations and bars. Looking out, I sort of knew where I was, but I didn't feel home. I figured I'd be home when I kissed my wife and pet my dog.

We went in through Lejeune's side gate, which is about ten minutes away from our battalion area. Fifteen, I told myself, way this fucker is driving. When we got to McHugh, everybody got a little excited. And then the driver turned on A Street. Battalion area's on A, and I saw the barracks and I thought, there it is. And then they stopped about four hundred meters short. Right in front of the armory. I could've jogged down to where the families were. I could see there was an area behind one of the barracks where they'd set up lights. And there were cars parked everywhere. I could hear the crowd down the way. The families were there. But we all got in line, thinking about them just down the way. Me thinking about Cheryl and Vicar.

And we waited.

When I got to the window and handed in my rifle, though, it brought me up short. That was the first time I'd been separated from it in months. I didn't know where to rest my hands. First I put them in my pockets, then I took them out and crossed my arms, and then I just let them hang, useless, at my sides.

After all the rifles were turned in, First Sergeant had us get into a no-shit parade formation. We had a fucking guidon waving out front, and we marched down A Street. When we got to the

edge of the first barracks, people started cheering. I couldn't see
them until we turned the corner, and then there they were, a big
wall of people holding signs under a bunch of outdoor lights, and
the lights were bright and pointed straight at us so it was hard to
look into the crowd and tell who was who. Off to the side there
were picnic tables and a Marine in woodlands grilling hot dogs.
And there was a bouncy castle. A fucking bouncy castle.

We kept marching. A couple more Marines in woodlands
were holding the crowd back in a line, and we marched until we
were straight alongside the crowd and then First Sergeant called
us to a halt.

I saw some TV cameras. There were a lot of US flags. The
whole MacManigan clan was up front, right in the middle, holding a banner that read: OO-RAH PRIVATE FIRST CLASS
BRADLEY MACMANIGAN. WE ARE SO PROUD.

I scanned the crowd back and forth. I'd talked to Cheryl on
the phone in Kuwait, not for very long, just, "Hey, I'm good,"
and, "Yeah within forty-eight hours, talk to the FRO, he'll tell
you when to be there." And she said she'd be there, but it was
strange, on the phone. I hadn't heard her voice in a while.

Then I saw Eicholtz's dad. He had a sign too. It said: WEL-
COME BACK HEROES OF BRAVO COMPANY. I looked
right at him and remembered him from when we left and I
thought, "That's Eicholtz's dad." And that's when they released
us. And they released the crowd too.

I was standing still and the Marines around me, Curtis and
O'Leary and MacManigan and Craig and Weissert, they were
rushing out to the crowd. And the crowd was coming forward.
Eicholtz's dad was coming forward.

He was shaking the hand of every Marine he passed. I don't
think a lot of guys recognized him, and I knew I should say something but I didn't. I backed off. I looked around for my wife. And
I saw my name on a sign: SGT PRICE, it said. But the rest was

blocked by the crowd and I couldn't see who was holding it. And then I was moving toward it, away from Eicholtz's dad, who was hugging Curtis, and I saw the rest of the sign. It said: SGT PRICE, NOW THAT YOU'RE HOME YOU CAN DO SOME CHORES. HERE'S YOUR TO-DO LIST. 1) ME 2) REPEAT NUMBER 1.

And there, holding the sign, was Cheryl.

She was wearing cammie shorts and a tank top, even though it was cold. She must have worn them for me. She was skinnier than I remembered. More make-up too. I was nervous and tired and she looked a bit different. But it was her.

All around us were families and big smiles and worn-out Marines. I walked up to her and she saw me and her face lit. No woman had smiled at me like that in a long time. I moved in and kissed her. I figured that was what I was supposed to do. But it'd been too long and we were both too nervous and it felt like just lip on lip pushed together, I don't know. She pulled back and looked at me and put her hands on my shoulders and started to cry. She reached up and rubbed her eyes and then she put her arms around me and pulled me into her.

Her body was soft and it fit into mine. All deployment I'd slept on the ground, or on canvas cots. I'd worn body armor and kept a rifle slung across my body. I hadn't felt anything like her in seven months. It was almost like I'd forgotten how she felt, or never really known it, and now here was this new feeling that made everything else black and white fading before color. Then she let me go and I took her by the hand and we got my gear and got out of there.

She asked me if I wanted to drive and hell yeah I did, so I got behind the wheel. A long time since I'd done that too. I put the car in reverse, pulled out and started driving home. I was thinking I wanted to park somewhere dark and curl up with her in the back seat like high school. But I got the car out of the lot and down McHugh. And driving down McHugh it felt different from the bus. Like, this is Lejeune. This is the way I used to get to work. And it was so dark. And quiet.

Cheryl said, "How are you?" which meant, How was it? Are you crazy now?

I said, "Good. I'm fine."

And then it was quiet again, and we turned down Holcomb. I was glad I was driving. It gave me something to focus on. Go down this street, turn the wheel, go down another. One step at a time. You can get through anything, one step at a time.

She said, "I'm so happy you're home."

Then she said, "I love you so much."

Then she said, "I'm proud of you."

I said, "I love you too."

When we got home she opened the door for me. I didn't even know where my house keys were. Vicar wasn't at the door to greet me. I stepped in and scanned around and there he was on the couch. When he saw me he got up slow.

His fur was greyer than before, and there were weird clumps of fat on his legs, these little tumors that Labs get but that Vicar's got a lot of now. He wagged his tail. He stepped down off the couch real careful, like he was hurting. And Cheryl said, "He remembers you."

"Why's he so skinny?" I said, and I bent down and scratched him behind the ears.

"The vet said we had to keep him on weight control. And he doesn't keep a lot of food down these days."

Cheryl was pulling on my arm. Pulling me away from Vicar. And I let her.

She said, "Isn't it good to be home?"

Her voice was shaky, like she wasn't sure of the answer. And I said, "Yeah, yeah it is." And she kissed me hard. I grabbed her in my arms and lifted her up and carried her to the bedroom. I put a big grin on my face, but it didn't help. She looked a bit scared of me, then. I guess all the wives were probably a little bit scared.

And that was my homecoming. It was fine, I guess. Getting back feels like your first breath after nearly drowning. Even if it hurts, it's good.

I can't complain. Cheryl handled it well. I saw Lance Corporal Curtis's wife back in Jacksonville. She spent all his combat pay before he got back, and she was five months pregnant, which, for a Marine coming back from a seven-month deployment, is not pregnant enough.

Corporal Weissert's wife wasn't there at all when we got back. He laughed, said she probably got the time wrong, and O'Leary gave him a ride to his house. They get there and it's empty. Not just of people, of everything: furniture, wall hangings, everything. Weissert looks at this shit and shakes his head, starts laughing. They went out, bought some whiskey and got fucked up right there in his empty house.

Weissert drank himself to sleep and when he woke up, MacManigan was right next to him, sitting on the floor. And MacManigan, of all people, was the one who cleaned him up and got him into base on time for the classes they make you take about don't kill yourself, don't beat your wife. And Weissert was like, "I can't beat my wife. I don't know where the fuck she is."

That weekend they gave us a 96, and I took on Weissert duty for Friday. He was in the middle of a three-day drunk, and hanging with him was a carnival freak show filled with whiskey and lap dances. Didn't get home until four, after I dropped him off at Slaughter's barracks room, and I woke Cheryl coming in. She didn't say a word. I figured she'd be mad and she looked it, but when I got in bed she rolled over to me and gave me a little hug, even though I was stinking of booze.

Slaughter passed Weissert to Addis, Addis passed him to Greeley, and so on. We had somebody with him the whole weekend until we were sure he was good.

When I wasn't with Weissert and the rest of the squad, I sat on the couch with Vicar, watching the baseball games Cheryl'd taped for me. Sometimes Cheryl and I talked about her seven months, about the wives left behind, about her family, her job, her boss. Sometimes she'd ask little questions. Sometimes I'd answer. And glad as I was to be in the States, and even though I hated the past seven months and the only thing that kept me going was the Marines I served with and the thought of coming home, I started feeling like I wanted to go back. Because fuck all this.

The next week at work was all half-days and bullshit. Medical appointments to deal with injuries guys had been hiding or sucking up. Dental appointments. Admin. And every evening, me and Vicar watching TV on the couch, waiting for Cheryl to get back from her shift at Texas Roadhouse.

Vicar'd sleep with his head in my lap, waking up whenever I'd reach down to feed him bits of salami. The vet told Cheryl that's bad, but he deserved something good. Half the time when I pet him I'd rub up against one of his tumors and that had to hurt. It looked like it hurt him to do everything, wag his tail, eat his chow. Walk. Sit. And when he'd vomit, which was every other day, he'd hack like he was choking, revving up for a good twenty seconds before anything came out. It was the noise that bothered me. I didn't mind cleaning the carpet.

And then Cheryl'd come home and look at us and shake her head and smile and say, "Well, you're a sorry bunch."

I wanted Vicar around, but I couldn't bear to look at him. I guess that's why I let Cheryl drag me out of the house that weekend. We took my combat pay and did a lot of shopping. Which is how America fights back against the terrorists.

So here's an experience. Your wife takes you shopping in Wilmington. Last time you walked down a city street, your Marine on point went down the side of the road, checking ahead and scanning the roofs across from him. The Marine behind him checks the windows on the top levels of the buildings, the Marine behind him gets the windows a little lower, and so on down until your guys have the street level covered, and the Marine in back has the rear. In a city there's a million places they can kill you from. It freaks you out at first. But you go through like you were trained and it works.

In Wilmington, you don't have a squad, you don't have a battle buddy, you don't even have a weapon. You startle ten times checking for it and it's not there. You're safe, so your alertness should be at white, but it's not.

Instead, you're stuck in an American Eagle Outfitters. Your wife gives you some clothes to try on and you walk into the tiny dressing room. You close the door, and you don't want to open it again.

Outside, there're people walking around by the windows like it's no big deal. People who have no idea where Fallujah is, where three members of your platoon died. People who've spent their whole lives at white.

They'll never get even close to orange. You can't, until the first time you're in a firefight, or the first time an IED goes off that you missed, and you realize that everybody's life, everybody's life, depends on you not fucking up. And you depend on them.

Some guys go straight to red. They stay like that for a while and then they crash, go down past white, down to whatever is lower than "I don't fucking care if I die." Most everybody else stays orange, all the time.

Here's what orange is. You don't see or hear like you used to. Your brain chemistry changes. You take in every piece of the environment, everything. I could spot a dime in the street twenty yards away. I had antennae out that stretched down the block. It's hard to even remember exactly what that felt like. I think you take in too much information to store so you just forget, free up brain space to take in everything about the next moment that might keep you alive. And then you forget that moment too, and focus on the next. And the next. And the next. For seven months.

So that's orange. And then you go shopping in Wilmington, unarmed, and you think you can get back down to white? It'll be a long fucking time before you get down to white.

By the end of it I was amped up. Cheryl didn't let me drive home. I would have gone a hundred miles per hour. And when we got back we saw Vicar had thrown up again, right by the door. I looked for him and he was there on the couch, trying to stand on shaky legs. And I said, "Goddamn it, Cheryl. It's fucking time."

She said, "You think I don't know?"

I looked at Vicar.

She said, "I'll take him to the vet tomorrow."

I said, "No."

She shook her head. She said, "I'll take care of it."

I said, "You mean you'll pay some asshole a hundred bucks to kill my dog."

She didn't say anything.

I said, "That's not how you do it. It's on me."

She was looking at me in this way I couldn't deal with. Soft. I looked out the window at nothing.

She said, "You want me to go with you?"

I said, "No. No."

"Okay," she said. "But it'd be better."

She walked over to Vicar, leaned down and hugged him. Her hair fell over her face and I couldn't see if she was crying. Then she stood up, walked to the bedroom and gently closed the door.

I sat down on the couch and scratched Vicar behind the ears and I came up with a plan. Not a good plan, but a plan. Sometimes that's enough.

There's a dirt road near where I live and a stream off the road where the light filters in around sunset. It's pretty. I used to go running there sometimes. I figured it'd be a good spot for it.

It's not a far drive. We got there right at sunset. I parked just off the road, got out, pulled my rifle out of the trunk, slung it over my shoulders, and moved to the passenger side. I opened the door and lifted Vicar up in my arms and carried him down to the stream. He was heavy and warm, and he licked my face as I carried him, slow lazy licks from a dog that's been happy all his life. When I put him down and stepped back, he looked up at me. He wagged his tail. And I froze.

Only one other time I hesitated like that. Midway through Fallujah an insurgent snuck through our perimeter. When we raised the alarm he disappeared. We freaked, scanning everywhere, until Curtis looked down in this water cistern that'd been used as a cesspit, basically a big round container filled a quarter way with liquid shit.

The insurgent was floating in it, hiding beneath the liquid and only coming up for air. It was like a fish rising up to grab a fly sitting on the top of the water. His mouth would break the surface, open for a breath and then snap shut, and he'd submerge. I couldn't imagine it. Just smelling it was bad enough. About four or five Marines aimed straight down, fired into the shit. Except me.

Staring at Vicar it was the same thing. This feeling, like, something in me is going to break if I do this. And I thought of Cheryl bringing Vicar to the vet, of some stranger putting his hands on my dog, and I thought, I have to do this.

I didn't have a shotgun, I had an AR-15. Same, basically, as an M16, what I'd been trained on, and I'd been trained to do it right. Sight alignment, trigger control, breath control. Focus on the iron sights, not the target. The target should be blurry.

I focused on Vicar, then on the sights. Vicar disappeared into a grey blur. I switched off the safety.

There had to be three shots. It's not just pull the trigger and you're done. Got to do it right. Hammer pair to the body. A final well-aimed shot to the head.

The first two have to be fired quick, that's important. Your body is mostly water, so a bullet striking through is like a stone thrown in a pond. It creates ripples. Throw in a second stone soon after the first, and in between where they hit the water gets choppy. That happens in your body, especially when it's two 5.56 rounds traveling at supersonic speeds. Those ripples can tear organs apart.

If I were to shoot you on either side of your heart, one shot . . . and then another, you'd have two punctured lungs, two sucking chest wounds. Now you're good and fucked. But you'll still be alive long enough to feel your lungs fill up with blood.

If I shoot you there with the shots coming fast, it's no problem. The ripples tear up your heart and lungs, and you don't do the death rattle, you just die. There's shock, but no pain.

I pulled the trigger, felt the recoil, and focused on the sights, not on Vicar, three times. Two bullets tore through his chest, one through his skull, and the bullets came fast, too fast to feel. That's how it should be done, each shot coming quick after the last so you can't even try to recover, which is when it hurts.

I stayed there staring at the sights for a while. Vicar was a blur of grey and black. The light was dimming. I couldn't remember what I was going to do with the body.

4

THE WAVE THAT TAKES THEM UNDER

Brian Turner

THE LANDSCAPE GLOWS COLD AND BLANK in the cracked lens of the moon. An ascent. A decline. The motion repeated dune after dune. With each step, Henderson's boots sink mid-calf deep. It's as if the desert itself is pulling them down to an absolute low, he thinks, to be buried in sand when the wind picks up. He pauses at the crest to catch his breath and take in the sweep, the dusty sea rolling to the horizon.

The platoon stretches out in staggered wedge formations. The fire teams move like the silent wings of birds in slow motion, one "v" following another with single-minded intention. Alpha team is out front with Sgt. Reyes on point. Henderson watches how easily Reyes gives in to the dune's steep pitch: he leans back with his weapon muzzle-up at the moon, then slides down the dune on his back in a fluid, unbroken sweep. The rest of Reyes's team—Royce, Caldwell, and Ong—follow him, Royce yelling, "Tits up, fuckers."

Sgt. Gould huffs up behind Henderson, the rest of Bravo team in trail. "Any word from the LT?" Gould asks. He flicks old chew to the ground and brushes his hand on his fatigues.

Henderson shakes his head while Royce helps Caldwell to his feet in the shadows below.

"I'm sure something'll come down soon . . . Fucking shitbags up at brigade, man. They just sit on their asses punching the clown all day." Gould spits and sucks water from his CamelBak.

"You jealous? You want to get promoted up to a desk?"

Gould wipes the last flecks of chew from his lips with the back of his hand, smiling. "Well, I'd sure have a helluva lot more time to do what I love best."

Henderson waits for it.

"Punching that god-damned clown."

*   *   *

After 0200, a slight headwind picks up, lifting the finest grains from the dune crests, catching sand in little twists and pockets of air, swirling into widening cones and dropping into hollows. It reminds Henderson of the beach near Half Moon Bay, the flats where the tide pulls back white foam. Anna, asleep in a mummy bag with her hair tangled by salt. Breathing. The breakers' white-caps rolling in from out of the darkness while the wind lifted the spray from the peaks of the falling waves. The cool mist on his face when he closed his eyes beside her. For a moment, Henderson can almost taste it. He's back home again. He's with her. Anna. He says her name under his breath to make her real. "Anna. Anna."

He looks up the slope to his right, about 150 meters away, to where Lt. Novotny and his radioman, Griggs, struggle against the dune, leaning into the wind and sand that pours down on them as they near the top. Henderson slides his goggles down from his Kevlar and pulls them tight to his face. A voice crackles over the radio on his chest, but the transmission's too faint to make out.

*   *   *

"Everybody always says it's like a bad dream," Royce says. "But it ain't like that at all. I mean, if this was a dream, there'd be all kinds a weird shit out here, you know? Like your fucking mom would be out there or something. Fucking sand just goes on forever and forever."

Ong says, "Yeah. Like, if this was my dream, over every dune you'd see some crazy shit, you know? Like a giant fishbowl with seaweed and big orange Nemos with goofy eyes like they're gonna blow up or something."

"There's definitely weed in your fishbowl, Ong, but it ain't seaweed," Royce says. "How the fuck you ever pass a piss test?"

*   *   *

Henderson and Reyes hear the wind-muffled laughter of the squad rising up from below. He wonders how long their humor will last.

"What do you think?" Reyes asks.

"I think we're fucking lost," Henderson says, staring off at the clusters of soldiers strung out along the dunes. "I'm thinking vehicle coms are down, and maybe they're waiting for us in the wrong spot. Plus, I'm thinking we should sit tight and wait for this sandstorm to blow over, link up with the vehicles, then get the hell out of Dodge."

Reyes motions to Lt. Novotny and Griggs off on a far dune. "And him?"

Henderson shakes his head, exhaling deep and slow. "I don't know. I think our Lord Farquaad's gonna keep pushing forward." Henderson wipes his lips with his shirtsleeve. "Double-check the weapons and make sure your guys haven't oiled them down too much. I don't know how in hell to keep them from getting all gunked up, but do what you can."

"Do what I can?" Reyes tilts his head and tries to shake the sand grains out of his earlobe. "Right. Do what I can. Sure."

*   *   *

05:00 . . . 11:40 . . . 19:07 . . .
    The turning of day nearly indistinguishable from night.
Oh-dark-thirty. Oh-dark-hell.
Bringer of the wave that takes them under.

*   *   *

The platoon moves forward in fits and starts as the wind drives
hard against them, soldiers falling back or tumbling down dunes
to roll into pits where the sand seems determined to bury them.
Henderson can see Sgt. Gould yelling, but his voice barely registers above the wind's cry and the crack of sand against his goggles. He thinks maybe Gould is cursing the sky itself, as close as
any of them might come in their argument with God, or maybe
he's calling out to the men disappearing around him, yelling to
be heard over the din of the world in its gritty erasure.
Henderson would yell, too, but what difference would it make?
It would fill his mouth with sand to even try. And Caldwell?
Ong? Royce? Each is driven to his own silence, whole and com-
plete. Henderson imagines Sgt. Reyes still on point somewhere in
the storm, moving forward, and hears the *pop pop* of small arms
fire from a squad in the distance. Now Sgt. Gould, the last man
Henderson can see—though he's only a form in the wind and
sand blowing over now, more shadow and movement than man
or a soldier named Gould with a family, someone from Rhode
Island, no, nothing more, a blur—is running off sideways along
the shear of the wind into the sound of gunfire. Something
breaks inside. In some essential place of order far deeper than the
architecture of the brain, the body discovers its rope-held panic
and cuts it loose. Henderson's legs stumble forward until the
dune gives way, and he tumbles in the swirling dust the way a
man might fall to the very bottom of his life, the carbine torn

from his firing hand, coughing as he falls and spins and twists before slamming against another body slumped on the low ground. Half-buried in the sand beside him, the body is curled up on itself. When Henderson pushes him over, he discovers it's the radioman, Griggs. A red chem-light in his left hand signals a world that only recognizes a man when it breaks him down to his most elemental form, though Griggs would never have thought of it that way. Griggs would most likely have said something like "Oh, fuck" or "I goddamned thought so." No matter. He speaks the grammar of sand now, Henderson thinks, and the wind will break him down to dust.

* * *

The sand buries the moonlight.

Henderson sits in the darkness with his back curved against the inexorable. And as the sand gathers around him, he thinks *the world feeds on us all.* This thought surprises him. He doesn't know where it came from, but as he sits hunched over, the wind and sand shape a dune around him, a transient barchan moon. He takes off his helmet, sets it in his lap. It is a bowl of shadow, filling with the inscrutable world.

He thinks of home, of Anna, of sand pouring in their bedroom window. The slow tide of it all pours in, wave by wave, as the ceiling fan spirals a thin cloud of dust over her. The painted lines on the streets outside begin to disappear. Streetlights dim and go dark. Anna calls out to him in her sleep.

As the wind picks up around him, he opens the door and walks into his home. He snaps a chem-light, which is like holding the last cold remains of a fire, holding it out and away from his body. Anna sleeps in the wreckage, sand erasing her image in the far mirror. Henderson traces her body in the soft light. Sand sparkles red on her eyelashes and the fine soft edges of her lips. He touches her face, but he cannot wake her, and she cannot hear him when he says her name. He can only watch as her features, yielding, disappear beneath the gathering dune of their bed.

Henderson cups his hands over his face to block out the dust.

He remembers a time from twenty years back, when he was just a kid. Poolside. An apartment complex. Summer smoke and distant helicopters. Laughter. His bare feet on the curving concrete lip of the pool as old man Kelman startled him with what he must have thought was a playful gesture. And Henderson, not knowing how to swim, fell backward wheeling in slow motion. The old man had turned away, not recognizing how the cool waters of the deep end displaced Henderson's small frame before curling back over to push him down, as deep into that blue and unlivable world as his body could go.

5

The Train

Mariette Kalinowski

On bad days she rides the subway. She knows the bad days from the somewhat OK days by the tightness that inches slowly across her skin. On bad days the tightness overwhelms her and forces her onto the 7 line, its simple out-and-back path through Queens soothing her a little. Riding back and forth on the train gives her time to think. Watching the western skyline of Queens backed by Manhattan gives her a swinging backdrop to the narrative of her memories. One trip between Times Square and Flushing averages forty minutes. About five months ago, on one of her worst days yet, she rode back and forth thirteen times, before the claustrophobic press of rush hour forced her off. She watches buildings and neighborhoods flow past the window first one way then the other. The blur of outlines and colors soothes her, hypnotizing in a way that numbs whatever follows the constriction and headaches. The tightness announces the flood, those images and emotions lurking beneath the surface of everyday life, the soft buzz from a mistuned radio. A normal day is when she can make it through class and work, but when the tightness comes on, she knows it's not going to be a normal day.

Today, she's on her way to Penn Station to meet her mom for a long trip north to Vermont. It was her mom who decided they would take this trip, a month away from the city. She decided that the two of them should spend a month together at the house, hiking and swimming and "catching up, just us girls."

"It'll be good for you, honey," she'd said. "You're so alone in the city, and I'm worried about you. You need fresh air."

Ten hours on Amtrak to the small town where her mom has a summer home, a barn-like house built in that odd Vermont continuous manner, with one room followed by another and unexpected doors and thresholds appearing out of the shadows drawing a person through the house, floating along without wanting to. She drifted along whenever she was in that house, the rooms choosing her direction for her. She had spent most of her time drifting through the house that last summer before boot camp. Her memory of that summer, hazy in the same way the dust rolled in over the base and made her feel like a goldfish trapped in a bowl, everything looking curved and surreal. She had wanted to go to her bedroom but found herself in the short entryway instead, looking at family photos and small landscapes bought in local shops. The crumbling scent of dried flowers hung around her as the air shifted with her movements. The house was deserted most of the year, cleaned every three months by a woman for hire. Only their possessions there proved that they visited, no other lasting mark. She touched her fingertips gently to the bottom of one of the photographs, a bright fiery orange one, her and her mom shadows against a campfire. If another person ever came through the front door, if they took the time to look at the pictures in their frames, hold their nose close and take in the details, the swirled marks of her prints would distract the eye away from the captured intensity of the flames.

Outside, on the single concrete step, she leaned against the front door and tried to remember why she was there. A smudge of blue flannel caught her eye. She saw her mother standing in the old cornfield. She walked slowly across the field to join her mother, stumbling over the rough earth. With each step she expected her mother to turn around, to wave and smile like she always did, but she remained where she was, staring at something at her feet. Even when she scuffed to a stop next to her, she didn't move.

There was a dead bird on the ground. She wanted to say something to her mom, but kept her mouth shut at the look on her face. The bird lay on its back, its wings gently spread and feet curled up to its belly, looking for all the world as if it had simply fallen out of the sky, body frozen midflight. A few wing feathers shivered in the breeze, a line of ants moved around the beak and open, staring eyes. Her younger self tried hard to understand why the death-eyes of the bird felt so familiar. She tried to remember where she'd seen them before. And then her older self remembered for her: eyes staring up into the cloudy Iraqi sky and a body so still and she wishing and wishing that the eyes would blink and the mouth say "Gotcha." There wasn't a single hole or mark on the bird. She couldn't figure out what kind it was; something about the size of a cardinal but dark brown and speckled all over. She imagined it flying some great distance, maybe from the top of Canada, south along the curve of the earth and looking down at the shifting landscape below. The methodical beat of its wings leveraging against the wind, gravity, matching the beat of its heart, maybe became too much. The small, gradual movement along its path too tiring and it simply gave up, let its wings go slack and tumbled to the ground.

Her mother spun to face her. Her eyes were big, scared. "I don't know how to—" she choked out. She didn't finish. Instead, she turned away and crossed back to the house, staring at the ground.

She was the one who buried the bird; she carried the bird before her, the dark body on the spade of the old shovel she leveled in front of her body, feeling the rough wood and splinters digging into her hands. She couldn't not look at the bird as she walked to the tree line. Her short steps across the fallow field and the shovel swinging slightly with the shift of her hips. Her mother should be with her (she was probably watching from a window) to hug her shoulders and finish what she had started to say. An unfinished sentence. An unfinished migration. She kicked the bird into the shallow hole with her toe and packed dirt over it. Even after so many years she could still feel the soil beneath her foot as she tamped it down. A soft giving beneath the shovel that had the hollow sound of the rusty steel. She wonders what that would sound like from below, from beneath the soil. So often she's thought about it: death. So often the idea fills her head while she's awake that she hardly remembers anything else. Expansion of that single thought until there is no room for others and she is fastened onto the idea of being down, *beneath*. To be underground. To be where Kavanagh was.

She'd been away from Vermont for so long. So much had happened since she'd left. Going back meant catching up with her mom. Catching up meant talking about the four years she had been away—away from Vermont and away from the city—and the two times she'd gone overseas. But open air is always too open. She recalled the spinning dizziness of the desert on a clear, bright day, a vertigo growing deep behind her forehead, standing on the flat-packed sand in the middle of nowhere and feeling like she was the epicenter of the earth's rotation. On those days she felt like a figure skater: extending her arms would slow the spin and manage the dizziness, while pulling her arms close would spin her faster, faster until her body pulled apart.

The train lurches along a curve in Long Island City and the centrifugal force pushes her gently into her seat. She remembers how Vermont feels in the summer, the days cool, the noise of the cicadas high, and she and her mom sitting on the screened-in porch to watch the thunder clouds roll in over the mountains.

Remembering that last summer in Vermont, the dead bird, was so simple for her, just a mere flick of her thoughts and she was back there floating through the last real part of her life. The last solid part of her before the edges of her experience faded into that questionable fogginess of memory, that state in which a person could no longer be sure that what they recalled was true, or even their own. At times, when she was consumed by the tightness of Iraq and barely conscious on the train, she wondered if what she was feeling was even her own, as though she were living someone else's memories, transforming into another person. The tightness could be a metamorphosis, a twisting and reshaping of her body from the inside out until one morning she would walk past the vanity in her bathroom and not recognize the face reflecting back. She wants so badly to remember everything about that day, some clear part of that memory that stands out in a clear way, a part that she can call true. Too much of what she recalls feels false somehow, fabricated or drawn from some other part of her mind. She remembers the cold winter wind blowing unhindered across the open desert and feels her skin erupt in goosebumps as the memory makes her shiver, even in the dead of summer. But everything else about that day seems misplaced, drawn from every other day she spent in Iraq. Every recollection spins together flashes from every part of her tour, flashes of hajjis lining up to be frisked at the ECP, the world swept away beneath a roiling red cloud of sand, the staccato of an M16 firing or the distant *thoomp* of artillery firing that is felt deep in the chest more than heard. Frozen, each of these images floating across her memory, photographs that confuse the true progression of events. Reality on that day couldn't be trusted, because she was no longer sure which parts should be kept, which discarded. There was very little variation from one day to the next. Wake up, shuffle across the chilled sand in her shower shoes to the head. Grains of sand slipping under her toes and caking around the drain of the shower. In the mornings she was often the only one awake. She enjoyed the quiet and stillness, the vast purple sky with stars just before the sun rose, because it was the calmest part of her days. Nothing to worry about, yet. Every day filled with the crouching and clutching at bunches of clothing. Frowning and snapping at women to stand still, stop talking while she manipulated the fabric of *hijabs* and *chardors*, feeling through linen along the braids in their hair and beneath their breasts for weapons or bombs.

And standing around. The long stretches of time with no women showing up and her feet and back hurting while she and Kavanagh talked and smoked to feel busy. But always shifting her feet and body, hand never far from her pistol grip. Every day feeling like every other and she began to feel stuck, unable to keep track of the weeks turning into months. Holidays surprised her. She was shocked the day she realized she had only a couple of months left in her deployment. In those moments she fought hard to pick out something from the persistent forward blur of days, the memory of anything that stood out from the routine of her life. But all she saw was gray. Looking across the short distance to where the men shuffled one behind the other, their worn-out clothes beginning to look like the gray sky and gray sand. The men's faces beginning to look like the gray sand, and she couldn't discern them from the desert, from every other hajji she'd seen.

Gray surrounded the one day that stood out in sharp relief. A dense, rainy gray that pressed down close over her head, compressed her body into the sandy ground. The low clouds blocking out the sky over the base gate were the clearest part of her memories—the only part that seemed to come back to her whole. The gray clouds that winter day hung so low, and the glare made her squint and tear up.

She stood at the Entry Control Point for the main gate of the base. The ECP was a wide, sandy lane leading out from the main gate, about 100 meters long and framed on both sides by Hesco barriers, tall, canvas and wire baskets filled with sand built to stop shrapnel and small arms fire. About ten meters from the main gate, concrete barriers narrowed the lane of approach, corralling visitors into two files, all the hajjis coming in and out, going to their jobs at the chow hall, laundry building, or wherever, had to pass through the ECP. The men lined up along one side, shuffling patiently as each waited to be frisked by a pair of male Marines.

In her memory the corridor narrowed and stretched for miles and miles, the Hescos rising into the air, reminding her of the skyscrapers along the spine of Manhattan, like the entire world that day was the ECP and nothing else existed.

She stood on the other side with Kavanagh, watching for women coming through. There were never that many and almost all of them had children with them. Most came to visit their husbands or brothers or fathers who were being treated in the hospital for injuries. On that morning, as the hajjis lined up for work, Kavanagh argued with an Iraqi woman who'd brought her kids along, a boy and girl, trying to make it clear to her through an interpreter that she couldn't come on base because she didn't have the right documents. The woman kept insisting that the medic who took her husband said everything was in order. Kavanagh turned away from the woman and said, "Hey, get the hospital on the radio, see if we can unfuck this."

She nodded and moved off. With each step across the sand and gravel, her M16 knocked gently against her chest, making a hollow thump against the ballistic plates in her flak jacket. She couldn't help but feel edgy. That worry hovered all around her and in her mind until it became the standard sensation, until a day without fear was a bad day. On that particular day, with its heavy clouds and stretched-thin feeling, she glanced over at the line of hajjis queuing up for their pat down, and an alarm somewhere inside her went off, her fear screaming loud and long, leaning into her gut, making her wonder, making her *think*. There: a man of medium height, with a full head of shiny black hair combed and parted. He looked normal, but something wasn't right. He wore a clean white robe and no coat despite the cold. His eyes fixed on the back of the man in front of him, his gaze focused on the stripes on the man's jacket. She saw the man's lips move, a slight trembling of words in a language she'd never understand. Then she saw how, for such a slight man, his belly protruded in a strange way. His torso was too big for his body. As her thoughts clicked into place, she felt her body tense up. He was only the second man in line now and wasn't more than a few meters from the other Marines, and yet no one had noticed the hajji's weird bulge.

Fear had made her stop that day to look back at the hajji. Fear that something wasn't right with the man and the determined set of his face so different from the bored passivity of all the other men. Fear had spoken up in a soft voice in the back of her mind and she paused long enough to let the emotion grow into a tightness across her body that almost itched with its pull on her skin. That was the first time she felt fear come on with the tightness; it was her fear of the past and the memories of that day that first drove her to ride the train.

Fear seems to be the only thing she feels anymore. She remembers the first time the fear threatened to spill over after she returned to the city. How the fear started as only a worry. Sitting in her empty apartment in her ratty chair and trying to ignore the two-year-old in the apartment above banging her feet against the floor. She could feel worry growing somewhere inside her, deep, a tiny worm that twisted and writhed only enough to be noticed. She grew stagnant, numb against this fear until this worm grew and grew and dug into her and finally she felt compressed, constrained. She felt squeezed between the past and the present. She could feel Iraq everywhere, feel the dusty film of the desert covering every object and surface, her skin. She couldn't wash the desert away and all she saw was gray: gray sky, gray tinted sand, gray movements of bodies rushing. Or lying still. Darker gray pools spread across the ground. She smelled flesh and sweat and bile and she couldn't tell if these sights were solid or ghosts.

The fear consumed her until the two-year-old in the apartment above was no longer just an annoyance, a bratty child who stomped on the floor and would soon tire out, but a pounding through her skull. In that pounding her body remembered the concussive blow that threw her down, the reverberation of that day through her skeleton over and over. The fear and the pounding brought on the tightness like a hand across her face, her neck, and squeezing all her breath out until spots danced before her eyes. In a panic, she bolted, ran out the door, down the stairs, up the short hill to the subway and into the turnstile. Her hands shook so much she couldn't swipe her card right, first too fast and then too slow, the little screen repeating "please swipe again" over and over with that shrill beep needling at her.

"If you can't do it right, step aside and let other people go." The voice behind her was sharp, commanding. The woman stood with her arms crossed and glared hard at her. More people drifted up with curious looks. Most of them kept their distance.

"I'm trying," was all she could manage.

"And failing," the woman snapped. "Now get out of the way." The woman approached and prepared to shove through.

"Hey!" A muffled shout came out of the MTA booth through the weird microphone speaker. Everyone stopped and looked at the large black man glaring through the security glass. "You wait your turn ma'am!"

"She ain't getting through anytime soon."

"Yes she is," there was a click from the turnstile. "Go on through, miss."

She glanced back nervously. Nodded her thanks at the man and pushed through. The other woman stalked up to the booth and confronted the man, "Why the hell you let her through? You gonna give all of us a free ride?"

"You don't concern yourself with who I let through," she heard the man say as she took the stairs two at a time up to the platform.

She knew she had to wait for only a few minutes, but she trembled, panicked, worried she wouldn't make it. She might stop breathing, pass out, tumble forward onto the tracks, two solid, silver shining lines below, only seven or eight feet below, carrying the train along, wheels locked in and rolling fast and heavy. The fall wouldn't be bad, just a couple of bruises and scrapes, maybe a sprained wrist. All she had to do was pitch forward, lie across the tracks, and wait. The train would probably hurt less than the fall. All she would have to do was let her knees go slack and let her shoulders slump under the compulsion of gravity—the single most powerful law of the universe, pulling always down, down across the tracks and beneath the mass of the train. Down beneath the sweet, loamy surface of the soil, where her body could finally rot where it belonged. Rot, just like Kavanagh's. She felt the gentle tug of gravity, of downward force on her body, and she almost believed that she wanted to give in to this desire and be below, beneath where she belongs. And, yet . . . and yet. The silver lines swelled in her vision, glinting in the sun, and she stared, fixed, as the world shuddered and gusted in her face, steel explosions, the train. She stepped in and collapsed into a seat, her entire body clammy and cold, shaking, the train and the city and the bodies around her blurred with sweat and tears. She didn't care which way she was headed, but only watched the large clouds float past the train, focusing on the clear baby blue behind them and the way it made her feel a little better.

She thinks about that hajji all the time now, his face and the way the wind pulled at his robe, the weird shape underneath, and tries to pick out what she could've seen sooner. She remembers the look in his eyes, the resolve in that flicker of a glance he gave her as she stopped and turned back under the gray clouds hanging so low in the sky. In that brief look she knew, the feeling in her gut smashed wide open and she *knew* exactly why the mother-fucker was there. She felt her mouth open, felt her weapon rise up in her hands, felt her voice erupt in warning as the Marines turned their heads in her direction. The last thing she felt, the last *real* thing she remembered feeling in her body was the constriction of her finger around the trigger, cold and firm.

The earth closes around the train. The clatter of the wheels and joints grows more persistent, closer. The lights of each station flashing past the windows then streaking and finally stopping with the alignment of the train. She is only a few stops away from her transfer downtown: Hunter's Point, Vernon-Jackson Boulevard, Grand Central. Bryant Park came after and that's where she should get off, walk the long tunnel beneath the city. She sees in her mind the glistening white tiles and the long-winding mosaic roots leading people, one foot in front of the other. Each step forward would take her one step into the future, should take her one more step away from Iraq, but really took her directly into the past. Circling about, retracing scuffed footprints wearing down into a track, and she witnesses again and again that clear, determined look in that hajji's eyes, an explosion through the center of the earth, flames licking at the darkness and sending new stars whirling up into the night. Existence is circular, the world built in the round: clocks, horizons, galaxies, and always the earth swinging wide and then close, around and around the sun and always at some moment striking a point at which it has already been. At any given moment she exists in the very same place that she existed in Iraq, the exact same instant that she stood over Kavanagh bleeding out, or the moment she snatched her weapon up, or the instant before that when she should've already been snatching her weapon up.

No, she can't walk through that tunnel, not today, not yet. She can't walk beneath the words pleading *telmetale of stem or stone*. She could tell a tale, but one of dusty red and fear. "Tell me a tale," she almost hears her mom's voice in her head, in the air all around her in the same stricken voice as the day of the bird, "tell me something, please." Questions about her being *over there* that already hang beneath every phone conversation. But she won't answer those questions. Ever. She doesn't want her mom to know the truth about her new life. Her life after Vermont. She wants her mom to hold on to that young, untainted part of her life, the one that shines through the tall fire in the picture in the front hall. She wants her mom to want to look at that picture and remember the heat on their faces and their hands while they held marshmallows to the fire, and the early spring air with the remnants of winter cooling their backs. Such a good and clean memory. She doesn't want the way her mom looks at that picture to change. "I want to know," her mom might say. But to know about something, to understand what happens and why, changes a person. She still doesn't understand what her mother said that day over the bird. Her mom wouldn't understand about the girl and her kicking leg. No, she won't go to Vermont.

She woke against the Hescos, contorted and slumped, and took a minute to figure it out. Her head ached and her ears rang. Her sling was up around her collar, pulling against her throat, her weapon twisted awkwardly around her sling, the barrel jammed into the sand. Her face ached and she tasted blood in her mouth. Later, when she returned to the States, two of her teeth had to be replaced: her left incisor had shattered to the root and her left canine was completely knocked out when the blast threw her M16 into her jaw. She never found the missing tooth, figured she'd swallowed it.

She managed to push the sling away and sat up with a groan. She felt a sharp, knifing pain in the back of her neck and where the lower edge of her ballistic plate dug into her kidneys. She looked down at her feet. Sticky brown smears on her boots and trousers smelled faintly of hamburger. Her gut wrenched hard in the instant before she turned and vomited. She thought about wiping it off but stared helplessly at her bare hands.

A medic worked on Kavanagh, whose helmet lay a few feet from her head. She'd always complained it was too big. Next to Kavanagh lay the Iraqi girl. Her legs kicking in weird spasms, her right leg swinging slowly to the sky and back down like she was playing soccer. She could never remember how long the girl took to finally lie still. Some days it lasted only a moment, other days it lasted hours. She sat there against the Hescos and watched that thin, brown leg swing and fall and twitch and finally, shuddering, stop.

She finally pulled herself to her feet, gritting her teeth as she stumbled over to Kavanagh. Kavanagh was on her back, blood splashed all around her body. She looked only at Kavanagh's face, somehow untouched, pale and brushed with those Irish freckles so many guys liked. She didn't interrupt the medic's work. She wanted to stop him but she couldn't move, couldn't raise her hands, the cold tingling spreading through her body and keeping her still. For several minutes, for such a long time, she could only watch. A soldier passed with an armful of body bags, and she took one from him, then found a pair of surgical gloves in the medic's trauma bag. She lifted the young Iraqi girl in her arms—five, six years old?—cradled her and slid her awkwardly into the body bag, head and shoulders first, then her broken torso, then the legs, that leg cool and pliant in her hands. The girl must've shielded her mother, who sat nearby, wailing and cradling her son.

The pitch of the train air brakes matches the sound of the wailing mother in her ears and she looks up through the windows to a crowd of bodies. Above their heads she reads, 42nd St–Bryant Park. She jerks to her feet, knowing she should get off, followed quickly by the anxiousness, the need to be away from Vermont. She thinks of the tunnel, the dusty memory of Iraq a movie in her head, rolling, rolling like the earth spinning constantly into, out of the sunlight. A single scene with the girl's kicking leg and Kavanagh's blank stare and the pathetic urge to get drunk. She eases back into her seat, reassured by the firm plastic, and watches the flood of bodies crushing in. She is still, almost calm, her hands resting in her lap. She isn't sure what she'll tell her mother, but in this moment she's not ready to exit the train.

The cleanup at the ECP lasted through nightfall. When she finally climbed into the back of a seven-ton truck to be taken to the base hospital, her body aching with pain and fatigue, she realized she was famished. She asked one of the corpsmen for food and was handed a Styrofoam box with cold, greasy fried chicken, string beans, and mashed potatoes and gravy. She took one look at the fried chicken and gravy and vomited all over the tray and her lap. "I'm sorry," she wailed as the orderlies started cleaning her up, "I'm sorry, I didn't mean it."

She was kept under observation in the hospital for three days, for head and spinal trauma: her impact against the Hescos left large bruises along her back and the doctors were concerned she might have internal rupturing. They gave her Percocet for her missing teeth and blinding headaches. She was thankful for the way the meds helped her forget Kavanagh's brown eyes staring up at the sky, her blonde hair blowing out of her bun.

She spent another four days on bed rest in her quarters. On the second day, a young, skinny girl was shown into her room by a staff sergeant saying this is Warren, your new roommate. She didn't answer the girl's shy smile and "hello." Instead, she replaced her headphones and tried to ignore Warren as she unpacked her things. She could see the small piles of clothes and DVDs growing on Kavanagh's old bunk. Kavanagh, everything had the touch of her, the slack look of her face disrupting everything she did and thought. A racking wave of tightness moved through her gut and pulled her away, dragged her back to California; a quick tug from behind her navel and she was no longer in TQ but in her quarters so many months before where she lay across the width of her bed, her hands clasped behind her head and the lights off. Looking out the open window at the full moon hanging just above the ridge glowing in the light and the face of the moon looking back at her. Leaves outlined against the sky and a faint smell of smoke from a brush fire. It was a week before deployment and her room was empty of her belongings, most of them in storage. Only her toiletries on the sink, her sea bag and rucksack propped in a corner remained.

She jumped at the hollow metal banging against her barracks door. She found Kavanagh outside, a twelve pack of beer hanging from her hand.

"Heard you were staying in," Kavanagh said as she walked into the room. "Why were you sitting in the dark?"

"I was starting to fall asleep."

"Do you want me to leave?" But Kavanagh had already cracked open two beers and was throwing the rest into the fridge.

"No, it's OK." She took the beer and sat on the corner of her bed. "Don't you usually go up to L.A. on the weekends?"

"Yeah," Kavanagh sat in a chair, "but I've gotten a little sick of it. Besides, you said you wouldn't go."

She nodded and drank from her beer. The large window reflected her face and Kavanagh's profile in gray casts, a charcoal-and-ink sketch of the two of them in the room, waiting.

She turned back to Kavanagh, "Are you scared?"

Kavanagh didn't answer, only looked at her feet.

"I mean about Iraq."

"I know what you mean," she ran the back of her hand across her chin where a drop of beer slid down her skin. "That's just not a question you ask." She looked at her reflection in the plate glass.

And even then, sitting in that room with Kavanagh and talking about everything but Iraq, the questions kept circling. The room filled with a heaviness that constricted her lungs, constricted her brain, and the mere thought of seven months nearly drove her insane. And she hadn't even gotten there yet. Seven months in the desert filled her with such unease, such giddiness that she spun between the two, orbiting between the two thoughts until she was caught, and Iraq and everything that followed her stepping onto the tarmac on al-Taqaddum sunk away into a black hole that pulled her down and through her own life.

In that moment she wanted to be held by her mother. When Kavanagh ignored her first question, making her wonder if her corporal really was scared, and growing scared at the thought, all she wanted was to hug her mother. Whisper to her that she was scared and that she wasn't sure she could do it. Wasn't sure she would come home. Her mom's voice whispered back to her, "I don't know how to—" *What?* she asked back. *What don't you know how to do? Be strong for me? Watch me go away? I want to know, too.*

Kavanagh kept talking and laughing and opening more beers until almost the whole pack was finished and the two of them had fallen asleep. Kavanagh never mentioned Iraq again. Not even when they were on the plane bound for that fucking place and sitting next to each other as the plane crept farther across the arc of the earth. Kavanagh calm and bored enough with the idea of a second tour to sleep most of the trip. She could still see Kavanagh sitting on her rack reading magazines, or dressed in her gear and smoking a cigarette. But thinking about Kavanagh always ended with her on her back and bleeding out into the sand. The gray clouds reflected in her open eyes. Kavanagh lying in the sand, and now Warren would be lying in Kavanagh's bed. She grew angrier with each item Warren placed on the bed, wanted to shout at her that she would be sleeping in a dead woman's bed. Instead, she turned up the volume on her music and turned to the wall.

On the final night of her bed rest she couldn't sleep. Sometime in the very early morning she shuffled slowly out to the burn barrel on the outskirts of the compound, carrying her bloodied cammies, clutching them to her chest like she had the Iraqi girl. When the flames burned hot and tall, she threw in her uniform and boots. She crept as close to the flames as possible, feeling the sharp heat on her face, neck, and chest. She wanted to get even closer, to climb into the flames and curl up at the corners into ash the way her cammies did, feel the flames eat into her skin in widening holes until she was consumed like her boots, melt away into the embers of the fire, feel her bones flake and rise up on the heat of the flames into the empty black sky where their last sparks would drift like spinning stars.

Then, finally, with a concussive exhale, the train comes to the end of the line. She rises calmly and crosses the gap with ease. Walks beneath the sign: Times Sq–42nd St. Feels her feet move easily across the platform and her body move in and out and around the people on the platform. The dead bird, her mother's words, coming forward in her thoughts and mixing with the people, with her movement. She should've died with Kavanagh. She shouldn't be walking across the platform trying to reach the escalator. She shouldn't be in the city at all. She had tried to forget everything; had tried to sink into drunkenness, into meds, tried to stay awake in fear of the dreams, burrow into some dark place that would give her a break from the memories, from the ECP that would come when she inevitably fell asleep. The pain of self-abuse still felt better than the guilt. Guilt drove it all. Anger that things had gone so wrong. "I don't know how to let you go," she thinks her mother wanted to say. She understands her mother, understands the need to hold on to whatever you can of a person who leaves, who is gone, the fear of the gaping hole that person creates and the way pain seems to fill it. She carries Kavanagh with her. Always the still and bloody Kavanagh that didn't fly home with her. Rarely the quiet sketch of her in California. And she tries to change the ending. Tries to make it so Kavanagh walked away from the ECP and Warren never moved in. Tries to make it so she shouted sooner or squeezed, squeezed the trigger until she felt her weapon buck into her shoulder; pink mist clouding from the dead hajji. But even if she changes things in her mind, they were still the same in reality. So she rides the train.

She steps onto the escalator. Her shoulders rock back with the first motion upwards. She'll get out of the subway, she thinks, find a bench or someplace to sit and call her mom to tell her to not expect her. She's not sure exactly what she'll say to her mom or whether she'll make any sense when she tries to describe this need, this understanding inside her that she shouldn't go to Vermont, not right now. But she knows that if she takes her time now that there would be more time in the future. No more calling at the last minute to cancel coffee or dinner plans. She could see her in a little while, sometime soon maybe, calling and saying that she was coming up to the summer house. She imagines sitting next to her mom and rocking back and forth in the old wicker rocking chairs and watching the thunderheads building and the energy rippling through the air. She smells ozone. The beer sweaty in her hand. She watches the opaque gray clouds darken the summer sky prematurely into a false twilight, the overcast sky looking so much like the one over the ECP. And she looks at her mother. Her mother looks with heavy lids at the distant Green Mountains and is just rocking, rocking. Then the wind picks up and blows through the screened porch and she feels herself lifting, rising buoyant on the heat rising into the air and swirling into the clouds.

And she is rising, climbing the escalator up from underground, going up and up and seeking out the sun, seeking out the open air, a place where she can sit down and call her mom. She pushes through the turnstile, steps quickly up the steps in choppy, scuffing steps to the street. She blinks in the sunlight in such contrast with the artificial glow underground. She looks at the small crowd gathering on the sidewalks, walking and chatting and ignoring her. She flips her long hair away from her neck to let fresh air breathe along her skin.

There is a second flash of hair flipped away from a twin neck. She turns to face her reflection in a shop window, pale and colorless in the sunlight, but still there. So different from the solid gray lines of her image in the barracks window beside Kavanagh's. This one barely draws a figure in the smoky shape of loose jeans and T-shirt, greasy hair hanging over one shoulder, her hands shoved deep into her pockets. She wasn't always like this, lost and hurt and wanting nothing else. She used to want more for herself. She used to want bigger things.

"Oh, whatever, you know I'm doing the best I can!" A second vague shadow appears at the far end of the window joining the loud, nasal voice. A tallish woman, slim through the hips, in big sunglasses. She's dressed neatly, but the low cut of her tank says she wants to be looked at. She runs fingers through her hair. "I can only do so much until things are out of my control, you know," she snaps into her cell phone.

Cute shoes. She looks at the sandals on the other woman's feet. Strappy with a faint gold sheen. She could see herself wearing those shoes with a light sundress.

The woman sighs dramatically and leans in to check her lip gloss. "Fine, yeah, I know. I'll try. I love you, too, mom." The woman flips her phone closed and struts away.

Just that simple: I love you, mom. She could say those words and calm her mom and reassure her that she'd be OK on her own for one more summer. She'll explain why she's not on the downtown train, why she won't be on the train with her to Vermont.

But she will also say that she will be here in the city in a month when she gets back. She knows that she'll be ready to try then. She will promise coffee or lunch. They will talk. Maybe Iraq will come up, but she won't talk about it. Not until she's ready. She turns left without choosing to. Thinks only of finding a bench. She walks in a calm way, a certain way, one foot in front of the other.

6

RAID

Ted Janis

I NEEDED TO GET THE HELL OUT OF THE COMMUNITY. Bin Laden was fish food, but we were still chasing targets, hunting down low-level pipe swingers in the name of GWOT, an acronym and a concept that belonged to last decade. Two deployments ago, I drank the Kool-Aid—drank it like it was the blood of Christ.

Two deployments was a long time ago.

Now it was all about the ritual. Just like back home, sitting in pews, doing call and response. I'd hoped to find something new here, but it was just another church and just another creed, and I never was believer material. At least I get to jump out of planes. The Mormon Elders might look into that as a recruitment tool.

Meanwhile, Sergeant Deke was getting all up in my business: "Doc, you fuck up your brief one more time I'm gonna smoke the ever-loving shit out of you. That was amateur hour."

This idiot. I turned and stared at him. Same ol' square jaw, same ol' beady eyes. I didn't know who I felt worse for, his dog or his wife.

"Roger, Sergeant. Won't happen again."

"It better not. As much as you think this whole gig is beneath your precious fucking intellect, MEDEVAC HLZs matter."

"Understood, Sergeant."

I walked out of the briefing tent, flicked on my headlamp, and aimed for the ready room. My eyes were still adjusting when I stumbled into Omar.

"How's my favorite Afghan?" I asked. "Ready to go murder some of your countrymen or what?"

"That's funny, Doc. You know Afghanistan's not really a country, right? It's just a hole where other countries send their retards to die."

"Whatever you tell yourself to get to sleep, rock star."

"I told you, Doc, I just translate. You're with the trigger-pullers."

"Hah. Sure. That's why I carry all these Band-Aids."

"So who's the target tonight?"

"That Jaweed guy again. Objective Charon 7. Seventh time's the charm and all that."

"I hope you're right. It'd be good to finally get that bastard."

"Whatever. He's just another dude making a buck. Just like you."

"Doc!"

Ah, shit. Sergeant Deke again. He'd had it out for me ever since he found my spice stash back at Fort Lewis. The only bastard who checked pillowcases.

"Stop polluting the locals' heads, Doc. Get to the ready room."

"Roger, Sergeant."

The terp and I followed him to the ready room tent, a temple of light surrounded by deep, black still. The golden glow emanating from the doorway revealed outlines of devotees entering and exiting, donning armor, priming their souls, weapons in hand. I was one of these men, I reminded myself. I was a Ranger.

Sergeant Deke veered off to the side to join the other squad leaders and the lieutenant. With them out of earshot, I went on.

"You gotta understand, Omar, in our country, no one ever thinks about death. It's completely removed from our lives. At worst, it only registers as a slight speed bump before an even more perfect afterlife. But then we come over here and it's in our faces. Over here, death is life. So you see these big motherfuckers like Sergeant Deke coming over seven, eight, nine times, you better believe they dig it. They love it. They worship it. Death."

Omar frowned and shook his head. Even he didn't buy my bullshit.

"You've been deployed a couple times, too, Doc, haven't you?"

We walked on, the crunch of gravel underfoot providing cover.

"I re-upped back when I believed. These days we create more insurgents than we kill. I'm done. As soon as my contract is up, I'm out. Goodbye and good riddance."

"That's a pretty story, Doc. You know, my people have been at war for thirty years. Thirty years. One thing you learn is some motherfuckers kill, and some motherfuckers die. You Rangers are on the killing side, most days. That's not bad."

I had no answer to that. We got to the ready room, where all doubts were replaced by hustling, sweaty bodies and the metallic thud of magazines being slapped into place. The mission would continue with or without my approval. Omar just smiled and shook his head. I lost myself in the ritual of preparation.

*　*　*

The helicopters approached our waiting platoon, screaming their chorus of kill-kill-kill-kill through the darkness. I felt a surge of adrenaline shoot through my body. It was that time again.

I flipped on my night vision and the world turned green. We filed to the birds one at a time, counted in by Sergeant Deke. The helicopter shuddered under our weight as it strained to pick up, then found its rhythm, and we were off into the Afghanistan night.

Blood pulsed through my veins as we sped through the mountain passes to the HLZ. Tightly packed in on the floor of the Chinook, we looked to each other, energy passing from man to man. This moment was our one release. Together. I got the togetherness here. Once we got back things changed, but here, I got it. The mission. The only chance to leave the bullshit behind. Without women or alcohol, without cars or drugs, we had only this.

The three-minute call started at the front with the lieutenant and was repeated down the line. I mouthed a prayer as my eyes stared past the rear ramp at the jagged, sinister mountains behind us, their peaks cutting into the heavens.

" . . . the Power and the Glory, Forever and Ever, Amen."

* * *

We finished the walk to the target compound. It must've been nearly eight kilometers, not an inch of it flat. We had left the highlands and entered a broad, tiered valley. In the distance, the ruins of an old fort rose on a faraway hill. Its weathered walls appeared like a sandcastle waiting for the tide to melt it back into the land.

"This is 2–6, I copy: isolation set, moving to the breach."

The target house was on the near side of the village below. With disturbing speed and even more disturbing silence, the platoon separated into fire teams and set the trap—a standard point raid. Lasers danced on the walls of the compound, coming to rest on doorways and windows.

From an adjacent grove, on overwatch with the lieutenant and the rest of his gaggle, I waited for the ambush to unfurl. I scanned the village, so mute and ignorant of the violence about to play out. I thought of the time in high school when that Jack Mormon dealer down the block got busted by the cops and we watched through the dining room window; my mom had been so upset. "His poor mother," she kept saying. "His poor mother." Out of the corner of my eye, I saw Omar lean against an ancient, gnarled tree and pick at his fingernails.

The deafening crack of the earth being torn apart echoed into the night. An instant of hopeful silence followed. Then a shriek. Shouts reverberated from cluster to cluster back to us. Even before I could make out the words, I was in full sprint down the valley.

"Doc!" "Medic!" "Man down!" "DOC!!!"

I skidded to a halt at the group of huddled, bent bodies, pushing them aside.

Just one, that was lucky. Most of his left leg was gone, the femur exposed. The right leg bled profusely. Must have been a pressure plate.

Clearing space for my medical pack, I grabbed the nearest Ranger. I couldn't tell who it was. Too many shadows, too many noises, too much going on. It didn't matter who it was.

"We need a tourniquet on the right leg too, have to stop that bleeding. Anybody working on the 9-line?"

"I'm on it, Doc."

"Roger, sir." When the hell had the lieutenant got here? "I think HLZ Rooster is closest."

"No. HLZ Rock. Sergeant Deke's securing it now. Get him prepped for movement."

The wounded's screams became moans and were accompanied by rifle fire and the shock of grenades from the compound. Third squad, bringing the fight to the enemy. Don't look at his face, I reminded myself. Don't look at his face. Don't look at his face.

"You lose him?"

"He's unconscious, sir, but still got a pulse."

Both of the tourniquets were secure. My hands caressed the wounded's body, probing for tears, holes, lumps, any sign of further injury.

"Looking good, Ranger, looking good. Got those legs to stop bleeding, everything should. . . . Shit, shit, shit. FUCK."

I felt a wet puddle just below his plate carrier. I pulled my hand away—my glove was completely red. Please God, I prayed, tell me it missed his organs.

"Doc, let's go! MEDEVAC's in a holding pattern, just waiting for the target secure call. We gotta move him."

"Sir, I found another wound!"

"Roger 2–7, I copy: compound clear and secure, be advised I'm bringing in the MEDEVAC birds. DOC! Let's fucking go!"

I sat back on my heels as two Rangers stepped in and scooped the wounded onto a litter. In an instant he was strapped in, and the three of us sprinted toward the HLZ. The Rangers strained with the load until Sergeant Deke appeared and grabbed a handle. We ran faster then. I held the IV bag high, ashamed of its paltry weight.

I forgot myself and looked down. It was Peters. I found it strange that his screams had been indistinguishable from the others.

* * *

I approached the lieutenant's entourage in the courtyard of the target house. With the raid over, everyone had gathered to listen to the radio chatter.

"Line four: two EKIA, two AK-47s, two PTT radios, eight pressure plate boards," the lieutenant reported. "One room with leather straps, chains, electric prods, pliers, hammers, saws."

Two EKIA. At least the hunters would be happy.

"Line eight: Requesting HLZ Rooster for exfil, nothing follows. Over."

What had it been, two hours? Three?

"Roger, I copy: Dead on arrival. We're moving to the exfil. 2–6 out."

That was Peters. The mountains seemed to fade in the distance, like wine dissolving into water. Everything got tight on me, my armor, my face. When I found I could breathe again, I realized I couldn't look at the other Rangers, so I turned around and looked for Omar. He was off to one side, sitting on a stone ledge, arms crossed, watching the proceedings.

He must have noticed something when I came over and sat down next to him. "What happened?" he asked.

"Peters" was all I could say.

"God grant his soul rest. He was a warrior."

"He was a motherfucking Ranger, you traitorous piece of shit."

"Alright, Doc. He was a motherfucking Ranger." Omar stood up. "You know what's funny though?"

I looked up at him, thinking what it would feel like to have his neck clenched in my hands.

"Charon 8."

"What?"

"Charon split, Doc. We'll be back."

"Fuck me. Who were the two EKIA?"

"Associates." Omar smirked. "Some motherfuckers die."

Then he walked off and I just watched him. Then the men moving around me. Then the stars glimmering watery in the distant, icy black, feeling the air go out again, amazing, the second time in one night. That was new. Then Sergeant Deke knocked me on the helmet and said time to move. The platoon filed out of the compound. I followed the body in front of me because I was a Ranger and that was what Rangers did.

We arrived at the HLZ. As if cast down, the heavy birds materialized from the pitch-black sky, singing their unearthly refrain. They were coming to take us home. Home, where Peters lay waiting.

7

PLAY THE GAME

Colby Buzzell

THE HAT'S GOT THREE RIBBONS embroidered on the front, which all pretty much get handed out to everybody now: a National Defense Service Ribbon, a Global War on Terrorism Service Ribbon, and a Global War on Terrorism Expeditionary Ribbon. Though inside the tag read "Made in China," I thought it looked kinda cool anyway. I especially liked how it read in bright yellow: *OPERATION IRAQI FREEDOM COMBAT VETERAN.* I went ahead and tossed it in my shopping cart and pushed toward the PX checkout.

Days later, as main post receded in the rearview one last time, I caught a look at myself in that hat. My blue infantry cord dangled from the mirror, somehow sad, like a limp-hanging flag. Was I making a mistake?

Fuck it, I thought, then turned on the radio. It was this song I'd never heard before, something about how there was this girl and everything was different now. I chuckled to myself, thinking about how my platoon sergeant kept hassling me those last months, trying to get me to re-up, always asking what kind of job I thought I'd get once I got out, if I was gonna put "shoot, move, and communicate" on my résumé, and saying, "You'll be back. I was just like you once, I got out too, and guess what happened? That's right. You'll see."

* * *

Six months later, I got out of bed and stumbled over to the window. Out on the street corner stood a little blonde-haired girl, dressed like she was on her way to Sunday school. Was today Sunday? I thought about that a minute.

Wearing nothing but a pair of boxers, a black metal bracelet around my right wrist with some names and dates engraved onto it, and my dog tags, I watched the little girl as she started to cross the street.

Out of nowhere, a beat-up Ford pickup whipped around the corner and slammed on its brakes, smashing right into the girl and sending her flying onto the pavement.

The truck idled for a couple seconds, then started to move again. Slowly it turned onto a side street and drove off. I tried to catch the license, one of those old black-and-yellow plates, but it was too late. It was gone before I could make the numbers.

I looked back at the girl again, and stared at her lying there in the middle of the road. Then I felt kind of tired, so I got back in bed and went to sleep.

* * *

The next morning I woke up with a throbbing headache. I reached out and picked up my grungy cargo shorts and an empty beer bottle to use as an ashtray. Thank god I still had a couple cigarettes left in the pack half-crumpled in my shorts.

Just as I was starting to feel the smoke get inside me, my cellphone buzzed. The screen read RESTRICTED NUMBER.

When I pressed call, the guy on the other end said, "Hello, is this Specialist Dunson?"

I paused and said, "Let me guess, you're Army, right?" He laughed and said he was. He introduced himself and asked how I was doing. I told him I'd been fine until he called. "What you need, Staff Sergeant Jessup? You low for your quota or something, you gotta call up med discharges?"

I couldn't figure out what was so goddamn funny about that as he chuckled. Then he wanted to know how things had been going since I got out.

Now I'm pretty sure when this guy signed up, he didn't request to be put on that shit detail, so I let him do his spiel about inactive ready reserve and the National Guard and all that. When he asked me if I was in college or what, I asked him how he got put on this assignment.

He let out a sigh and said, "You know how it is."

Yeah, I laughed. I know exactly how it is.

We went back and forth for a minute, but when he realized there was no way in hell I'd come back, he got all confrontational and started saying if I didn't sign up for the Reserves, the Army'd probably call me back up anyway, and if I didn't go then, I'd go to jail.

That was when I hung up on him. I stubbed out my cigarette and made my way to the window and stared at the street for a while.

*   *   *

I live up on the fifth floor of one of those weekly-monthly low-rent hotels you find all over Los Angeles, one of the old-school ones with the rusty neon signs hanging down the corner of the building. Liquor store on the corner, gang graffiti on the walls, homeless human trash leering over the bus stop bench all hours, church a block away, basically an "up and coming" neighborhood, ripe for gentrification.

It's temporary. Soon as I get a job, the plan is, I'll move someplace nice.

On my way down the stairs and out my building I salute the girl working behind the front desk. She sits there behind bullet-proof glass chain-smoking like she does all day.

Outside the warm sun felt good hitting my skin, and after taking that in for a second I lit up. That's when I noticed my car wasn't parked across the street where I'd left it. I walked over to the empty spot where I always parked and looked around like I'd find some kind of a clue.

No evidence of theft, like shattered glass, car parts, or a hostage note, just a huge oil stain on the ground, either from my POS or from junkers long gone. I could have sworn I parked it here, but maybe not. Maybe I parked it somewhere else and for-got, which I'd done before, I think, I'm not sure. I went looking, up and down every single street around my hotel, two or three times each street just to make sure, and an hour and a half later concluded that my car must have been stolen.

* * *

The nearest precinct was just a few blocks south of world-famous Hollywood Boulevard. The sidewalk is set up just like the Walk of Fame, only instead of stars immortalizing famous people like Michael Jackson, Frank Sinatra, and Donald Duck, they have stars for cops nobody ever heard of.

Inside, the walls were covered with LAPD recruitments posters, no doubt putting grand ideas in the mind of the room's one non-cop inhabitant, a Hollywood runaway in a filthy blue hoodie sitting on a duffle bag. The kid looked up at me with hate-ful eyes burning in a greasy, acne-scarred face, and I gave him a little salute.

The blond officer working behind the counter eyeballed my OIF hat and sat up a bit in his seat, puffing out his chest, and said, "Nice hat."

I nodded. What the fuck do you say to that? Then he tried again: "Were you *over there?*"

"Came back about nine months ago," I said. Then he told me how he had some buddies over there right now, Reservists who got called up, and asked me what branch I was in. I said Army, and he shook his fist at me and shouted back: "Hoo-ah!"

Runaway teen looked over, confused.

I didn't know what to say back—I sure as hell wasn't going to return the hooah—so I just got down to business, the status of my vehicle. We went back and forth and he asked me if I was sure, and I told him positive, I'd checked every street in the neighborhood and it wasn't anywhere, and I'd called downtown and had them run the description and it came back negative.

As I was explaining all this to him, I couldn't help but notice the silver airborne wings clipped to his left shirt pocket. This confused me because, even though the LAPD sometimes ran like a military outfit, I was almost positive they didn't have an airborne unit. After he directed me to the Missing and Stolen Vehicles Department, I pointed at his pin and asked when the LAPD started jumping out of airplanes. He chuckled and told me no, but he'd gone to Airborne school years ago, when he was in the National Guard.

"LAPD lets you wear military badges?"

He sort of hemmed and hawed and said no, not really, but at the same time nobody ever said anything. So I asked him, "You think if I became a cop, they'd let me wear my CIB?"

Standing in front of that recruiting poster, he turned serious. "Why? You interested in being a police officer? We could use men with your training."

"Yeah, I don't think so," I said. "I'm gonna go back to school one of these days. For now I just want a part-time thing, just something to keep me busy."

He shrugged and told me to think about it.

* * *

The Missing and Stolen Vehicles Department office was decorated with movie posters: *Dick Tracy*, *Beverly Hills Cop II*, *Red Heat*, *Miami Vice*, all framed. Then there was a marker board with make, model, location, and date of a bunch of missing vehicles.

Some mustached Tom Selleck–looking guy in civilian clothes greeted me: "How can I help you?"

I told the same exact story I told Airborne, and Tom Selleck pulled out some forms and the two of us went through them. Basic questions like what type of car, when and where did you park it, and so on, and does anybody else have keys?

You could tell he'd done it a million times and could probably do it in his sleep. When he was done he handed me his card and a photocopy of the paperwork so I could file an insurance claim and said if for whatever reason the car did turn up, to not touch it, but to immediately call them, so they could run prints on it. If they found the vehicle they'd call me. He repeated himself: "We'll call you."

Then he said that's that.

I asked what my chances were of getting my car back. He told me you can't predict these kinds of things. "Sometimes a couple days, sometimes a couple months, sometimes never."

* * *

On the way home, I got some coffee and sat in the park, taking a moment to reflect on how shitty my day was going. I was just beginning to wonder if there was maybe something wrong with my life, or with me even, when a large, filthy, middle-aged woman carrying eight or ten plastic bags filled with clothes and trash sat her fat ass on the bench next to me.

She stared at my hat for a minute then asked if I'd served in Iraq. I nodded yes and lit another smoke. She said, "You shouldn't do that," and I threw her a *please, lady, don't fucking talk to me* vibe. Then I took a sip of coffee and she said, "You shouldn't do that either."

I turned and stared. "Can I help you?"

"I'm a vet, too," she said. "I was in the first Gulf War, back in '92. I came back all messed up, and it took 'em three years to figure out I had PTSD and Gulf War Syndrome. How you like that? Three years! Now the goddamned VA's all I got. I bet you smoked a lot in Iraq."

"Yeah," I said. "So?"

"And I bet you drink more coffee now than you used to, huh?"

I thought about that, then told her I did—I was drinking at least a pot a day.

She said I looked hung over and asked if I drank more booze now. I told her, "Yeah, I drink a hell of a lot more now, but maybe that's because I didn't drink at all for a fucking year and now I'm catching up."

More nodding. Then she said to me that when she was getting treated for PTSD at the VA, she learned the reasons why I drank, smoked, and caffeinated so much more since coming back. She explained that while I was in the combat zone, my body, without me knowing it, was releasing a ton of endorphins and adrenaline, even when we weren't doing anything. When I came back, my mind and body were still on that high. My body still needed those endorphins, she said. And so I was seeking out stimulants like caffeine, nicotine, and alcohol to compensate for having lost that feeling.

I thought about that for a second. I wanted to ask her if she was a fat, homeless slob because of the endorphins, but I didn't—

maybe if I'd been drinking whiskey instead of coffee. She told me she missed the war and wished she could go back. I wanted to ask her what she could've possibly done in that bullshit conflict that had anything to do with me, but I just thanked her for her time and excused myself.

As I walked off, she yelled at me that I should get some counseling. "It'll change your life!" she screamed.

*   *   *

Later on that evening, sometime after my sixth or tenth beer, I started hearing them again.

The first couple nights I moved in, I couldn't sleep until they went away. I'd lay down in bed with my eyes closed and just listen. Laughter, giggling, females, conversations, carrying on . . . every now and then you'd hear somebody drop their glass, shattering it into a million pieces, and then they'd laugh.

The nightclub is down on the first floor next door. It has one of those monosyllabic names that's in all lowercase and in the back they have an outdoor patio smoking section . You can't see it from my window, but you can definitely hear it. Last call is always the loudest part of the night, and shortly after that the noise fades and finally disappears. You get so used to the noise, some nights the silence wakes you up, but mostly you just learn to sleep through it. After those first couple nights, I got used it; it was just background noise I hardly paid attention to, like the news about Iraq on TV, but every now and then I'd tune in, wondering what it was like.

Over cigarettes and another beer, I debated for a couple of minutes whether or not to go down and check it out. Finally I said fuck it.

*   *   *

As the harsh light burned into my sleeping eyes the next morning, I decided to work through my hangover by finding a job. A friend of mine had told me about a website that specialized in helping vets get work, which I thought was a brilliant idea and a great way for people to support the troops. My screen flashed with potential:

Cashier (gas station) $8/hr; Telemarketer (must be bright, cheerful and helpful, and punctual!) $11/hr; Office Assistant (Candidate must have prior office experience and possess a professional appearance and attitude) $9/hr; Shipping & Receiving Clerk (Use safety gear, gloves, ear and eye protection in accordance with Company policy) $9.50/hr; Assembly (entry level candidate must be mechanically inclined, have a working knowledge of hand tools, and have the ability to solve simple math problems) DOE Immediate opening!; Warehouse Workers (must have experience working in warehouse) $9–11/hr DOE.

The website also had a feature where you could post your résumé and employers would contact you if they were interested. I set up a profile, posted my résumé, and spent the next hour or so applying for nearly every job posted, then checked out some other listings on Craigslist. I spent most of the day online and slowly, one by one, each one e-mailed me back to tell me the position had been filled, or I didn't have enough experience. Some of them were kind enough to thank me for my service and wish me luck on my search. Some said they'd keep my résumé on file and contact me if anything opened up.

The next day I logged on to see if I'd received any messages. There were two. The first was from the Army National Guard. "Subject: Make Your Next Job the Adventure of a Lifetime!" The other was for a part-time weekend position that paid $9 an hour, holding a sign by the side of the road. "Get paid while listening to music!"

The message said to call if I was interested, so I did. They asked if I could start this weekend. I told him I could. Basically they needed somebody to hold a sign on a street corner downtown to try to get people to stop and look at the open house for these new condos. The job paid cash at the end of the day. They asked if I was interested in this particular line of work, and I said yeah, it sounded great.

They said they needed somebody who was enthusiastic and had a positive attitude, so I told them I possessed both those personality traits. They said that was great and told me where to be on Saturday morning at 8 a.m. They said they looked forward to meeting me. I said I did too.

That night I celebrated by drinking most of a bottle of Dewar's.

* * *

The hangover wasn't as bad as having to get on the bus with the 7 a.m. work crowd. All these Mexicans and black guys and women going to their shitty jobs, looking at me like I was some kind of stain. I closed them out and sipped my coffee and tried to ignore the lurch in my gut every time the bus stopped. Who rides the bus? I pulled my hat down low over my eyes and stared at my feet.

By the time I got off at my stop, I was feeling a little better. I walked two blocks and then through the visitor parking area of Future Sun Condos and into the administrative building where I met Assistant Deputy Manager Marco. We shook hands, and he thanked me for coming down. He also thanked me for my service and said he loved it when he could hire a veteran. I said that was great. He nodded and told me it was good PR for Future Sun Condos. He asked me if I needed anything. I told him I was fine. He said there was some coffee brewed, and I should help myself.

He went and got all the shit for the day, then came back, handed me a red sign with two handles on the back, and told me to follow him. He also had a backpack, which he opened and showed me, saying everything I needed was in there: a pair of gloves, a couple bottles of water, a bottle of sunscreen, and a red T-shirt and baseball hat with FUTURE SUN CONDOS on them. He told me the shirt and hat were my uniform, so I threw on the red shirt and replaced my OIF hat with the FUTURE SUN CONDOS one. I folded my real hat and stuffed it in my cargo pocket with my cigarettes.

"You look great," he said. "A real go-getter."

He led me out to his Range Rover and drove me two blocks to where he wanted me to stand, not far from the bus stop I got off at earlier. On the way, he gave me a detailed briefing on my job responsibilities: "Okay, your job is to stand here on this corner and hold the sign up so people driving by see that we're having an open house. Now the reason why we're paying you nine dollars instead of eight dollars is that we don't want you to stand there with the sign like a lump, but be really animated and dance around, twirl the sign around or do whatever you have to so you grab people's attention, got that?"

He said the gloves were optional, but I should wear them to keep from getting blisters. He took the sign from me and showed me his technique, whirling it and lifting it and shoving it out in front of him like he was a cheerleader. Then he handed it back to me and told me to show him my stuff.

He said, "You should be good at this since you were in the army, and it's just like when you twirl your rifles around and stuff at parades."

I thought for a second about twirling his head off his neck but instead just spun the sign around and did a little quarterback dance. He grinned at me. "Good job, you'll get the hang of it yet. Just keep at it, kid."

I held the sign and moved it around some more, and he told me that was good, but he wanted more feeling, more soul, and I should really go all out. "That's why we let people listen to their Walkman or whatever, so they get in the mood. It's like, just rock out. Like in *Top Gun*."

I nodded.

Then he made sure I had my cellphone and told me to call him if I needed anything. He said he'd be by in a couple hours to check on me and see how I was doing. "Great, thanks," I said, and as he drove off, I stood there on the corner wishing all the kids who thought I was a loser in high school could see me now.

Still, job = money and money = cigarettes, and it got me out of the house, and it was only temporary anyway, so I remembered what the drill sergeants always told me: "Play the Game." I lit a smoke and listened to some music and waved the sign around. It was a great feeling standing there moving my sign up and down like a retard, while cars I'd never be able to afford drove past ignoring me.

At first I jiggled the sign and swung it around, shuffled my feet, tried to pretend I had some dignity, then after a while I just stood there with the sign and jerked up and down. I did that for a couple hours.

When the juice on my iPod ran out I started thinking of movie quotes: "Nothing is over! Nothing! You just don't turn it off! You asked me, I didn't ask you!" "Stanley, see this? This is this. This ain't something else. This is this. From now on, you're on your own." "For me this life is nothing! We had a code, you watch my back, I watch yours. Back here there's nothing!" "Back here I can't even hold a job PARKING CARS!" "June twenty-ninth. I gotta get in shape. Too much sitting has ruined my body. Too much abuse has gone on for too long. From now on there will be fifty pushups each morning, fifty pullups. There will be no more pills, no more bad food, no more destroyers of my body. From now on will be total organization."

Just then a silver Range Rover pulled up to the corner, and it was Marco, looking all pissy. "Hey!" he shouted. "What the hell's going on?! I'm not paying you good money to just stand there! You gotta move that goddamn sign around like I told you! You got that?"

"Roger," I said.

He shook his head and told me he'd be back to check up on me again, and I'd better have that sign moving when he does.

I nodded and started dancing the sign around, then when the Range Rover turned the corner I went back to just standing there. I sorta spaced out, staring at the horizon where the long boulevard and the streetlights and the low smog haze all seemed to melt into a shitty gray nothing, like not even static but just the smear of existence out there on the edge of the concrete. Maybe that was tomorrow, like it was yesterday, even though I kept telling myself that tomorrow was something else, even if I didn't know what it was. The edge of the sky in Los Angeles looked just like the edge of the sky in Iraq, near the cities, the way the oil towers burned off into the air, and the handle on the sign almost for a second felt like the grip of my 240, and I almost felt the Humvee rolling underneath me down the MSR.

Then a white SUV pulled up to the light and I heard this kid ask his J.Crew-looking dad, "Daddy? Why's that man holding a sign?"

J.Crew looks over at me, then looks away, then the light changes, and they drive off.

I can hear him chuckle, driving away: "Why's he holding up a sign, son? Well, he's holding up that sign because that's what happens to people who don't go to college. That's what happens to people who don't have a plan." Or something like that, anyway.

There was a homeless guy pushing a shopping cart full of empties up the street, so I called him over, waving a couple dollar bills. I said I had an emergency to go take care of, and I'd pay him to hold the sign for me. I told him I'd be gone for an hour and when I came back I'd give him another five bucks. He said that's cool, so I gave him the two dollars and handed him the sign and the red hat and the backpack with the sunscreen, and gave him the same instructions my boss gave me. He really went at it, right off the bat, twirling the sign, dancing, jumping, the whole works, a hell of a lot better than I ever could. I told him he was a natural, great job, keep it up.

I put my OIF hat back on and took the next bus back to Hollywood.

* * *

A couple days later, I noticed a 1964 Mercury Comet Caliente parked right across the street from my hotel. I rubbed my eyes, then with my eyes refocused stared at the vehicle. It looked almost exactly like mine. Same color and everything. Only difference was this one had a parking ticket on it, but then when I saw the blue infantry cord hanging from the rearview mirror, I was like *holy fucking shit.*

I raced toward the vehicle to see if there was any damage, and surprisingly there wasn't any. The doors were all unlocked and my duffle bag full of clothes was still right there in the back seat. The only thing I noticed different was that there was pigeon shit all over the hood. That was new.

I pulled out my cellphone and called the number on the card the detective at the station had given me. The cop on the line asked for my location, and I gave him the cross streets. He advised me to wait right there and not touch anything, and they'd send a car down as soon as possible.

I took a seat on the curb and waited patiently. A Mexican lady watered her dead lawn with a hose. Five cigarettes later, a black-and-white rolled up and two of LA's finest stepped out. Both female, and not hard on the eyes either: one dykey-looking brunette and a black chick with a bubble butt.

With her hands on her hips, the black chick asked, "You the guy who found his car?"

"Yeah," I grinned, "that's me."

She asked me what the situation was. I explained, "Well, the situation was, I was just walking down the street, and I looked over and I saw this car parked here, and I was like holy shit, that looks like my car. Then when I walk up to it, I'm like holy shit that *is* my car! And like I checked it out, and I don't think it was stolen or anything because the doors were all unlocked and my duffle bag's still in the back seat."

The brunette cop asked me where I lived. Without even thinking, I turned and pointed, "I live right there, on the fifth floor."

They both stood there and stared at me.

"You mean to tell me that you live in that building right there, on the other side of the street, and you don't remember parking your car here?"

Searching for the right words to explain to them the situation, I said, "I know, I know this looks bad, but I swear to fucking god, I didn't park my car here."

The black chick cop walked over to my vehicle and looked inside of it and asked, "Do you drink much?"

I started to say I didn't drink, not really, when out of nowhere the brunette cop asked, "You in the military?"

After a second I realized I had my OIF hat on and said, "Yeah. I was. I'm out now. I'm an Iraq vet." I pointed at the hat.

The two of them nodded together like they just solved a Rubik's Cube. Black chick cop shook her head. "All you guys come back, get drunk, get DUI's, or get so wasted you don't even remember where you parked. Then when you find your car, you waste our time by having us come down and do all the paperwork. That's some shit, soldier. That's what they teach you in the army?"

"Officer, I swear to fucking god, I did not park my vehicle here."

But they just rolled their eyes and asked if I knew a guy named Jim Evans. I told them no, and the brunette said that's funny, because they got a call from him just that morning saying he found his car, and when they showed up, he was like, "Oh, I just got back from Iraq. I got so wasted I forgot where I parked it. Ha, Ha. Sorry!"

Then we filled out the paperwork on the hood of their car. We chatted a little more, and I couldn't help but think about their hair all pulled back and that tough-ass attitude, and the way the black chick cop's butt filled out her uniform trousers. Maybe I should look into becoming a cop.

I asked the black chick cop, "So, you have a number I should call if something comes up?"

"9-1-1, hero," she said. "Don't drink and drive, alright?"

"Roger," I said. Then they got in their car and drove off.

I got in mine, rolled down the window, and grabbed the parking ticket off the windshield. I started the engine and turned on the radio. There was this song I'd never heard before, talking about some girl and how things were gonna change. I lit a smoke and rolled out, headed for who knows where—somewhere, anyway.

Down on the floor of the passenger side, I noticed some In-N-Out wrappers. At first I didn't pay too much attention, but then they started bugging me. I didn't even eat at In-N-Out, couldn't remember the last time I went there. I started to wonder if maybe some kids had jacked the car to go joyriding and pick up some drive-thru. Then while I was idling at a red light it slowly dawned on me, bits and pieces of this dream I had the other night where I walked into this In-N-Out totally wasted. I demanded that they super-size my meal, and the hajji dude behind the counter kept on telling me they didn't do the "super size." I kept arguing with him then finally got my food and smashed my Coke all over the floor and shouted, "Fuck this shit!" Then it had this weird part, the dream, where I stumbled out of the In-N-Out while everybody else in line just stared at me, and it was just like when I got back from Iraq and there was the same line of staring faces saying welcome home.

8

TELEVISION

Roman Skaskiw

IT'D BEEN A DAY SINCE THE ATTACK, and Lieutenant Sugar had not had a chance to see if Joe was okay. Sergeant Joe Zabitosky, aka Sergeant Alphabet, was a squad leader in Lieutenant Sugar's platoon. He and his squad were hit with an IED after picking up a scout team and returning along Route Lion. It demolished a windshield and rang eardrums, but there was no follow-up ambush, there were no secondary IEDs, and it was just a single blast between trucks—not a daisy chain of detonations. No one was hurt, just a local kid they shot.

Lieutenant Sugar wasn't there when the IED went off because he and his two other squads were guarding a knot of highways called "the Mixing Bowl." It had been getting more dangerous for convoys rolling through, and his platoon had been working in shifts, watching cars go by and waiting for something, anything, to happen. When Sergeant Alphabet's squad was hit, Lieutenant Sugar got his map board out and waited for a break in the radio chatter to see if they needed support. They didn't.

Lieutenant Sugar sat there drinking warm water from a dusty bottle and watching traffic while he thought about his squad leader and about his own role as a newly minted officer. Of course Sergeant Alphabet could handle it, but still, Lieutenant Sugar felt responsible. He didn't know if guys would take it hard, like they do on television. They'd been in the country for five months now and their big moment of truth hadn't yet come. Maybe this was the moment. And maybe he just missed the whole thing.

Since taking over the platoon, Sugar struggled with his third squad leader—the big, loud staff sergeant named Joe Zabitosky, Sergeant Alphabet. The guy came on too strong, pushed his soldiers too hard—in physical training, in the cleanliness of their weapons, in being at the right place at the right time. All these were virtues, sure, but his soldiers were scared of him. They were timid. And he was defensive too. "Don't talk to my men," Sergeant Alphabet once told Sugar, "talk to me. I'm their squad leader."

It happened during a field problem back at Fort Bragg. Sugar had just taken over the platoon, and Alphabet said it loud and angry in front of the soldiers. Sugar made the mistake of not settling it then and there. Instead, he raised the issue with his platoon sergeant, Sergeant First Class McPherson, who had a talk with Alphabet. Humiliating. Sugar felt determined to not let it happen again. Not now. Not here, in Iraq.

Lieutenant Sugar didn't see what happened with the attack, and he didn't see what happened afterward, but he had a sense of it. After five months of other companies and platoons seeing action of their own, he had a sense of how things worked.

* * *

When the attack was reported over the radio, a breathless private sprinted from the Tactical Operations Center to the Aid Station where the battalion surgeon, Major Roscoe, watched a DVD with the medics. Scraps of cardboard shaded the windows of their hooch, and the blue light from the television shone on their faces. Two medics watched from their cots, a third sat in a plastic lawn chair. Major Roscoe sat in his camping chair. He lifted the DVD remote from a mesh cup holder, paused the movie, and faced the private. He asked how long ago it happened, how many people were hurt, and what injuries there were. All the medics looked up.

He couldn't answer. He sprinted back to the Tactical Operations Center holding his slung M4 carbine against his hip with one arm, and swinging the other as he ran.

Major Roscoe and the medics turned back to the movie, but it wasn't there the same way it had been. When the private returned and told them a local boy was coming with a head wound, they turned off the television and walked to the bay to prepare for the boy's arrival.

* * *

As Sergeant Alphabet's patrol re-entered the wire, one of the scouts held a bandage against the boy's ear. The other had gotten an IV started and held the bag up to keep the drip going. Guys from Alphabet's squad saw the boy show his teeth. His shoulders climbed up to his ears, and his feet and hands curled into tight claws and stayed that way.

After giving the kid to the medics, Sergeant Alphabet had to see the battalion intelligence officer, who kept him waiting in a corridor, then sat down next to him with a legal pad and, in a tired voice, asked him what happened. He took occasional notes and twice reminded Sergeant Alphabet to limit his explanation to observable facts. "It looked like he set it off," Sergeant Alphabet said, "so I shot him."

Sergeant Alphabet was directed to the Colonel's office.

"He wants to see me?" Alphabet asked.

"He wants to see every patrol leader who makes contact," the intelligence officer said.

The Colonel was a small, neat, aggressive man. He ate a riblet dinner from a paper tray, dipping spoonfuls of corn into a bright red sauce. He spoke between bites and hurried because of the staff meeting he'd called to prepare for the big upcoming mission. They planned to bring everything on this one: Apaches, fixed wing. This would be the biggest one yet.

The Colonel apologized for having to hurry and wiped his lips many times with a napkin. He told Sergeant Alphabet how important it was to get these guys when they hit us. "Hit them right back," he said, "or else they'll keep coming." And while he made it very clear that Sergeant Alphabet did nothing wrong, he encouraged him to think about what he could have done differently, if anything at all, that would have resulted in getting these guys, or in not hurting the kid, unless of course the kid set off the IED. "In that case," the Colonel said, "shooting him was the right answer."

"Yes, sir," Sergeant Alphabet said. "Yes, sir. Yes, sir. Yes, sir."

"It's like we're a bunch of pussies," Sergeant Alphabet later told his platoon sergeant, Sergeant First Class McPherson. "I do my job and everybody acts like I pissed in their Cheerios."

The tired intelligence officer wrote a number on a red sticker and pressed it onto a satellite image already marked with many red, yellow, green, and blue stickers. Neither he, nor the Colonel, nor Alphabet, or Lieutenant Sugar, who was still at the Mixing Bowl, heard the medevac helicopter touching down, or, seconds later, lifting off with the kid. It was just another sound, and not one of the important ones like the whomp of incoming.

The last person to talk to Sergeant Alphabet about the incident that day was the Sergeant Major, the senior enlisted man at their base—what had once been an Iraqi meat processing plant and was still known to both locals and soldiers as "the Chicken Factory."

The Sergeant Major was the rare kind: his knees and back weren't destroyed despite having been a paratrooper for as long as many of the battalion's soldiers had been alive. He could still run and move. He was a big man who probably landed hard on jumps, and that made his vitality all the more impressive. He wasn't quite as tall as Sergeant Alphabet, but thicker. He had the muscled forearms of a major league shortstop and put one of those tattooed limbs around Sergeant Alphabet's shoulders. He pointed at Alphabet's chest with his other hand.

"If you ever have any doubts about what's the right thing to do," he said, "just remember that your job is to bring these boys home. None of us got hurt. That's the important thing."

Sergeant Alphabet said, "Roger that, Sergeant Major," and the Sergeant Major clapped him on the back and told him to get some sleep.

The colors of evening drained from the sky and the night was chilly. The last call to prayer sounded from a nearby mosque, a distant wail, and a wind rattled loose sheets in the tin roof of the warehouse.

The next day at about thirteen hundred, Lieutenant Sugar pushed aside the canvas flap of Sergeant Alphabet's tent and saw him lying on his cot, his size thirteen boots pointing to either side. He wore headphones. A CD-player rested on his chest, and his hands were interlocked over it.

Two fluorescent bulbs lit the tent. There was a row of cots on each side, cardboard box nightstands, and equipment under the cots and hanging from nails in the wood tent-frame. At the far end of the tent, Specialist Tommie slept on his side wrapped in a sleeping bag. Sergeant Alphabet's eyes were closed.

"What's going on?" Lieutenant Sugar asked, and when no one heard him, he said louder, "What's going on, Joe?" pretending that he just entered and was asking for the first time.

Sergeant Alphabet saw Lieutenant Sugar. He pulled a headphone from one ear and said, "Oh, not much, sir."

After a pause, Lieutenant Sugar asked, "You doing okay?" Alphabet startled at the question. "Of course I'm doing okay."

"The boss says I have to go make nice with the kid's family."

"Great," Sergeant Alphabet said.

"I want you to come with me."

"You want *me* to go?"

Lieutenant Sugar nodded. He didn't want to explain every decision to his subordinate. That shows a lack of confidence, he thought.

Sergeant Alphabet shrugged. "Just say when, sir."

"Probably tomorrow. Early. So we can get back inside the wire and prep for the big mission."

Sergeant Alphabet nodded and when Lieutenant Sugar didn't say anything else, he put his headphone back in and pressed a button on his CD Player.

Lieutenant Sugar sat on an adjacent cot and flipped through the small stack of CDs on Sergeant Alphabet's nightstand, pretending to be interested.

"Ser-geant Alph-a-bet!" The voice of their platoon sergeant, Sergeant First Class McPherson, boomed from the other side of the warehouse.

At the far end of the tent, Specialist Tommie lifted his head and listened like an alert deer. The whole chain of command had been on his case ever since he lost accountability of some spare weapons parts.

"Ser-geant Alph-a-bet!" Sergeant First Class McPherson called again, his voice closer.

Confident he wasn't needed, Specialist Tommie lowered his head and went back to sleep.

Sergeant Alphabet rotated up on his cot, setting his big feet on the floorboards. He removed the headphones from his ears and wrapped the cord around his CD Player. He placed it gently in the shoebox beneath his cot, then took his M4 carbine from where it hung on a nail and exited through the canvas flap.

Sergeant First Class McPherson had just been told about an upcoming issue of cold-weather clothes and needed to update the platoon's roster of sizes. He communicated this to Sergeant Alphabet who said "roger" and went to find his squad. His guys were taking their turn on the wire, and he would make the rounds and double-check their sizes.

The tent felt empty. Lieutenant Sugar walked to the far end where Specialist Tommie slept, then back. He listened to his footfalls on the floorboards.

He's a rough one, Sugar thought, but he's got a soul like everyone else. He'll go with me and not talk back. It's a tragedy, this thing, sure, but my duty is to make the Iraqis understand that we've come to help them with freedom, and honor, and duty. Courage, Sugar thought.

A little plastic dog tag printed with the Army values dangled from Sugar's neck, beside the stainless steel ones bearing his name, social, blood type, and religion.

Sugar exited and walked to his own tent where he lived with Sergeant First Class McPherson. He reread a letter from his girlfriend. It was chatty and all wrong. He read carefully, looking for an undercurrent of pity and longing. The hell with that, he told himself. I have responsibilities to worry about. I have people relying on me. He read the letter again. It was all wrong.

* * *

On the way to dinner, Lieutenant Sugar and Sergeant First Class McPherson spoke about the upcoming mission. Rumors had been circulating about their platoon being the main effort. They'd supposedly be going after two high-value targets. The similar mission they'd done turned out to be a dry hole, but that didn't stop everybody's anticipation, nerves. "This might be the one," Sugar told his platoon sergeant. "Whether it is or it ain't, let's make sure the boys are ready," said McPherson. Together, Lieutenant Sugar and Sergeant First Class McPherson led and ran Second Platoon. Sugar was glad he could speak freely to his platoon sergeant.

They ate their riblet dinners, mopping up bright red sauce with dry pieces of Wonder Bread, then filled their pockets with packets of peanut butter and jelly, grabbed a loaf of bread, and returned to their hooch.

Lieutenant Sugar asked his platoon sergeant if he felt like a little *Halo* action. He did, and they set up. Lieutenant Sugar carried over a pair of plastic lawn chairs and switched on the television and Xbox.

It'd been great since their forward operating base got a second school-bus-sized generator. Power was now reliable enough for long games of *Halo* on Xboxes, or *Madden* on PlayStations. But now more soldiers found reason to travel the thirty miles out of their way during patrols to the big base at Baghdad International, where they stuffed themselves in fancy KBR chow halls, ogled the many female soldiers, and returned with satellite receivers, televisions, DVD players, game systems, and all the junk food they could carry, and the load was showing signs of being too much for even the two school-bus-sized generators that hummed 24/7 between the warehouse and the wall of the base.

SFC McPherson poured hot water into two mugs and the room filled with a warm, sweet smell. Sugar used a pen to stir the cocoa smooth. He pulled off his boots. This, finally, was living.

Sugar let his platoon sergeant get the first few kills because he wanted to keep things competitive. After the previous night, he didn't want SFC McPherson to become discouraged and quit their semi-regular games. Soon, they were both laughing and cursing and swaying their bodies as their characters ducked, ran, and threw hand grenades at one another on the television screen.

Eventually, Sergeant First Class McPherson went to sleep, and Lieutenant Sugar turned to a newspaper he'd received in the mail. He just looked at it and didn't read. Then he folded it along its original creases and set it atop a plank of wood that rested on two cinder blocks and served as a shelf. He placed it atop novels sent by various friends. Novels he really did intend to read. He put his boots back on and went outside.

Tommie was in the motor pool dragging a heavy plastic chest out of the quadcon. He wore a headlamp that illuminated his nose, lips, and chin, and had a cigarette in the corner of his mouth. His M4 carbine lay on the ground beside the connex, resting on his uniform blouse. He wore a T-shirt and sweated in the chilly night. He was in trouble all the way up to the Sergeant Major for losing accountability of the spare weapons parts.

"What's up, Tommie?" Lieutenant Sugar called.

Tommie dropped the chest. He had a habit of grinning that made Lieutenant Sugar do the same.

"I heard you and the Sergeant Major having a chat a little while ago. Something about weapons parts."

"Oh you heard that did you, sir?" Tommie giggled. "Yeah, old Willie and me were having a talk about the importance of proper accountability of Army equipment. He wanted me to blow it off, but I think I talked some sense into him."

Lieutenant Sugar loved Tommie.

"Is that what he wanted?"

"Yeah, sir. I really had to put my foot down. I said, 'Look here Willie, I'm gonna find those parts, even if it takes me all night.'" He giggled. "It's a good thing he backed down too. For a second there I thought I was gonna have to get loud with him."

Tommie offered Lieutenant Sugar a cigarette. He took one and lit it with the lighter from his pocket and inhaled the harsh smoke into his lungs, then blew it out through his nose. He didn't cough.

"There," He said. "How did that look? I've been practicing"

"Not bad, sir. I'll have you addicted in no time. But it'll take dedication."

"Oh, I'm dedicated."

"That's good, sir. Speaking of which, I got some weapons parts to find." He got up, and began carrying more things from the connex: windshields, bags of uniforms, an enormous box of toilet paper.

Lieutenant Sugar smoked and watched him. Tommie worked inside the Conex with his headlamp while he sucked the cigarette without pulling the harsh smoke into his lungs.

He sat on the plastic chest and looked at the rows of Humvees and five-tons in the motor pool. A soldier from his company paced back and forth with an axe handle on his shoulder. They suspected the guys in Alpha Company of swiping parts from their vehicles but had yet to catch the dirty bastards in the act. A row of tracers rose slowly in the sky and winked out one after the next, and Lieutenant Sugar watched for more but didn't see any. It was nothing.

"I want you to come with me tomorrow morning on a little mission I got. You'll be my driver."

Tommie was dragging another chest along the concrete. He set it down. "Hoo-ah, sir. You know I'm gonna be looking for those weapons parts all night."

"I know," said Lieutenant Sugar.

"You say run, Tommie say how far. You say shit, Tommie say what color."

"We're leaving at oh-six-hundred. You'll drive me in Delta Six," Lieutenant Sugar said, naming the commander's vehicle.

"And then Tommie will polish that turd and put a ribbon on it and pretend it smells like roses."

Tommie continued unloading the connex, and Lieutenant Sugar finished his cigarette.

"Need a hand?"

"Nah, sir, this is supply work. I don't think you infantry guys could handle it."

Lieutenant Sugar saw his grin lit by the downward light of his headlamp.

"That's why they sent me," Tommie continued, "to look after you all, and keep you out of trouble. I don't know what this company would do without me."

"I don't either, Tommie."

* * *

Lieutenant Sugar wore his watch when he slept, and when he woke at three, morning was still infinitely far away. He went back to sleep and forgot about the kid and the mission. He fell asleep imagining his girlfriend unbuttoning his uniform, then woke up at four thirty with morning too close to ignore and lay there, trying to sleep until he heard the company radio guard walk hesitantly into the tent.

"Sir?" he said, "I was supposed to wake you, sir."

Lieutenant Sugar rose from his warm sleeping bag and dressed quietly in the darkness so Sergeant First Class McPherson's sleep wouldn't be disturbed.

The ponchos bungee-corded around the heavy weapons to keep the dust out were removed and tucked away in the beds of the gun trucks. Heavy boxes of ammunition were mounted to the gun cradles beside the automatic grenade launchers and heavy machine guns, and the belts of ammunition were draped into their chambers. Shoulder-fired anti-tank rockets, which could also destroy bunkers and knock down structures, were lifted from the bed and fixed with their shoulder straps around the open hatches of the gunners' turrets.

Sugar tied his boots and walked to the motor pool where Sergeant Alphabet had his trucks running and his men ready to go. Tommie was there too, wearing a tired grin.

Lieutenant Sugar dropped his kit in the passenger seat of Delta Six.

"I'm going to get the terp. Meet me at the gate. I'll be right there."

"We got to go, sir," Sergeant Alphabet said.

"I'll be right there."

Sergeant Alphabet directed the four Humvees to the gate, and Lieutenant Sugar went to wake Stuttering John.

He opened the door of the interpreter's hooch. A battery-operated lantern cast shadows about the room. It hummed on the floor beside one of the interpreters who prayed on his rug. Stuttering John was asleep. Despite his grey hair and wrinkled face, Stuttering John looked like a young boy as he slept. Another interpreter prayed, and Lieutenant Sugar said nothing to him. He shook Stuttering John's shoulder and the old Iraqi man woke. Lieutenant Sugar watched him sit up and put his feet on the floor. He wore long underwear and looked around like he didn't know where he was.

"Are you awake?"

He nodded.

"I have a difficult mission. I want you to come with me. You. No one else. I need your help." Lieutenant Sugar spoke in short phrases, in the tempo of an Arab's broken English.

"Would you like some tea?"

"There is no time."

"No breakfast?"

"No time. I have an MRE for you in the truck."

Stuttering John found his glasses. "I need to pee," he said, and rubbed his face.

"There is little time. We leave as soon as you are ready."

Stuttering John nodded again and looked back and forth, as though he'd lost something.

"It is a difficult one. I do not like this mission."

Stuttering John dressed, his face puffy and expressionless.

"We have to find the family of a child and speak to them," Lieutenant Sugar said. "We shot the child yesterday. Sent him by helicopter to the hospital. I'll talk. You just translate. I need you because you are the best."

Stuttering John was the best. He translated, and almost never entered into his own conversations with locals.

He buttoned his shirt and put a cap on his head. He stood up straight, stomped one foot on the floor, and raising his chin said, "Sir, I am ready, sir." The other interpreter continued to pray by his lantern.

The two gate guards spoke with Sergeant Alphabet. They probably heard about the IED. "This is bullshit," Lieutenant Sugar heard Sergeant Alphabet say. "First these fuckers try to kill us, and now we got to drive down that same fucking road to kiss their asses."

* * *

Outside the main gate, a row of laborers sat on the ground against the wall, waiting for the escort who would watch them spend the day spreading piles of gravel over the field. The cooks worked busily over stoves beside the chow hall, and in the motor pool, a mechanic leaned all his weight against a torque wrench.

Lieutenant Sugar climbed into Delta Six and called a radio check with Alphabet.

The SAW gunners clipped drums of ammunition to their weapons and kept at least three more drums on their persons. Riflemen, including Sergeant Alphabet and Lieutenant Sugar, opened their optics and adjusted the size of the little red dot. They slapped magazines into their weapons. Frag grenades fit into pouches specially designed for the body armor, or beside the magazines in the old-style pouches some soldiers still used. Concussion grenades didn't fit anywhere and were often reinforced with hundred-mile-an-hour tape and tucked by their spoons into the loops on a soldier's body armor, or else they were kept inside the vehicles with their spoons around a taut piece of five-fifty cord that ran along the windshield. Smoke grenades were kept in a similar way, arranged by color so they could be quickly found—or as quickly as is possible in the confusion of the mysterious event called contact.

A gate guard scribbled some marks in his ledger, then dragged the strand of concertina wire out of the way.

The gate lifted. As they rolled through, SAW gunners slid the charging handles on their machine guns back and forward and each rifleman let the bolt of his carbine slam forward, chambering a round. The gunners in the turrets slammed the feed tray covers down on their heavy machine guns and automatic grenade launchers. The gunner on the lead vehicle waved his palms toward the traffic on the highway until it came to a stop, and the convoy rolled into the middle lane of Route Lion.

A few locals were already out in the market. The first merchants removed the thatched grass mats from the fronts of their stalls. White chickens fluttered in their cages and a cool dampness hung in the air. Stuttering John pulled his cap lower and didn't look out the window.

They veered off Route Lion after the market and drove along dirt roads, snaking between farms. Sergeant Alphabet was in the lead vehicle looking at his GPS. They came upon two mud houses partially concealed by a small grove of date palms.

Sugar saw their thick, sturdy walls. The houses were all by themselves and surrounded by fields, which was good. Soldiers could see far in every direction. The Humvees drove to two adjacent corners and all the soldiers but the gunners dismounted. Tommie cut the engine of Delta Six and dismounted with the shotgun.

Two Iraqis ran toward them from far out in the field, and Lieutenant Sugar asked Stuttering John to exit the vehicle. The figures dropped their shovels as they ran and lifted their legs to make progress in the soft, loose ground. Sergeant Alphabet stood beside Lieutenant Sugar.

Their backs were to the little houses, but Tommie covered them with the shotgun.

The first of the two was a woman. She stopped several meters from them. Lieutenant Sugar could see she had tears in her eyes already.

"Well, fuck me," said Sergeant Alphabet.

Sugar was thinking that too. He removed his helmet so they could see his face and clipped it by the chinstrap to his body armor. He removed his ballistic sunglasses and stuffed them into a cargo pocket.

The woman clapped her hands together and shook them at Lieutenant Sugar. She was saying something. She canted her head and kept saying it in a loud, wailing voice with her hands clasped together like she was begging. The second of them, a man, put his hands on her shoulders and turned her away from them. They exchanged words as Lieutenant Sugar watched. He glanced at Stuttering John and saw by his expressions that he understood everything they said.

"Is this the piece of shit whose feelings we hurt?" Sergeant Alphabet said.

The woman wore a shawl over her head and layers of rags wrapped thick around her legs and held with pieces of wire. The man was lightly dressed for the morning's cold. His skinny legs and bare feet were grey with the mud of his field.

The man held his woman by the wrist and called to Stuttering John who said something back to him and gestured with an open palm toward Lieutenant Sugar. Lieutenant Sugar was familiar with this gesture. It was time for him to say something.

The field was bare, and the earth was broken and soft. It extended some distance to an irrigation canal where tall thick grass rose from the mud. Route Lion could be seen beyond it. The farmers both looked at Lieutenant Sugar.

He stepped toward the man. Stuttering John and Sergeant Alphabet came with him, the three of them advancing in a rank.

"Are these the parents?" Lieutenant Sugar asked Stuttering John.

"Sir, I am sure of it," Stuttering John said without having spoken to the farmer.

Lieutenant Sugar offered his hand to the man, they shook, and Sugar put his hand over his heart in accordance with Arab custom. The woman began shouting again from behind her husband, and he said something over his shoulder at her.

"Tell him my name is Lieutenant Sugar."

Stuttering John told him.

"Sir, he want to know how is his son."

The farmer had a thick mustache and a deeply furrowed face and two hard eyes.

"Tell him that I was not here when it happened, but I know what happened, and today I drove here to meet him face to face and to tell about his son."

"He says thank you and praise be to God and like this, and he want to know about his son."

"Tell him that we sent his son to the hospital."

The farmer's eyes still looked at Lieutenant Sugar. Behind him a car drove down Route Lion past the big gash in the road.

"Tell him that we sent him to the best American hospital."

Stuttering John told him.

"By helicopter," added Lieutenant Sugar. He was glad for the helicopter.

The woman had a lot to say. She said it loud and without any holding back.

Stuttering John hesitated, said something back to her, and she replied with the same ferocity.

"Sir," he said to Lieutenant Sugar, but the woman was not finished.

She was waving her hands all over the place, and Lieutenant Sugar and Sergeant Alphabet watched her hands. Sergeant Alphabet asked Lieutenant Sugar if he wanted him to control her.

"No, not yet," Lieutenant Sugar replied. "Tell him that I want to just speak with him."

Stuttering John told them, and the woman quieted again.

"No, tell him that I want to speak with him alone. I don't want her here."

There was a debate between the farmers, and the man took the woman to the house. She pleaded with him, using the same gestures as she'd used with Lieutenant Sugar earlier. When the farmer returned, Lieutenant Sugar took out two cigarettes he'd bummed from Tommie and offered one. He lit his own, then passed the lighter to the farmer who cupped his hands to shield the flame from the breeze.

Sergeant Alphabet kept an eye on the house where the woman was.

"Sir, he say you can speak with him honestly. He only wants to know only what is the truth. How is his son? Is he alive? Is he dead?"

"Tell him he is wounded seriously. Tell him that is why we called the helicopter."

The man asked again if his son was alive.

"Tell him he was alive when he left the Chicken Factory."

"Sir, he want to know how is he hurt?"

"I don't know," Lieutenant Sugar lied. "Tell him he was shot, that's all I know. He was shot because soldiers think he set off the bomb. Tell him that I wanted to come here and talk, even though I think his son set off the bomb."

The farmer who'd been looking intently into Lieutenant Sugar's face with his two hard eyes turned toward his fields when

Stuttering John finished. He smoked. Lieutenant Sugar pulled on his cigarette without inhaling the harsh smoke. Sugar wondered if the kid had, in fact, set off the IED.

They looked across the field, over the irrigation canal to Route Lion. It was black and straight where it showed between the reeds of the irrigation canal. Most of the field had dry stalks ploughed into the grey earth. In spots, they stood crooked in the ground. The two of them looked for a long time and smoked.

The farmer turned back and said something and Stuttering John replied in Arabic, and they went back and forth.

"Sir, he says it is good for you to come. And he says like this that it is a very bad thing, but good for you to come and if you will have tea, and I told him you are very busy, and he says if we can come sit inside."

"Tell him no tea."

There were bundles of dried reeds beside the house. The trucks outside could see far in every direction. Lieutenant Sugar asked Sergeant Alphabet to make sure he had communication with the trucks through his hand radio. In their body armor, they brushed both sides of the low, narrow doorway.

A young boy who looked like he'd been suddenly awakened stared at them with wide eyes and open mouth. He looked torn between fear and curiosity. Their eyes adjusted to the dim light, and more of the room became apparent. There was a crooked bench along one wall, two chests, and a pile of blankets on the floor that looked like they'd just been slept in. The far wall did not quite reach its adjacent one, and the space served as the doorway to the next room from which they heard a woman's sobbing.

The farmer gestured lavishly toward the bench, and Stuttering John and Lieutenant Sugar sat down. Sergeant Alphabet remained standing by the entrance. The boy stared at all his equipment. He watched Sergeant Alphabet speak into the radio on his shoulder to do another commo check with the vehicles outside.

The farmer removed a ball of cloth from the hole in the mud wall, which served as a window. A little bit of cold morning light shone through. He placed a lantern on the floor, kneeled beside it, and pumped it vigorously. It lit and he stayed on his knees in front of Lieutenant Sugar and Sugar felt like coming inside was a mistake. He didn't want hospitality from a poor farmer whose son they'd shot.

The farmer looked from Sugar to Stuttering John and spoke.

"Sir, he says again for you to have some tea."

"Tell him no thank you, we have a busy morning."

The farmer said something again, and Stuttering John answered, shaking his head. The farmer paused a moment and said something.

"Sir, he say how can he go see his son."

The sobbing from the next room quieted.

Lieutenant Sugar knew the names of the towns between here and the base to which the boy was likely sent, and he explained it through Stuttering John.

"He knows now," said Stuttering John. "If I could suggest something, sir."

Lieutenant Sugar nodded.

"Maybe a note he can show the soldier at the gate, so they will let him go."

The boy leaned over the heat of the lantern and looked from Lieutenant Sugar to Sergeant Alphabet with his mouth open. Sergeant Alphabet stood by the front door. He rolled his shoulders under the weight of his body armor.

Lieutenant Sugar pulled a notepad from his cargo pocket and the farmer watched him scribble a note. He signed it with his name and rank and dated it, then tore it from his notepad.

"This is bullshit. You should tell him that if his other kid ever tries to blow me up, I'll shoot him too. And if I have to shoot that little fucker, I'll make sure I kill him so we don't have to go through all this shit."

Lieutenant Sugar handed the scrap of paper to the farmer who folded it carefully and held it lightly between two fingers.

Stuttering John looked at Sergeant Alphabet but didn't hold his gaze when Sergeant Alphabet looked back. No one said anything and the farmer held the note.

Lieutenant Sugar asked Sergeant Alphabet to leave.

"Hooah, sir. I'll be outside," he said.

Lieutenant Sugar made a second note with his name on it and told Stuttering John to tell the farmer that if he has problems, he should come to the Chicken Factory and show this to the guard. Lieutenant Sugar said goodbye in Arabic and put his hand over his heart.

Stuttering John touched Lieutenant Sugar's arm as they exited the farmer's home. "You are a good man," he said. Lieutenant Sugar's mind was elsewhere. He went outside and saw Sergeant Alphabet walking from one gun truck to the other. He could tell by his stride and by the way he carried his weapon that he was preparing the guys for the trip back.

That's why they sent me, Lieutenant Sugar told himself. Sometimes you're handed a piece of shit and the best you can do is put a ribbon on it and pretend it smells like roses.

During the return trip, Tommie talked about those grey, wrinkled sausages they served in the chow hall and how they sounded pretty good about now, and Sugar felt glad he brought him as a driver.

He thought about his girlfriend. It'd be nice to sit down with her and hear her voice for a little while. She was very beautiful, and he wanted to look at her and spend a little time with her before the big mission. It'd be nice to go for a slow walk on that sandy trail beneath the pines, as they had in North Carolina before he left. He decided that as soon as he got back inside the wire, he'd re-read the last letter from her.

*   *   *

At eleven hundred local time, Lieutenant Sugar received his mission from Captain Yona. He made a plan, and two hours later, gave his operations order to his squad leaders. He sat on his cot and referred frequently to a map and satellite photos spread on the floor between them. He pointed to his first squad leader's chest.

"Task," he said, "provide security for the main effort. Purpose. Facilitate their movement to building zebra one one."

"Third squad." He pointed at Sergeant Alphabet's chest. "Task. Clear buildings zebra one one through zebra one four."

Sergeant Alphabet wrote intently in his notebook.

Lieutenant Sugar pointed at him again. "Purpose. Kill, capture, and deny sanctuary to insurgent forces."

Lieutenant Sugar completed his order and asked if there were any questions. There were none. His squad leaders gathered their M4s and boonie caps and pocketed their little notebooks and pencils. No more distractions, Sugar thought. Everybody's thinking about doing their jobs and staying alive. A small part of him was excited at the possibility of finally making contact with the enemy, finally seeing what war was all about.

9

NEW ME

Andrew Slater

I JOINED THE ARMY AFTER MY GIRLFRIEND RENEE drowned because I felt that some people in my hometown would be unable to not blame me. Something would have seemed wrong with the world if they didn't. The Army was a way for me to leave Elberton for good without seeming like I was making a big spectacle out of it. Renee's dad called me up about a week after the funeral to ask me why I didn't go in after her. His voice was calm on the phone when he said it. It sounded like he was reading the question off a piece of paper he was holding with both hands. I think he'd been trying to not say it for a while.

By the time I realized she must be down river I couldn't see her at all. I had just got back to the riverbank from my car with a pair of foam water noodles and a CD player. I had been scrounging around in the back seat of my Corolla trying to find a CD, something I wanted her to hear. I stood there staring at the flat top of the river, unblemished blue-brown between the cat tails, a foot or two higher than normal with the past week's rain, but the water was quiet that morning. There was a clear, quiet sky. I never made sense of it.

She picked that spot of the river because it was on her bus route in fifth grade, before her parents got divorced and she moved into an apartment with her mom. It was our tenth date, and she used to put her hand on my arm and lean in to tell me some thought that had struck her in a way that meant a great deal to me. The spot she picked was a sunny bend of the river below the pastures, miles of flat grazing land in all directions dotted by round, browning bales, and she had always wanted the bus to break down there so all the kids could go swimming and miss school. Some fishermen found her on a sandbar a few miles down, and the paper put "All-State Swimmer" on her obituary, like that wasn't adding insult to injury.

* * *

Nine years later, I was finally discharged from the brain injury clinic at Walter Reed. Before I was leaving, I had a final, obligatory meeting with my overworked neurologist that was more of an informal send-off than a working session. I had told him that I originally enlisted because my favorite uncle served as a Seabee in Vietnam, which was only partially true, because he wasn't my favorite. The neurologist arrived at our meeting wearing a referee uniform that was a size too small because he was on his way to his daughter's soccer game, and he said that all the parents had to share the same uniform.

We met at a picnic table in a courtyard I had never been to before. He said he enjoyed the cherry trees there, but I found the people and noise around us a bit distracting. I had forgotten the question I wanted to ask him, which was maybe not a question as much as it was a list of things that still did not seem to make sense. Instead, I just started describing my latest dream.

"So this time we were driving across the Atlantic Ocean in our gun trucks, all the way back," I said.

"You mean, over a bridge across the Atlantic or something?" he asked. "I should mention this would be a great starting point for your new therapist when you get to your new home in Virginia, but you might find it more helpful to focus on your daily life with him. Or her, of course."

"No, it wasn't a bridge. We were driving over the ice. The whole Atlantic was frozen over. There was this flat sheet of ice we were driving on, and you could feel it vibrate because of the waves underneath the ice. We were driving real slow since the traction was bad, even with chains on our tires. As far as you could see it was just ice. And then there were these shantytowns we were driving past on the ice, which had palm tree chimneys whose roots reached under the ice, and you can see them stretching down. Our trucks were airtight so they stunk like diesel."

"This is with the no-mouth people again?" he asked. "You should actually take comfort in the fact that your short-term memory is retaining your dreams so vividly. That's probably encouraging."

"No, I never see any people this time," I told him. "But the reason we're afraid of the bombs is not because they will kill us directly, but because we'll fall through the ice. My truck hits this bomb—I hear a bang and there's water spray and bubbles everywhere—and the back end of my truck falls through a hole in the ice. I look out through the windshield and I see the bottom of the ice above me as we're sinking into the sea. I can see the bottoms of the tires of the other trucks making impressions on the ice. There's a depth gauge in the truck for some reason, and I watch it cross the redline. The hole we fell through is bright and it keeps getting smaller and smaller and the air keeps getting tighter and tighter in the truck. Then crunch, I wake up with a headache."

"I think we should stay focused, Aaron. Let's talk about your sleep quality. Your new doctor can put you back on the Ambien for short periods of time, if that's what it takes. That seemed to help you before."

"I was actually hoping there was something different than Ambien. I still had bad dreams on Ambien, but I couldn't wake up out of them," I said.

"What kind of different? What are you looking for?"

"Well," I said, "I was hoping there was something that lets you sleep without dreams for a while. Like a dark and quiet place in your head you can go to all night. Something like that."

"Are you taking your clonazepam before you go to sleep?"

"Yeah," I said. "As much as I'm allowed to. It kind of wears off before morning. Around two-ish. I was thinking maybe I could take mefloquine again, those malaria pills. They always gave me wild dreams. Maybe that would just clear all the dream problems out at once. Mix things up a little."

He didn't say anything, but I saw him underline something on the clipboard more strongly. Just then his cell phone rang.

"Well, good luck," he said. "I have to take this."

And he walked off to answer it after shaking my hand, heading in the direction of the hospital. When he did not return, I realized about thirty minutes later that our meeting was over.

*   *   *

On the drive to our new home from Walter Reed, Emily admitted that she had been telling everyone we were engaged. She only did this, she explained, so a family friend would have a job waiting for me at the Tractor Supply. And also other reasons. After she explained anything, Emily had a habit of staring at me and smiling until I smiled back at her to signal that I understood what she was saying. I just got into a habit of smiling and nodding just about whenever she looked at me. I knew I should feel lucky to have such a patient woman.

"This is going to be the start of a new life," she kept saying, and I knew that meant something different to her than it did to me.

They had a welcoming party for me at the Unitarian Church across the street from her parents' house, right on the lawn for the whole town to see. I pretended that I recognized everything and some of it was vaguely familiar. A lot of things are vaguely familiar now. I had no idea how many times the old me had been to this town. I had been walking without the cane for a couple weeks, but Emily thought I should bring it along just in case. She explained to the minister that I would not be giving a speech to the small crowd that came, so I sat in a folding chair while people walked by to shake my hand, like I was visiting royalty from the poorest country in the world.

I met the man who would be my boss, Gerald, and he said there was no hurry for me to start work, and I thanked him for the job. I meant to ask him what kind of job it was, but I was afraid he had already told me. He had the kind of large rings on his hand that make handshakes painful. A woman with enormous sunglasses told me Emily used to babysit her son who was now a Marine in Afghanistan, and I said that I had never been there.

"He says you shouldn't believe all the bad news in the papers," she told me.

When the owner of the Mazda dealership offered to put up part of the down payment on a house for Emily and me, I said okay, and the local paper contacted me to provide a quote about it. "I was real touched" was the best I could come up with. It was a blue house at the top of a hill that looked out over our whole treeless development, a bright sea of lawns and aluminum siding. We even got a used Mazda for under Blue Book, since I had trouble driving stick now and had to trade in my old truck. Emily said to get the Tribute since it was big enough for when we'd have

kids, which was the first she'd broached the subject, and I guess I
said that was fine.

Since I wasn't sleeping, and Emily got up early to open the
pharmacy, I stayed downstairs all night and unpacked our things
as quietly as possible. I get easily distracted now so these nights
were not always productive. I got my army stuff down to about
two black Contico boxes and a rucksack of stuff I couldn't bring
myself to throw away yet. I took naps during the day on the futon
chair on the patio because I seemed only able to sleep soundly in
indirect sunlight. Once I started working at the Tractor Supply, I
slept in my car during my lunch break and went to bed right after
work. I was not looking forward to the long nights of the winter
months.

*   *   *

My afternoon naps were filled with the sound of neighborhood
lawnmowers. It seemed as if people mowed their lawns every day,
like brushing your teeth. In the lawn-mowing dreams, I was mow-
ing the wide shoulder of the state highway with the rest of my old
squad, which was six guys before I got hit. We were driving zero-
turn Kubota mowers, because there was good clearance in front to
see hazards in the grass. These were a big seller at the Tractor
Supply. We had a dozen lined up on the front berm at the entrance to the shopping plaza. Our other job in the dream was to
gather up the roadkill, which was everywhere, dogs and deer
mostly. We had these fishing rods with little grappling hook ends,
because we all knew that if there was a bomb in the roadkill, it
would safely detonate while we were dragging it.

I would crouch behind the mower and cast my line over and
over until I'd hook a deer on the side of the face or the shank and
reel it back in to where I was. Sometimes I spent most of the
dream casting the line over and over without success. This part of
the dream got rather tedious.

The deer had the usual power-drill holes in their joints and skulls and cigarette burns on their legs. Some had illegible confessions stapled to their bodies. Most dogs had been beheaded and hog-tied with fence wire, but we never seemed to find any dog heads.

*   *   *

They had a card table and a chair for me by the main entrance of the Tractor Supply—which was the Super Tractor Supply, the flagship store of the state—right in front of the big windows, and it was so bright in the mornings I had to wear sunglasses and sunblock. After my first day at work, Gerald called Emily at home. She said I should wear my Georgia Tech hat to work, which I guessed was on account of the scars. I had meant to grow my hair out long enough to comb over the scars, but I wore the hat like she said. After a week, I had the initials "STS" from my polo shirt lightly stenciled in un-tanned skin onto the left side of my chest. The shirt was made of thin material. They made a placard that said "Three-Time Iraq Veteran Sergeant Aaron Ferguson, Combat Engineer and Tractor Supply Super Specialist," which was awkward because I was not very good at answering tractor supply questions. I kept the store catalogue in front of me and studied it when no one was talking to me, which was just about all the time.

After my first week, Emily came home from work—she got off a few hours after I did—with a bucket of fried chicken and a bouquet of flowers.

"Who are those flowers for?" I asked.

"They're for you, baby. It's congratulations on your first week," Emily said and handed them to me.

"They smell real nice," I said.

"So, tell me, what is your favorite month of the year?" she asked.

I thought on this a while.

"December, I guess. Because of the holidays."

"That's not a great month for an outdoor wedding. How does early October sound?"

"For a wedding?"

"Yeah."

"October is fine too," I said.

After the first few weeks it became apparent that there was not much greeting for me to do, and I spent half of the work day at doctors' appointments, so I asked what the previous store greeter did with his time. Gerald admitted that I was the first greeter they had hired. He could see I was uncomfortable with the lack of work, so I started to make delivery runs with a young guy named Ramon down to their store at the County Mall. It was only small inventory—tools and outdoor gear—but customers would place orders for larger items and we would move the orders from our warehouse down to the mall before it opened.

Ramon let me drive and I'd watch the truck while he unloaded goods onto a dolly at the service entrance. The main food court did not open until eleven, so we would have a breakfast of pretzels and iced tea at the Auntie Anne's and talk about the strange, jobless, non-housewife people that shopped at the mall on weekday mornings. Ramon did not have much work to do back at the Tractor Supply either, or so he told me.

* * *

In my mall dream, the County Mall was attached to the side of the granary building on the Tigris. At the far side of Belk's, the aluminum silos ran up alongside the parking garage. When rockets hit the silo walls, the grain dust blew out in red clouds, little burning clumps of falling grain smoldering. The fire seemed like an intentional part of the building to me, a kind of theme park fixture. It burned constantly, like the waste gas flame over the south Baghdad refinery. We had to open up all the stores before daylight.

I ran my fingers over the store locks in the dark, to see if they were tampered with, to see if men were waiting inside. The dark corridors of the mall were filled with grain-fattened pigeons, and their fluttering was all we could hear. We were casting our gun lights over the penny fountain when the neon lights turned on in the food court.

"It's coming from Arby's," someone said.

The Arby's front window was spider-webbed with bullet holes. A shopping cart from Sears sat by the entrance, filled with artillery shells and sweaters with a wire running up into the ceiling. There were mannequins at the registers wearing Arby's uniforms and suicide vests. It smelled like someone was cooking fries.

"That's probably the decoy," I said.

As we scanned around us, I felt two of my grenades tumble out of a pouch on my body armor. I had to whisper loudly, "They're mine, don't worry, they're mine. I'll get them."

The two grenades rolled under the metal security curtain in front of Old Navy, which was propped up just a few inches. The curtain was jammed and wouldn't raise any further than where it was and it made a terrible racket when I pulled on it. I could see my grenades on the floor, just a couple feet away.

My friends were shouting about Arby's. There was someone in there.

"I have to get my grenades," I said. "Just hold on."

I got down on the floor and I tried to sweep the grenades back toward me using my rifle as a hook. I could just barely nudge them but was unable to sweep them any closer. I reached my arm in further, as far as it would reach. To do this, I had to turn my head away. Something inside the store pulled the rifle out of my hands. I was wedged under the curtain. I yelled out. My friends were gone. I woke up in my car to the sound of my phone alarm.

When I returned to work after the dream, I couldn't sit at the desk. All afternoon I did slalom weaves through the aisles, thinking about what Emily might say if I came home and said I quit the Tractor Supply. I flipped through the landscaping magazines until I started feeling short of breath.

* * *

When I came home that day, the screen on the front basement window was busted in. The day prior, I discovered a crack in our house's foundation where water had gotten into the basement during the storm, so I had left the basement windows open to help it dry out. It looked like someone had busted into the basement. The shades were drawn on the other floors to keep our AC bill down so I could not see into the rest of the house. There was a car I did not recognize at the end of the street, but I wasn't confident about not recognizing anything. I took my revolver out of the glove box and checked the rounds while I decided what to do.

It seemed like a reasonable reaction I was having, but I couldn't bring myself to call 9-1-1. There's something normal about this you're not noticing, I thought, something you would have noticed before.

When I came in through the patio door, it was hard to remember how things in the house had been arranged. I couldn't tell if the living room looked different. The furniture was all hand-me-downs from Emily's parents, couches with patched cushions. There was a creaky recliner that smelled like pipe tobacco. The stack of catalogues was still on the kitchen table where I had not touched them, things Emily wanted me to go through for the registry. None of the appliances seemed to be missing.

As I opened the door to the basement, I saw trash strewn on the stairs. I had to force myself to breathe through the tightness in my chest. I walked downstairs, feeling as if a slowly winding cable was pulling at my sternum. Every step felt like I was about to fall through the boards. All I could see was shredded army gear—uniforms and ponchos, things like that. When I turned the corner at the bottom of the stairs, I was alone in a room full of trash.

I guessed a stray dog had broken in, judging from the shit and the muddy paw prints on the workbench under the window. My old rucksack was busted open on the floor, and the chewed up remains of a two-year-old MRE that must have been buried inside were scattered all over. It was Chicken Tetrazzini. I could tell from the smell. Then the gun went off.

A lot of time must have passed while I was just standing there staring at the gun, my ears ringing. In all my months walking around with a loaded gun I never had an accidental discharge, not once. I couldn't even remember putting my finger into the trigger well of the revolver. It was hard to explain. I felt like reality had just cheated against me. There was a fat chip in the floor in front of me and another in the wall in front of it where the bullet sat mashed up on the floor. It looked like a tiny brass dolphin lying on its side, from where I stood.

The patrolman called to me from the window with his gun drawn.

"Mr. Ferguson, it's the police. Are you all right in there?" he called down.

I dropped the gun on the basement floor then put my hands up and turned toward the window.

"Don't shoot," I said. "It's my house."

"Sir, would you mind meeting me at the front door?" he said.

"Sure," I said. "It was a stray dog."

* * *

Emily ran up to the house in hysterics when she saw the police cruiser with the lights on. I had forgotten to call her. Officer Landau was just about to leave by that point anyway.

"What were you doing with that gun in your car?" Emily asked.

"I've always had a gun," I told her.

"But you can't have a gun anymore," she said. "You just can't."

"Officer Landau said to just be more careful. He said there wouldn't be any charges. I'll send some flowers over to Mrs. Morris in the morning. She was the one who called about the gunshot."

"We're selling that gun tomorrow," she said. "I'll pick you up on my lunch break and we'll go down to the pawn shop."

My bad ear was still ringing the worst. I couldn't tell how loudly she was talking. I had to judge from the expression on her face. There seemed no sense in arguing it.

"How about I just give it to you now so you don't have to cross town to pick me up? Anything over two hundred's a fair price," I said. "It's not a bad gun."

* * *

I threw the last of the .38 rounds from my driver's side window on the way to work the next morning, right off the side of a bridge. I made sure no one was within sight. I sped up just a little after I threw them. I think part of me thought they might go off on the rocks below and chase me down the road.

* * *

On the weekend, Emily and I went to the county fair with her brother, Joe, and his wife, Melissa. I enjoyed how loud Joe talked because he was one person I never had trouble understanding. It wasn't for my sake he talked so loud. I had forgotten what Joe did for a living, and it was far too late to ask, by at least a year. I might have blamed it on my condition, but I decided to just keep quiet. It involved him talking people into things they were too stupid to realize were in their best interest, I knew that much. In these stories, there were people who had to be humored like children, either customers or subordinates I think. Maybe his boss too. His stories made him sound frustrated and selfless, but he was sweet toward Emily. He called her Milly. He didn't seem quite as sweet on Melissa, and she was very pregnant then.

Since most of my friends were deployed or couldn't make the wedding on short notice, Emily had put this outing together for me to ask Joe if he would be one of my groomsmen. I must have forgotten to bring it up.

"You just let us know if this gets too much for you. All these crowds." Joe said.

"Aaron doesn't have a problem with crowds," Emily told him. "He's just got the sleeping problem."

"I can't dunk anymore either," I said.

"You used to dunk?" Melissa asked me.

"Missy, he's teasing," Emily said.

"Also, there's going to be fireworks once the sun goes down," Joe said. "That won't bother you will it?"

"He doesn't have a problem with fireworks," Emily said.

"I still like fireworks," I said.

"And it won't bother you if I get a beer will it?" Joe asked. "I don't mean to make you feel left out."

"Go right ahead. I'd join you if I could."

"Do you have to drink in front of Aaron? You can't wait until later?" Melissa asked him.

"What? He said it was all right."

"Go right ahead," I said. "Maybe get me a bratwurst or something."

Late in the afternoon we went over to the tractor pull on the edge of the fairgrounds, because Joe knew one of the drivers. I always liked the tractor pull when I was a kid, but I had to bow out once we got in the metal bleachers because the sound was amping up my tinnitus like a dog whistle. Most of the time it's just a little high-pitched whine that's always hanging around, mostly in my right ear. After the first tractor hit top rpms, it felt like a pair of tuning forks had been jammed into my skull. I didn't want anyone to feel bad so I said I was going to find a Porta John.

What caught my eye was the car fire in the parking lot. I saw the smoke beyond the Ferris wheel as the fire trucks first sounded in the distance, or what sounded distant to me. It had been dry for a week, and the parking lot to the fairgrounds was just an open field roped off. It had been laid with dry straw to keep the mud down. I figured somebody's hot manifold must have set off a patch of it and it set the car burning. From the dark color of the smoke I could tell there were tires on fire at least.

It was a Jeep Cherokee that was probably black before it caught fire, and there was an anxious man pacing nearby who clearly owned the Accord next to it. The Accord wasn't burning, but the heat was already peeling the paint. It came as a relief to see no one was sitting in the Cherokee, which should have been fairly obvious. The windows had all burst and the hood popped open in front of us with a black belch. As I watched the fire trucks trying to maneuver in around it, I realized that was the reason I had come over to look at the car fire in the first place, just to make sure no one was inside.

The strangest thing about watching people burn to death inside a vehicle is the fact that you don't have much choice about it. Once the fuel and the tires catch and it's hot enough, and it's full of things that explode, there's nothing to be done. You just have to watch. You can burn the skin off your hands trying to get that door open, but it won't budge. You might see someone inside looking like they're just sleeping and you can bang on the windows at them all you like. They're not waking up out of a concussion and lungs full of smoke, maybe something worse you can't see. Maybe it's better they don't.

If the truck burns itself out on its own, you could be waiting twelve hours for it to be cool enough to get close to if it's a hot day. It might be in a place you don't want to be for twelve hours. When you finally get into that truck you will realize that ants have a higher tolerance for heat than people do.

*　*　*

When we got home that night, Emily stood by the front door and refused to put the key in the lock. She didn't like scowling—she says it goes straight to your crow's feet—so I could tell she had made a conscious decision to do it. I could feel the sunburn glowing on my face. I was afraid it made me look angry. I was afraid to tell her I had a headache, a worse one.

"Aaron, when you just wander off like that it makes people think you're some kind of invalid now," she said. "Did you just forget about us?"

"I'm really sorry," I said. "I just lost track of time. I guess it was longer than I thought."

"Melissa was scared to death about you," she said. "She can't be getting stressed out like that in her third trimester."

"I'm sorry," I said. "I'll tell her I'm sorry next time I see her. I'll tell Joe too."

"I can take care of you, you know. I don't mind doing that," she said. "You just have to promise to give a shit."

"I know. I give a shit," I said. "I'll try harder."

"Is it trying that's the problem?" she asked.

"No. It's probably something else."

The automatic lights on the front porch went out with us standing there, staring at each other. We both made a flailing motion with our hands to get the motion detector to turn them back on.

*　*　*

In the county fair dream, I found myself searching for my rifle in all of the Porta Johns, constantly intruding on angry occupants. I would ask them politely if they could check the serial number on their rifle and get a door slammed in my face. One guy was eating a huge cotton candy on the john, and I thought, who is this guy to judge me?

There was a FOB gate at the edge of the fairgrounds, the edge of the base, and the gate guards would turn me back without a rifle. I would not be allowed to leave. It was Indian Country out there. Instead of fireworks, there were red-and-white parachute flares drifting down over the carnival rides in between outgoing mortar rounds. Emily was waiting for me back at the car, and I had made some lame excuse. I could tell she knew it was a lie and that I was missing my rifle. She could see that I didn't have it.

When I found Renee by the fried dough stand, I asked her if she had seen a small black rifle lying around. She seemed to have gotten older, but not as much as I had. Seeing her at the fair felt like I had found the simple answer to a problem I had made too complicated for too many years. She was counting raffle tickets and had an enormous pink stuffed bear.

"You might be able to see it from the top of the Ferris wheel," she offered.

"All right," I said, but I had my doubts.

She turned in a fistful of tickets, which let us bypass the line and board one of the two-seater cars directly. We were the last car to load. The Ferris wheel began to rotate, and Renee smelled faintly of fresh-cut grass. For just a moment I felt the skin of her knee against my knee. Then she climbed out of the car as we neared the top of our ascent.

"What are you doing?" I called out.

"Relax," she said. "This is the only way."

Hanging by the wheel spoke below me, she dropped the pink bear into the gear mechanism in the center of the Ferris wheel. It looked like the interior of an enormous clock. The gears slowly pulled the bear inside, its plush skin tightening until white stuffing burst from the seams of its mouth. The gears stopped with only the stretched pink bear head extruding in an expression of agony. The Ferris wheel made an ugly noise and came to a halt with our car stopped at the very top. Renee climbed back up to me. I grabbed her tightly by the wrist as she sat back down. I put her hand on my heart so she could feel how hard it was beating.

"Do you see anything down there?" she asked.

It was bright and blurry in the fairgrounds beneath us. There were too many shadows.

"It's kinda hard to tell," I said.

Instead of a tractor pull, there was a drive-in theater at the far side of the fairgrounds with a giant screen. I recognized myself on the screen and realized it was a homemade movie of my first tour, when I was just a private. I thought about Renee every night of that tour. I remembered wishing she could see me while I was over there. I wished she knew how sorry I was. Now I just felt embarrassed. We couldn't hear the sound so I had to explain to Renee what was going on, what people were saying. I hoped the movie would jump ahead to my last tour, so I could show her how bad things got, so she could see why I was like this.

"What did you say right there?" she asked.

"I think I just laughed a little. We were laughing."

"Was it funny?"

"No," I told her. "I thought it might be funny later, but it wasn't."

As the movie continued, I noticed that the lights of the Ferris wheel had turned off. People stuck in their cars were shouting out to people below them. They were very upset with us. I thought maybe something impressive might appear on the screen for her to see. I kept waiting for it.

"You seem so frustrated," she said. "Did you become an angry person?"

"No. I didn't. I swear."

"That's all right," she said. "I believe you."

"I just got so tired," I said.

"I wouldn't have wanted to be an angry person," she said.

"You wouldn't have been," I told her.

"Hey, I think I see your rifle," she said. "Over there by the ring toss."

I looked down at the ring toss booth. One of the prizes on the wall was an M4 rifle that looked like mine. It cost a thousand tickets.

"That could be anybody's," I said.

People were climbing down the skeleton of the Ferris wheel in the dark. I could hear them shouting out as they lost their grip. We would have to climb down. I was afraid she would mention this.

* * *

The nonrefundable tickets to Dominica had already been bought when we cancelled the wedding, so Emily and I decided to go anyway. We were both tense on the plane ride. Neither of us wanted this to be a catastrophe. I think her parents were hoping we would elope while we were there. I told her we should go see the boiling lake, and Emily said that sounded terrifying.

A tropical storm hit the island the day after we arrived and the power went out, which we found out later was actually from human error. The storm was mild, but the island flooded everywhere. Emily cried all day long in our dark hotel room, the two of us sitting on piles of towels in the bathroom since our room was facing the storm. I tried to reassure her. I told her we could go down to the beach tomorrow and pick through the debris. This will be a funny story some day, I said. I think it might have been funny if it had been a real honeymoon.

When we walked down to a general store in Rouseau there was a family putting a tarp over their collapsed roof. I showed their shirtless teenage son how to tie a bowline knot to a piece of rebar. Emily kept telling them how sorry she was. I was just happy that my hands remembered the knot and I kept tying it over and over.

The roads leading out of town had washed out and Emily was not willing to walk barefoot through the flooded streets, so we went back to our hotel room and played pinochle. Emily and I couldn't sleep that night and the following day was overcast and bleak. The toilets weren't working and Emily said she thought she was getting sick.

"You can use the ice bucket," I said.

"Not that end," she said.

"Oh."

"What am I going to do?"

"Let's go down to the beach. You can use the ocean."

"I'm serious."

"So am I. I won't tell anyone."

I dragged one of the hotel blankets down to the beach and laid it out while Emily sprinted into the surf in her two-piece. After I had it laid out, I stared down at the blanket like I was forgetting something. I picked up a blue piece of sea glass and turned it over for a second. I had forgotten about sea glass. A cold feeling came over me. I picked up the towel and ran down to the water. I still had my pants on and I ran in up to my waist after her and a wave knocked the breath out of me. Emily came up out of the water laughing with a guilty grin on her face, rubbing her hands with wet sand. The look on my face surprised her.

"Were you worried about me?" she asked.

I was about to wrap her up in the towel in my hands, but I realized it was now soaking wet.

"It's nothing," I said.

"Thanks," she said.

After Emily had gone to sleep that night, I left our hotel and made my way down through the dark streets to the beach. I stared up at the full moon until I fell asleep to the sound of the waves.

* * *

In the moon dream, the moon buggies looked like the Kubota mowers with mud tires. I was worried because I couldn't seem to get my body armor to go on over the helmet of my spacesuit. I asked the other guys how they got theirs on.

"We put our body armor on back in the spaceship, before we put our helmets on," they said, and I felt a bit foolish.

There never seemed to be any insurgents on the moon. I never saw any; I just assumed they were out there. When the bombs went off, they only had a small amount of oxygen sealed inside them, so the explosion itself was very small. The problem was, if it went off under your moon buggy it would create a large enough force for you to reach escape velocity. It would send you slowly hurtling out into space. The lunar sky was filled with the lost buggies of previous, stricken patrols if you looked carefully enough, bomb-struck mowers turning end over end until they reached some distant, settled solar orbit, the Earth and the Moon passing close to them just once a year. To try to prevent a "drift off," we had the fishing rods with grappling hooks again.

It was the truck in front of me that hit the bomb, just like in real life. I saw the moon dust bloom upward thin as chalk powder, rising out into space, and the moon buggy disappeared inside it. I heard them call us on the radio.

"My suit is leaking," the radio voice cried, with the hiss of escaping air. "We need space tape up here."

The space tape was a thick, chrome-colored reel of one-inch duct tape. I grabbed it and my fishing rod from the back of my mower and started bounding toward the explosion. Running on the moon is painfully slow. It was not until I reached the crater that I realized they were already above me, rising into space. I threw my line out at them over and over again as their moon buggy got smaller and smaller. It got very tedious.

10

POUGHKEEPSIE

Perry O'Brien

IT'S 0300 AND I'M SITTING ON THE SIDEWALK in front of Port Authority, trying to make a plan. I can't keep purchase on my thoughts with all this night traffic—taxis and limousines, garbage trucks, buses filled with vacant seats and harsh fluorescent light—this restless march of cars, all of them awake at crow piss and going somewhere. I was going somewhere, too.

It's raining a little, and the light from the television screens gets distorted in the wet air. Everything is sponged in a mist of color, even the smog from down below where passing trains rattle along the unchristly nethers of the bus station. Through it all I keep hearing Charlotte, her voice shingled by payphone static. "Medrick," she says, "what would you even *do* here?" She thought that was an explanation.

A female Reservist is guarding the entrance to the bus station. She's looking rugged in her plus-size digital cammies, and her pistol belt is decorated with big loops of plastic flex-cuffs. When the wind comes up, the plastic loops do a little dance on her hips. I caught her eye on me, one time, and a fat, black eel started squirming in my guts. What if she asks for my leave papers? With all the puddles and boogie darkness between every building, you'd think New York would be a good place for a man to hide. But the Army is everywhere. Look around, all you can see are porn shops, drug stores, and chain restaurants. Kill the illumination and it wouldn't look much different from Fort Hood.

*   *   *

This morning I met a coke dealer on the 10:45 from Columbus. His name was Ron, but he preferred I call him "Birdman." Ron liked my tattoos. He showed me the pieces he picked up inside, three black stars, scribbled together in a shot-group on his neck. In prison, you had to make your own ink by melting down Styrofoam cups, mixing the burnt slag with water. For a needle they sharpen a paper clip. Ron hadn't gone in for drugs, he did seven years for assaulting his wife with a soup can. Ron was surprised to hear the war was still going on. He showed me a picture of his wife, she was up in Saginaw and couldn't wait to start over. I showed him the photo of Charlotte. She said the picture was from freshman year, five young ladies crowded together on a blanket, all wearing volunteer shirts for the Catskill Folk Fest. On the back she wrote "I'm one of these," as if I wouldn't be able to tell.

*   *   *

Calling first, that must have been my mistake. I was just too excited. All the way from Texas I kept the surprise inside me, sleeping on buses and benches, shooting the shit with flatlanders and seed-folk, worrying, eating out of vending machines, imagining the look on her face. Charlotte always said she liked surprises. But she got real quiet when I told her I was coming to Poughkeepsie. I asked what was wrong, if maybe she was spooked by the idea of finally seeing each other. Then she got ugly with me. And now I'm sitting on my rucksack, stranded in this god-awful city.

* * *

I picture Poughkeepsie like a village from the Middle Ages. In her letters Charlotte described the big castles covered in vine, forests of respectable trees, stone bridges crossing rivers filled with swans and lake-fish. Charlotte said the gardens were the best part. She wrote about daffodils, pansies, foxglove, and some names for flowers I'd never heard before. My favorite of those is clouded geranium. You can't say the name of the flower fast, you have to slow down. It helped over there, sometimes. Go ahead and try: clouded geranium.

In the spring Charlotte started doing work study with the grounds team. Their job was to lay down seeds and mulch, trim the grass, and pick up fallen tree branches after big storms. She said she liked the work except for the rabbits. Someone's pet cottontail had escaped, back in the day, and I guess this bunny nosed out some kind of rangy, hard-scruff wild hare, and they must have procreated fiercely because now the whole campus was overrun. Other students thought they were cute, but for the grounds team these rabbits were like a plague from the Bible. They excavated fresh seed from the earth, left gnaw marks on bare roots, even scoured long strips of bark from the younger trees. Charlotte's team tried everything to get rid of the rabbits: cayenne pepper, clippings of human hair, even dried wolf piss. They wanted to use poison, but the environmental clubs said hell no.

What would I do in Poughkeepsie? I'd show the kids how to deal with rabbits. I've got a good knife and a poncho liner, everything you need to live in the woods. When I get to Poughkeepsie I'll climb into the trees and make a bivouac. From there I'll study the rabbits' movements. I'll watch where they eat, where they fuck, I'll chart out every tunnel on a laminated map.

My campaign will begin with overwhelming force. I'll plant snares in the rose bushes. I'll drop down on the rabbits from tree perches and break their little buckteeth. I'll chase snakes and weasels into their burrows, climb down there myself, yowling like a starved dog. The rabbits will be forced to dig deeper; they'll huddle in dark pockets of the earth and live off dead onions. Charlotte will discover the little mounds of charred rabbit-flesh I'll scatter around the garden, to make an example of anyone who pokes their head above ground. Just a few nubbles of blackened fur. Other than that, the gardens will be perfect.

Of course, I won't be able to stay hidden forever. Someone will see me, maybe a couple of kids out for a romantic walk. They'll pause on the bridge to look up at the fresh glint of stars, and they'll squeeze hands and whisper "forever" into each other's mouths. That's when they'll catch sight of me, wild and bent down among the cattails. Splashing blood from my hands and face. Questions will be asked, search parties will be deployed into the woods outside the castle. Eventually someone from the school newspaper will get a blurry photo: a pale body loping through the forest, wearing a hat made from lopped-off rabbit ears.

* * *

That female MP has been talking into her radio, like maybe there's a chance she's checking my description. I left everything at Fort Hood very carefully, all my gear stacked and folded in my barracks room, the full battle rattle except of course the boots I'm wearing. Supply Daddy told me they don't come after you if you leave all your shit behind. Still, if someone runs my driver's license it'll come up Absent Without Leave. Or maybe even desertion, since there's a war. They used to hang people for that.

* * *

It was the deaf box that made me realize I was leaving. When we got back to Hood they ran us through a battery of tests, checkboxes about our psychological health, blood-draws and knocking on our joints, x-rays to make sure we hadn't picked up any shrapnel. Finally you take a turn in the deaf box. It's a big glass chamber and once the door shuts, the silence is so heavy you worry about suffocating. You wear headphones and they tell you to listen for the beep. I didn't realize before then how long it had been since things were quiet. The silence was pressing on my ears, and all I was thinking about was Charlotte and her gardens because other things were coming up fast and it was better to think about the gardens. When I came out my hearing was fine, but I was blinking and snotty and there were wet trails on my cheek, and the tech guy looked away and said don't worry about it, happens to a lot of folks coming back. Probably something about the different pressure in the room. But I wasn't thinking about that, I was thinking about Charlotte.

Her first letter was addressed to any soldier. *Any soldier.* Imagine that, a million guys over there, and her letter happens to end up in the post Conex nearest my unit. Scrambled in with notes from church ladies and little kids' drawings of a dead Osama, and here was Charlotte, nervous about her junior year, writing about flowers. I'm not sentimental. I don't know about destiny or whatever, but you'd be dumb to give up on chances like that.

*   *   *

I grab my rucksack, pull my hood down, and go back around the corner. The payphone is decorated in curlicues of dripping black graffiti and half-peeled stickers. I punch in Charlotte's number and let it ring. And ring. Across the street they're advertising a new war game. Pictures flash across a display of television screens: soldiers crashing out of the waves at Normandy, soldiers wriggling under canopies of barbwire, soldiers hunkered down in muddy foxholes, waiting, chewing on all those broken promises. The phone keeps ringing. This time in the morning and she's not in her dorm. I want to yank the receiver out of its receptacle, swing it by the cord, and whip that phone up into the sky. I sit back down on my ruck and feel like crying. "You're on *my* time," First Sergeant used to say. Now that I'm on my own time, I don't know what to do with it.

* * *

So back to the rabbits. Once I've got them cowering in their burrows, I will return with an offer of peace. I'll explain that nibbling on flowers is beneath them; they could accomplish more with their lives. I'll spend a year training the rabbits. They'll learn small-team tactics, how to react to an ambush. We'll dig new tunnels together, deep down until we hit the foundations of those old castles. I'll show them how to make bombs out of garden fertilizer.

On graduation day, we'll take the school.

Charlotte will be a senior, posing for photos with her family. It'll be a warm, special kind of day. We'll wait until the perfect moment, when the celebrity is done with the speech about believing in yourself. Diplomas will be passed out, and everyone will throw their caps up in the air. That's when the castles will start exploding.

Big, billowy blasts from underground, the kind that rip up dirt and throw it for miles in the air. Those old castles will fall right into the ground. All the students and families and professors will be screaming and running, hundreds of black robes billowing and catching fire in the wind. That's when my combat teams of rabbits will pop out of their holes, biting at ankles, tearing at new black gowns.

The rabbits will eat everything. They'll gorge themselves on the gardens, tugging up whole root systems, mangling the tender vines and leaves and flowers, mashing delicate blossoms between their teeth. Their little black eyes will smoke with victory. Then they'll go for the grass, eating every green and living thing until Poughkeepsie is a desert of black graduation caps, ruined towers, and dunes of dried rabbit shit.

I'll find Charlotte. She'll be stumbling away from the fires, her robes all in tatters, makeup running with tears down her face. She'll demand to know why, why? And I'll say, "I needed something to do."

For a while I'll be named King of the Rabbits. Of course, my victory will be short-lived. With no food left, the rabbits will turn on me, unable to forgive my past abuses. I'll be chased from my own kingdom, set loose back into the world. On the run again.

* * *

Two taxis collide at the intersection up the street, the sound of tires screeching and smashing metal echoing off the block. The Reservist hustles over to the scene, where the drivers are already screaming at each other in two different languages. By and by, the day comes up. The mirrored buildings are casting sun down into the street, and for a second the millions of little glass pieces shine like gold around the wrecked taxis, but then the sun changes and the buildings return to the perfect indifference of an ocean, cold and black and flat-ass calm, bored by the day's violence. Seems like it's going to be a warm morning. The station will open soon, and a thousand buses will be gone before lunchtime, rumbling down concrete ramps, through traffic, and out into the country. The buses will go to Poughkeepsie and every other town, to airports where people are flying out to China, or Africa, or back to Iraq. I could be on any one of them. Or I could just sit here on my rucksack, watching the city fill up with sunlight.

11

WHEN ENGAGING TARGETS, REMEMBER

Gavin Ford Kovite

(1) ON THE ROAD

YOU ARE A UNITED STATES INFANTRYMAN. An Imperial Grunt. The emblem of American militarism. Your rank is: Specialist. It is late 2004, and you are behind a machine gun in al-Anbar, Iraq, swathed in bulky armor and expensive gear and sitting—almost reclining—in a wide nylon sling slung across the roof of a Humvee that's as cartoonishly bulky as you. Your job as a Humvee gunner is to provide rear security for a convoy of fuel tankers that's currently wending its way from the Baghdad airport to a Forward Operating Base one hundred miles east.

You're no fool; you're a college kid. You were just about to declare a poli-sci major at UC Riverside when you got the letter ordering you to active duty for Iraq, along with the rest of your California National Guard brigade. You're smart, and you get the joke. The fuel will be used to fill the vehicles and generators of the combat and combat support units at the base, whose main task is to secure the area around Kut, the security of which presumably increases the security of the country and then the region, which helps to secure the world in general and the United States in particular. It's tough to make a direct connection between what you're doing right now and the peace and prosperity of your hometown of Riverside, but that's no surprise because global security is all about action that's collective as well as synergistic, as far as you understand it.

As you think this, you reach into one of the nylon pouches of your vest. You pull out a Met-RX Big 100 protein bar and unwrap it with your teeth while your left hand rests on the handle of the Browning .50 caliber machine gun mounted to a swivel in front of you. The air smells of dust and burning garbage. The sky is eggshell white with brown and black highlights. You're about to see some action, although you don't know it quite yet.

At the front of your field of vision is the enormous black barrel of an M2 .50 caliber machine gun, a weapon that's longer than you are tall and that shoots rounds the size of small dildos. In the middle range of your vision, fifty meters away, is a pack of cars following your convoy. Any one of them could be a suicide car bomb, but they're probably just average Joes, day-to-day Iraqis trying to get somewhere. The reason they're all fifty meters away is that there's a large, white, bilingual sign affixed to your Humvee's rear that reads "US CONVOY DO NOT APPROACH WITHIN 50 METERS OR YOU WILL BE FIRED UPON," the Operation Iraqi Freedom version of the good old "IF YOU CAN READ THIS YOU'RE DRIVING TOO CLOSE." And of course, there's you, crouched in the gunner's hatch menacing everyone with the .50 cal.

It doesn't always work. Some hajjis are weirdly—almost nihilistically, you think—unresponsive to menacing. You wonder if nihilistic is the right word to use. Your PHIL 101 Intro to Western Philosophy course went over nihilism last semester, but thanks to the letter you got sending you here, you never finished it. Your PHIL 101 professor was nice about you leaving midway through, although he kept on saying he was, "So, so sorry," as if someone you loved had contracted a terminal illness.

Your thoughts drift. You know the importance of vigilance and constant scanning, but you are perhaps too imaginative for sentry work or rolling down Baghdad highways day in and day out. Consider: there is a large crater in the intersection outside your unit's walled-off living area on the edge of the Green Zone where a silver BMW exploded, beheading rush-hour commuters and landing a guy from 1st Cavalry Division in the ICU with "polytrauma," which is the new buzzword for injuries sustained in the kind of blast that would kill anyone lacking 100 pounds of Kevlar and ceramic armor and twenty-first-century surgical care. Thanks to a recent mop-up operation, you can now mentally produce a photorealistic image of what your own body would look like after such an explosion, and this image comes unbidden to your mind during long stretches of highway.

The protein bar is incredibly dry and needs to be washed down frequently with rubbery-tasting water from the hose of your CamelBak. You think about going back to UC Riverside and enrolling in ENGL 302 with no lower jaw or tongue, having to write out your conversation or type through some text-to-speech thing like a twenty-year-old Stephen Hawking, your old roommates looking at you with kindness and awkwardness and pity, no one really wanting to talk to you in that condition, and you not wanting to talk to anyone either. Sex with the Riverside coeds would be out of the question, with you looking like either the Phantom of the Opera or that Marine in the *New York Times Magazine* with his face and scalp totally burned off and scarred over, a too-scary-for-PG version of the guy in *Goonies*. And that's just what could happen to your head. A bomb could leave you dickless and castrated too, which would probably take at least one leg off pretty close, which would lead the few girls you have gotten with to suspect that it's worse than it looks and to have nightmares of what's become of you "down there." Your buddies wouldn't be able to take you out for drinks without acknowledging it and thinking about it, the worst thing that could happen to a guy, your catheter filling your bag with fluid after a few Heinekens and one of your friends, most of whom front like they're assholes but are actually really nice guys, changing it out for you, trying to decide whether wisecracking about it or refraining from wisecracking would make you feel worse.

You're not a worrywart, though. You cut that train of thought off and start mouthing Jay-Z lyrics while swiveling the Fifty around and aiming at cars and windows and the rooftops of the drab apartment buildings that line the highways. One interesting tidbit you heard from the 3rd Infantry Division troops, whom you relieved, is that some gunners have been ordered to crouch way down in the hatch, like too far down to really be able to see anything, since the main danger is IEDs, which you won't see anyway, but which will take your head off in a close blast or in a rollover if you're standing up tall and trying to scan this way and that.

In your (albeit limited) army experience, this is the kind of decision that sergeants or officers make for you, but you haven't been instructed either way, probably because your sergeants and officers, being new here themselves, either haven't thought of it or aren't sure whether it's wise. You figure you're probably justified in going either way, even though you're the rear security and are supposed to be keeping an eye out for threats coming from the rear of the convoy. You can crouch down low, popping up for a quick scan every fifteen or twenty seconds. You might miss the telltale lumps of a roadside IED that didn't detonate, but this also means you'd avoid taking the blast in your face if it does. All in all it seems prudent. On the other hand, there are things you know you don't know and things you don't know you don't know. And as long as you're crouched down, you're not watching the convoy's six.

DO YOU:

Crouch down in the turret and pop up to scan every twenty seconds? TURN TO SECTION (2)

Remain standing and scanning as before? TURN TO SECTION (3)

(2) TURTLE DOWN

Here's the worst situation: after having mulled over keeping your head down, you decide to keep it up, and then you get hit with an IED, which burns your face off or gives you the kind of brain trauma that disables you for the rest of your life but doesn't erase the memory of mulling over and then failing to take a simple precaution that could have saved you. You feel around for a comfortable sitting position and then settle into it, figuring out by trial and error the best method for hauling your heavily armored self up at twenty-second intervals for a quick scan. Your armor and equipment increase your body weight by about seventy pounds, and human nature and muscle fatigue being what they are, the twenty-second intervals become more like thirty seconds as the hours wear on. The convoy is keeping speed and making good time. The traffic is staying fifty meters away from you. You pass a billboard advertising Mr. Brown Canned Iced Coffee, which has actually become a personal favorite and is sold by the case by Ali at a kiosk he set up at the outskirts of your Forward Operating Base. Body armor is uncomfortable to move around in, but the immobility (along with the drone of the engine) can be somewhat sleep inducing in the heat, hence the regular drinking of Mr. Browns. The cartoon Mr. Brown himself looks jolly and avuncular. Popping back down into a sitting position on the turret's swinging foot-sling, you dig a strawberry-yogurt-flavored protein bar (that you've added for snack purposes) out of the extra ammo pouch on your flak vest and take a bite. Guardo, the medic, is sitting in the right rear seat looking troglodytic and pudgy-faced in his helmet and armor. Your boots have been resting on his trauma bag since you've assumed your new, protected position. Guardo does not seem to object to this. He holds a fist up, and you give it a bump.

The explosion sounds like a huge beam of hardwood snapping in half. The driver and your squad leader, Staff Sergeant Boyle, call out, "IED." Your gun truck runs over a large pothole almost immediately, smacking your neck painfully against the edge of the turret and pushing your Kevlar down over your eyes. Your platoon leader is yelling something indecipherable on the radio, and Guardo is yanking at the bag under your feet. You hear some of the gunners farther up in the column open fire. You untangle your feet and yank yourself back up behind the Fifty.

You are surprised to see a black BMW sedan passing you on the left at a high rate of speed and headed straight for the fuel trucks about fifty meters up in the middle of the convoy. Your Rules of Engagement (ROE) card, which you are required to keep in your left chest pocket at all times, reads:

THESE RULES APPLY AT ALL TIMES AND ON ALL OPERATONS

1. Positive Identification (PID) is required prior to engagement. PID is a reasonable certainty that the target you are engaging is exhibiting hostile intent or committing a hostile act. Once you have PID, you may use escalated force, up to and including deadly force, to eliminate the threat.

2. When engaging targets, remember:

a. Escalation of force. Always use the minimum amount of force necessary to eliminate the threat. If time and circumstances permit, use the following degrees of force when responding to hostile act or hostile intent:

- Shout verbal warnings to halt.
- Show your weapon and demonstrate intent to use it.
- Shoot a warning shot (vehicles only).
- Shoot a disabling shot (vehicles only).
- Shoot to eliminate target.

In bold is the caveat:

**NOTHING ON THIS CARD
PREVENTS YOU FROM USING
ALL FORCE NECESSARY
TO DEFEND YOURSELF.**

By the time you get the barrel swung around, the BMW has passed you. The time for warning or disabling shots is over, given that a shot going into the engine block at this angle would also go through the driver's head. You either engage the BMW or let it drive right into the middle of the convoy.

DO YOU:

Fire on the BMW? TURN TO (5).

Let the BMW pass into the convoy? TURN TO (6).

(3) LOOK OUT

You'll try and find a way to broach the subject with your squad leader tomorrow in a way that doesn't sound like you're just being a pussy. For now, your job is rear security and you have to be scanning at all times. You stay standing and facing the rear like a good trooper, only every once in a while allowing half of your mind to slip into a daydream about mom's kitchen or the Riverside coeds, and you wonder if thinking about whether you're a wartime cliché prevents you from being a wartime cliché.

About an hour after you made your decision to stand, an IED goes off at the front of the column. You can feel it as well as hear it: a pocket of stiffened air busting by with a sound like an enormous firecracker.* As soon as the IED goes off, your truck swerves slightly and hits a pothole, jolting you against the rear of the turret and pushing your Kevlar forward over your eyes. You push it back up and see that a black BMW about fifty meters away has floored it in the left lane and looks like it's going to try to pass you. After about a second's worth of deer-in-the-headlights hesitation, you remember your Rules of Engagement, which are printed on a small, yellow folding card that you keep in your left chest pocket. The card reads:

THESE RULES APPLY AT ALL TIMES AND ON ALL OPERATONS

1. **Positive Identification (PID) is required prior to engagement.** PID is a reasonable certainty that the target you are engaging is exhibiting hostile intent or committing a hostile act. Once you have PID, you may use escalated force, up to and including deadly force, to eliminate the threat.

---

*Most people have only seen large explosions in movies and so understandably assume that a large bomb makes a sort of loud but sort of wet and rumbly sound, because this is the sound it makes in theaters. But theater explosions are made by the vibrations of speaker cones, whereas an actual explosion is the sound of air expanding at like twenty thousand feet per second, which for obvious legal as well as technical reasons even the fanciest Dolby-surround-sound systems cannot reproduce. If you've never heard a large explosion go off nearby, just think of one of those little Black Cat firecrackers that tween boys like to light and throw on the street around the Fourth of July, then multiply it by a thousand or ten thousand until it's a loud, sharp, and pretty scary sound that you can feel as well as hear, and (because you can feel it) always seems surprisingly close.

2. When engaging targets, remember:

a. Escalation of force. Always use the minimum amount of force necessary to eliminate the threat. If time and circumstances permit, use the following degrees of force when responding to hostile act or hostile intent:

- Shout verbal warnings to halt.
- Show your weapon and demonstrate intent to use it.
- Shoot a warning shot (vehicles only).
- Shoot a disabling shot (vehicles only).
- Shoot to eliminate target.

In bold is the caveat:

NOTHING ON THIS CARD PREVENTS YOU FROM USING ALL FORCE NECESSARY TO DEFEND YOURSELF.

Many would have seized up in a situation like this, but you remember the ROE and go by the numbers as per your training, first yelling Hey and Stay Back. The meaning of this should be obvious by the context, even to non-English speakers, but the BMW keeps coming and is now within thirty meters. The next step in the ROE—Show (show your presence and weapon)—is a constant, given the huge DO NOT APPROACH sign, not to mention the enormous and unmistakable Fifty. Next is Shoot (a warning shot), which you now do, fully aware that gunfire at the rear of the column is going to freak out the rest of the group, but whatever, he's at twenty-five meters now, and you lower the Fifty and fire into the concrete behind your truck, not trusting yourself to be able to put it close to but not in the car, given that your truck's starting to hit potholes and swerve around, and a single round could take ten people's heads off if they were lined up right.

The car seems to hesitate for a moment, then continues ahead. It'll be past your bumper in a few seconds. You're probably within blast radius right now, and the thought that you should just duck pops into your head. You push it away. The ROE is all about your personal subjective threat assessment, an assessment that, given al-Qaeda's well-known tactic of impersonating civilians, is very hard to make. The ROE card makes clear however, that NOTHING ON THIS CARD PREVENTS YOU FROM USING ALL FORCE NECESSARY TO DEFEND YOUR-SELF, which is either a smart reminder of priorities or an end-run around the rules themselves. Your NCOs have made it clear to you that you are absolutely permitted and expected to light up a hajji that's intent on plowing into the convoy and won't respond to shouts, warning shots, and so on. The step now is to walk fire up into the engine block and then into the driver. You've just about committed to blow the BMW away when you remember the two-liter water bottle next to you and wonder if you can just fling it onto their windshield, like maybe the driver is too dense to realize that you're going to shoot him unless he stops, or is spooked and needs to be snapped out of it. You're out of time.

DO YOU:

Try and fling the water bottle onto the BMW's windshield? TURN TO (4)

Engage the BWM with the .50 caliber? TURN TO (5).

(4) WATER

You grab the water bottle in one of your green, fuzzy gloves and chuck it. Your aim is true. The bottle caroms off the windshield right in front of the driver. This would get a reaction out of you for sure. But instead of stopping, the BMW driver steps on it and speeds past you in the next lane while you're trying to get the Fifty around. There's no longer a question of warning shots, but you could still stop the vehicle before it reaches the tankers. If you blow it away, you run the risk of Swiss-cheesing a family. If you don't stop it and it's a VBIED and it gets to one of the JP-4 Tankers, it could wipe out half the convoy.

DO YOU:

Fire on the BMW? TURN TO (5).

Let the BMW pass into the convoy? TURN TO (6).

(5) FIRE

The M2 Browning .50 caliber machine gun was designed near the end of the First World War, and its design reflects its heritage. It is black and 100 percent steel and more than five feet long, weighing well over one hundred pounds loaded. Each round is almost half a foot long, and they are clipped together in long steel belts that disintegrate into shell casing and projectile with a sound that is described as "barking" but of course doesn't sound like anything else except for the repeated detonations of about 250 grains of propellant reverberating through a four-foot-long steel barrel. There is a widespread misconception among American combat soldiers that its use against human targets is banned by a number of treaties, and recruits have been told by generations of drill sergeants to aim a Fifty at enemy soldiers' "equipment" rather than their bodies. The persistence of this myth can probably be explained by the fact that while smaller bullets punch holes in humans, the Fifty takes them apart.

You draw a bead at the piece of concrete just in front of the BMW and depress the butterfly trigger. It is terrifically loud. You struggle to keep the muzzle from moving up and right as it spits out five huge slugs per second—the BMW is right next to the trucks and heaven forfend you put a round into one of your buddies or a tanker. Your grandmother used to say "heaven forfend," and the phrase is repeated in your panic brain in a queer voice that is somewhere between your grandmother's and your own. You quit firing after three bursts, unwilling to continue to shoot alongside (heaven forfend) your own column. You watch gratefully as another gunner a few trucks down opens up as well.

The riddled BMW swerves to the left and slows. Your ribcage expands, as it seems like a physical weight has been lifted. You have not killed your friends, either with a bullet or through inaction. No one will suffer polytrauma because of you, you think, and to know that after a few seconds of not knowing it gives you a euphoria almost palpably chemical, the dopamine hitting your brain and a wave of pleasure moving from your scalp to your balls.

The column is moving slowly forward and your truck follows. The BMW slows and lists to port. It has no remaining windows. There is no blood visible, though of course there must be a sea of blood. A Browning .50 caliber round puts a hole in a human body the size of a grapefruit. The hole is much larger than the slug itself because of the kinetic force of the slug hitting flesh at approximately 2,910 feet per second.

It is afternoon and the sun is at about a forty-five-degree angle from the ground and very bright. Through the lattice of complex shadows you can see what is probably a human body in the back seat. One of the silhouette's hands is up by its shoulder, as though it is calling a waiter. You can see into the car more easily because all of the bullets make the shadow cast by the car's roof and sides somewhat translucent. You are convinced for a second that the person sitting up in the backseat is alive and unharmed. There are now a few thin streams of blood running from a bullet hole low in the passenger door and onto the concrete. The smell of burned-up ammunition propellant is acrid and strong. You briefly remember that the BMW could still be a bomb and duck back into your hatch after making a quick 360-degree scan. You then pass the location of the IED explosion and are out on the open road again, picking up speed, the radio buzzing furiously.

TURN TO (7)

(6) DENOUEMENT (I)

You have about two seconds to make this decision. Your heart tightens up, and your thumbs clench a bit, but you do not press the trigger. Maybe you decided at the time that the statistical probability of any black BMW sprinting into a US convoy in al-Anbar being an actual suicide bomber was low enough that the risk of death should be borne by your comrades rather than the BMW's occupants. More probably you just froze up in the moment and couldn't bring yourself to fire on a human being—a normal enough problem for troops throughout history. You're a smart person, and you'll have years to rationalize the decision.

The BMW floors it up through the convoy until it gets to the fourth truck, where Boyce sees it and is faster on the trigger than you. He yells at the BMW and puts a few rounds into the concrete in front of it. The BMW keeps going. As per SOP, Boyce then puts down a steady stream of fire in front of the vehicle, and the car drives right through it like a pole of fresh timber though a mill saw. The car swings to the left and smashes up against the median. The convoy's radios are all going furiously. Drivers don't know whether to drive in the right lane closest to the IED and the dirt berm that was drawing the convoy's fire, or in the left lane closest to the now-smoking BMW that everyone assumes is a possible VBIED.

You have gone back to scanning the rear, but allow yourself a long glance at the BMW as it passes by your right shoulder. Aside from the scattered dents in the roof, it looks from the rear like the driver just parked it up against the median for some inscrutable reason. You think you see at least one other person in the vehicle besides the driver. Soon the convoy clears the IED, and the spread-out broken glass and parked-looking, corpse-filled vehicle recede into the distance as you pick up speed.

You'll be chewed out but good for letting some random car come right into the convoy like that. You'll get a lot of meaningful glances from the other members of your platoon, too, who also spend time thinking about getting their jaws or dicks blown off, and who depend on you to fend off bombers. The next morning, your squad leader informs you that he's swapping you out with the driver. You'll be behind the wheel for the rest of the rotation.

THE END

(7) DENOUEMENT (II)

They do not ask how you knew that BMW was a VBIED; the whole crux of the terrorist tactic is to take what looks like an innocent civilian family sedan or produce truck and rig it to blow. The idea is to use your own humanity against you—if you are fast on the trigger, you will end up stopping car bombers but killing civilians, doing al-Qaeda's work for it. If you hold your fire past the point of no return, you will start to get hit more often as al-Qaeda realizes that convoys are soft targets. It is the other asymmetry of this type of asymmetric warfare: heads they win, tails you lose.

It was a good shoot—the vehicle was speeding into the convoy. The LT arranges for you to see the chaplain anyway, because he suspects (with what you imagine is near certainty) that the BMW was full of civilians, the driver maybe having been spooked by the IED and thinking the thing to do was just step on it. Possibly he was drunk, unusual at midafternoon, but who knows? You shot them, regardless. You accept this, at first, as an unfortunate happenstance that is sort of the by-product of a landscape in which every enemy appears by design to be a civilian, which means that every civilian appears as a possible enemy. It will become a small hard nut of guilt and self-pity that you carry around, and that will, in subtle ways, color your opinions about yourself and the government and the people around you. You will find it hard to concentrate and your mind will frequently wander. You will stew in anger over insults that you imagine in daydreams. You will want to kill again, for a time. You will never quite be the same, although of course, no one can be certain whether or not this is a bad thing.

THE END

12

Big Two-Hearted Hunting Creek

Brian Van Reet

A FEW WEEKS AGO, SLEED AND I loaded onto a sleek tour bus. We filed behind a gaggle of other "wounded warriors"—the term the Army used to refer to us in official memoranda. I guess it's what we were, but the phrase was too cute to do our ugliness justice.

It was a beautiful May day, and we were taking the bus to Maryland to do some trout fishing. I had convinced Sleed to come along after seeing a sign-up sheet in the hallway outside my group's meeting room. I normally wouldn't participate in extracurriculars, but had fished the stream we'd be going to, years before. I grew up nearby in the city of Frederick and guess I took the trip because I wanted to revisit old stomping grounds—that, and I was going stir crazy in the barracks.

There were a bunch of guys like me at Walter Reed—severe burn cases, the faceless. You would think we would have hung out together, but we avoided it as much as possible. We all looked the same; being around one another was like looking in a mirror. None of us wanted that. We wanted to forget.

Sleed was not faceless. His was okay—a few scars—but mostly intact. Back at Camp War Eagle, he had been standing beside me in the awards ceremony, both of us receiving commendation medals from the Division Commander, when the suicide bomber ran up and exploded himself. Sleed lost his cock and balls and one of his legs above the knee. My privates survived the blast—my right leg shielded them—but I was never going to need them again, not with how I looked. I don't know how it was Sleed took most of the shrapnel while I got the brunt of the fireball. There's no explaining these things.

Sleed was served divorce papers shortly after returning to the States from the army hospital in Germany. His wife came bearing them on her one trip to DC from Toad Lick, Georgia, to visit her wounded husband. Turned out she had been cheating on him for most of the time he had been overseas and cited the loss of his reproductive organs, among other reasons, as grounds for divorce. She wanted more kids.

The whole situation was nightmarishly helpless, but there it was, our bodies transformed in a flash I could not remember. The only thing to do now was deal with it. Time was reckoned in two halves, before and after. I took a window seat on the bus. Sleed sat beside me. He was tall and ropey muscled, with freckled skin that tanned deeply in summer and paled to magnolia white in winter.

The air brakes released with a hiss, and we pulled out of the parking lot and onto Georgia Avenue. I thought it must be a painful reminder for Sleed to have to live on a street named after his home state, where his wife was probably hard at work trying to have more babies with her new boyfriend, a divorced first sergeant with two kids of his own. Sleed had sworn to fight his wife—"The Bitch," as he unfailingly called her—for custody of their three-year-old daughter, but the judge in the case had ruled the proceedings delayed until Sleed's medical retirement could be processed. In the meantime, Sleed had employed a private detective to gather dirt on his wife.

He had been raised in a foster home, surrounded by people he called his brothers and sisters, some black, some white. The way he talked about it, it had been rough, and he still hadn't rid himself of the bad habit that had resurfaced way back in the first week of our deployment: the liberal use of the n-word. The drill sergeants had broken him of this unfortunate tic in basic, but it had reared its ugly head again in Iraq and never gone away.

Sometimes, if we were in a public place, I would have to elbow him to silence his incessant rants about "that nigga that stole that fucking bitch and my kid." The thing was, his wife's new boyfriend wasn't black. Sleed wasn't a racist. He used the slur at random, sometimes affectionately, sometimes reproachfully, but never in reference to skin tone. Trouble was other people didn't know that.

He was one of those larger-than-life personalities, able to pull you out of your troubles and into his. Christmas morning, 2004, the bombed-out UN compound in Baghdad. In the muddy field on the other side of the wall, an Iraqi boy called up to my tower: "Mistah, Mistah, Merry Christmas! Chocalaté?"

Eight hours of soft and steady rain falling from a grey sky, soaking our body armor and black fleece, sucking the heat from our core. Along with myself, Sleed and the other members of 3rd Platoon pulled guard in the towers and bunkers encircling the UN. We were cold and wet on Christmas; engaged in the pointless activity of guarding an abandoned complex of buildings. Morale was especially low.

We carried walkabout radios, and Sleed came over the net thirty minutes into the miserable shift. He proceeded to tell jokes about our mothers for the better part of an hour, one after the other, a ceaseless string of insult: "Hey, Tower Seven, yo' momma so fat, she have to put on lipstick with a paint roller"; "Front Gate, yo' momma so stupid, when yo' daddy said it was chilly outside, she ran out with a spoon"; " . . . so poor, she hangs the toilet paper up to dry"; " . . . so greasy, she sweats Crisco"; " . . . head so small, she got her ear pierced and died"; " . . . so nasty, she have to creep up on bathwater." And once he had insulted all our mothers and exhausted his extensive repertoire, someone else came over the net and took up the banner. Trifling, moronic, and juvenile, yes, but in this way 3rd Platoon passed Christmas 2004.

Never at a loss for words, he was now unusually quiet as we traveled due north for a few miles before merging onto the Beltway. We passed out of DC proper and into Maryland, taking I-270. The scenery changed from urban to suburban. Million-dollar McMansions, quarter-million-dollar condos, strip malls, golf courses, and commercial parks lined the highway. Traffic lightened up—the cars all headed the other way, into Washington. Compared to Baghdad, everything looked so green. The vividness of it was like being on a mild dose of psychedelics, all the time.

Readjusting my sensibilities was a slow process, and I was also just getting used to not having my weapon with me. Call it "phantom gun syndrome." Like an amputee who still feels his limb tickle, I would find myself reaching down my right side, searching for the M4 carbine that should have been slung on my shoulder. I missed its reassuring heft, the way the charging handle dug into my hipbone.

We traveled for an hour. When we hit the clustered spires of Frederick, my old hometown, we switched onto US-15. Francis Scott Key's Frederick. John Whittier's. Lee's, Grant's. Located on the cusp of a pass through the Appalachians, the town had changed hands several times during the Civil War. Each time, the citizenry had filled the streets to cheer whichever conquering army happened to be marching through. This fact had always struck me as telling. Even during our most brutal, existential war, most Americans didn't care enough to stick their necks out for the cause.

We drove through the north side of town. I watched familiar scenes through the glare of my window seat: the ice rink where I had taken my first date and played countless games of hockey in high school, my favorite used bookshop, the liquor store owned by the Pakistanis who never carded. I caught a glimpse of myself reflected in a passing SUV. From a distance, I didn't look half-bad. The only thing off was the size of my head: swollen, as if it had been stung by a thousand bees.

On the horizon was a familiar set of industrial-looking buildings. I got Sleed's attention and pointed them out. "Fort Detrick," I said. "They do testing on monkeys there."

"What kinda testing?" he asked.

"Chemical and biological weapons. They have a big incinerator where they burn the dead monkeys."

"How you know that?"

"My dad works there."

"You never told me he was Army."

"He's not, anymore. Civilian contractor."

The first time my parents had come to visit after I'd arrived at Walter Reed, my father had given me a check for twenty thousand dollars. "Starting out money," he'd called it.

I lay on a hospital bed in a paper gown, recovering from the latest skin graft. Before entering my room, my parents had to scrub down like surgeons, donning hospital coveralls, masks, hair caps. My father placed the check on the nightstand beside the bed. He said it was the least they could do. He could hardly bear to look at me. My mom wept quietly. Nobody talked much. They visited often in the beginning, dutifully, every weekend. My mom went so far as to stay the first two weeks in a nearby hotel.

Five months later, the grafts had hardened nicely. I was a fast healer, and the risk for infection had returned to near baseline. Physiologically, I was out of the woods, off morphine and onto muscle relaxers for the pain. I had completed the initial course of therapy, and the Army had started the paperwork for a medical retirement. My parents were in town on yet another visit.

"So what are your plans?" my father asked.

"Live off the government," I said. "Get wasted." I was a little high on pills, or I wouldn't have been so bold. In Valium veritas.

"You don't mean that," he said, looking agitated. "You're just upset because of what happened."

"No shit I'm upset," I said. "Look, maybe you two should just leave. To tell the truth, I want you to stop coming here. This place depresses me enough without having to deal with this."

A month had passed since then, and they hadn't been back.

Now, to the west of the interstate, the bus ferrying me and Sleed along at a steady seventy miles per hour, I sighted the building where, for the good of the nation, my father infected rhesus macaques with smallpox, his lab only miles from the antiseptic home where my mother spent her days watching cable news and talking to the cat. I tried to imagine how it must feel to be a parent to a son in pain who doesn't want your help. I felt awful for them, but that didn't change the fact that I felt better apart. They were not rotten people—don't get me wrong—statistically speaking, they had been the best I could have hoped for: upper middle class, free thinking, well educated. I had been taken to art museums as a child, read to, enrolled in the finest preschool, kindergarten, et cetera. I had not entirely failed as a son, either. About the worst trouble I had ever gotten into was partying too hard and flunking out of school, and I remedied that dishonor by joining the Army a month after September 11. None of us had been bad people; we had simply made the wrong choices. How could they have known their values would lead me to this? That all that safety would push me into the fire?

I asked myself these and other unanswerable questions as we passed the borders of my old home, into acres of corn broken by the occasional exurban neighborhood, the new houses, trimmed in plastic, out of place in cul-de-sacs carved from cow pastures.

We turned off US-15 near the little town of Thurmont, onto a state road climbing into the Blue Ridge Mountains. The winding, two-lane road tunneled through a forest of oak, poplar, and hickory. The trees grew from a mat of ferns and decaying leaves atop a thin but rich soil broken by crags of limestone. A sign said we had entered Catoctin Mountain National Park. We drove a ways farther and then pulled into a gravel lot, where we filed off the bus. Sleed struggled down the narrow steps with his cane and prosthesis, which he was still getting used to. This had been a sticking point in his coming.

"How the hell am I going to fish?" he had asked. "I can't even hold a damn rod and stand at the same time. Let alone wade."

"You don't have to fish," I said. "You'll like it up there. Just sit down and relax by the river. It's beautiful country."

In the end, I had convinced him to come with the promise I would owe him, and as Sleed stepped off the bus and into Mother Nature, he said, "Well, Rooster, you weren't kidding. This is nice."

A short ways down the hillside, a creek gurgled through a rock-strewn channel. The rounded stones of the riverbed gave the water an amber tint. Manicured bluegrass ran down to moss-covered outcroppings lining the bank. My mammalian brain translated the white noise of running water into feelings of rejuvenation, nourishment, safety—a comfortable place to stay. I could feel it working on me. My shoulders sagged as a knot of tension buried in my upper back began to unravel. High overhead, songbirds built nests and called vigorously to rivals. Beams of sunlight streamed through leaves rustling in a gentle wind. The left side of my face was numb, but I felt the draft on the hairs of my forearms, the back of my neck. On the ground below, the breeze was no more than a stranger's breath. Any stronger and the air would have been too cool—but it was a perfect day. The fishing guide chartered by the Army had brought along the equipment we would need, and under his direction we unloaded the luggage bins beneath the bus. Once that was done, the guide gathered us around.

"Name's Grossnickle," he said. "This here's Big Hunting Creek. Y'all ready to do some fishing?"

A few of us answered with half-hearted yeahs, about as much affect as we could muster. Some joker said Big Hunting Creek didn't look so big. Unfazed, Grossnickle told us the stream became deeper and wider the closer it got to the Chesapeake Bay. Up here we were near the source. The Parks Service had designated this stretch as fly-fishing only, catch-and-release. Strictly for the purists.

He showed us how to set up a rod and gave us a quick clinic in fly-casting. I already knew how to do it and didn't pay close attention, absorbed instead by all the greenery, and the way the sunbeams reflected off bits of road dust floating in the air. After the lesson had finished and we were turned loose, I took my rod and hobbled off on my own, but not before asking Grossnickle to tie a fly onto my tippet. I was getting better at using my bad hand, but I'd never again have the dexterity to manipulate fishing line.

It took me awhile, but eventually I could flick the wooly bugger into the creek with some degree of accuracy. I cast, then gathered in the line with my claw-like left hand, jerking it erratically to simulate the movement of a wounded minnow. I wasn't even trying to hook a fish—just liked the look of the fly moving freely in the whiskey-colored water, its black feathers undulating like real fins. Cast and retrieve, cast and retrieve. There was something comforting in the rhythm of it.

After practicing for a while, I reeled in the fly, set down the rod, pried off my shoes, peeled off my socks, rolled up my jeans, took the rod, and waded into the creek to fish for real. The shallow water was ice cold. It rushed up my shins and around my calves with surprising force. My balls tightened and my toes numbed, but I kept my resolve and headed upstream in search of a pool suitable for big fish. Every so often I stood on a rock until my feet warmed and the feeling returned with pins and needles.

I had been wading about a half hour, casting into a few deep pools where falling water had eroded the earth between boulders, but still no luck. The farther upstream I went, the trees grew closer together and the canopy tightened, admitting less and less light.

I passed through a deep cut with steep and muddy banks. On the other side, the terrain flattened out, and the creek took a sharp bend, becoming much wider. A massive white oak had fallen and created a natural dam. Radiating from the main trunks like the brittle fingers of dead men, a tangle of limbs dipped under the foamy water, snagging floating branches, leaves, and plastic bags.

The bank around the oak was covered with a heavy growth of ferns and giant cattails. The downed tree had caused a web of rivulets to overflow the main stream and flood the low-lying surroundings. My feet sank to the ankles in cold muck as I hacked my way through the tangle of fronds. When I had bypassed the oak, which must have been nearly a hundred feet tall, I cut back toward the water. I emerged from the undergrowth to find a deep pool on the upstream side of the dam. The leaves lining the bottom of the pool leached tannins. The bed of decay colored the sluggish water dark, almost black.

I waded into the shallows at the head of the pool and cast my fly as near to the oak as I could without risking the line. Then, slowly, I retrieved it. I could not see my lure in the water but imagined how my movements would translate. When I jerked the line, the wooly bugger shot upward, top-lit at the surface, presented to any waiting predator—hopefully a trout, though I had inadvertently caught turtles in this creek. I paused, letting the fly fall through the water toward the bottom.

On my third try, the rod came alive in my hand. For the first time in a long time I felt a welcome burst of adrenaline, a better drug than booze or pills. The hair on my neck stood on end and my breath quickened. As it fought against a shadow much larger than itself, the fish's every burst of life was transmitted to me through the fly line via the tippet, a thread of nylon, microns thick, the whole process a kind of naturalistic Morse code. For such a small creature it was surprisingly strong, bending the rod in half.

I took my time and let the fish run, careful not to give it too much line for fear it would entangle itself on the submerged tree. When the fish tired, I headed to the bank and reeled it in, lifting it from the water. It flopped wildly and fell off the hook onto the mud, where it continued to thrash, opening and closing its gills, gasping. I pounced on it, picked up a rock the size of my fist, and thumped its head until it went rigid.

It was a big one—not the biggest I'd ever caught—maybe fifteen inches long, a couple pounds of lean muscle. It was a rainbow, a species once foreign to this water, introduced in the 1940s when the government stocked the river to satisfy the increasing demand of sportsmen. The native brook trout, more sensitive to environment than their larger, hardier cousins, had lost out.

It had been years since I had eaten trout of any kind, but suddenly found I really wanted to. I couldn't bring my catch back on the bus—the park service's rules and all—but I had my lighter and pocketknife. I decided the thing to do was to clean the fish, build a small fire, and cook it on the spot.

First, to cut off its head. I walked up the bank and flattened a patch of ferns to form a work area. I experimented with holding the knife in my good hand, but the fish was too slimy and kept sliding out from under the other. So I switched hands, now holding the trout in place with my right, pinching the knife in what remained of my left. I plunged in the blade just anterior to the pectoral fin near the gill cover. Clear fluid tinged with blood ran into the ferns.

When I hit the spine, I couldn't generate enough force between my three fingers to keep the knife from slipping as I tried to sever bone and the sinewy spine. It probably would have been wiser just to gut the thing and leave the head on, but my father had taught me how to cut fillets, and I had done it that way countless times before. Force of habit dies hard.

I gripped the knife in the palm of my bad hand and nicked the tip of the blade into the spine, balancing the knife perpendicular to the ground. I rammed downward with the heel of my palm. The knife shot sideways and sliced through the index finger of my good hand. I cursed and tried to bend it; it would go only halfway, exposing white bone as flaps of skin separated to reveal layers of red and yellow tissue. Then the bleeding started. Great. Now I only had five good fingers.

I let out a primal yell, grabbed the fish, brought it to my mouth, and wrenched its head the rest of the way off with one powerful chomp. As I pulled its tail away, stomach, liver, swim bladder, and intestines were stripped from its carcass and fell, a chain of organs, onto my chin. I spit them and the attached head into the water. Black wisps of blood eddied and curled in the shallows of the dark pool. Another trout shot to the surface to strike at the remains.

My anger was gone as soon as it had arrived. I laughed, tasting bleeding gums pricked by scale and bone, and threw the carcass as far as I could into the woods.

"Rooster! You okay? Where are you?" Sleed's voice called to me from somewhere within the ferns on the north bank. I answered and listened to his noisy approach, picturing him whacking away at the fronds with his cane. He punched through the bank too near the oak, nearly plunging through a marshy false-ground before catching his step. Seeing me, he skirted the pool and came around to the shallows.

"What the hell?" I asked. "You following me?"

"Naw," he panted, out of breath from bushwhacking. "There's a trail and a bench over there. I was taking a break and heard you."

"I cut my hand trying to clean a fish." I wiped blood, guts, and fish shit off my face.

"Damn, nigga, that's bleeding bad. Here, take this." He stripped off his T-shirt, literally offering me the shirt off his back. What a great guy—I wish I could peel his face off and take it for my own.

"Keep it," I said. "I'll use mine."

I got him to tear a strip off my shirt and wrap it around my finger. I applied pressure and elevated my hand above my heart. I sat down. Sleed lit a cigarette.

"You know you not supposed to keep 'em, right?"

"I know," I said. "But I wanted to eat it."

"How were you gonna do that?"

I bared my bloody teeth and felt a few rainbow scales still clinging to my gums. They must have glistened like mother-of-pearl in the half-light. Fish and human blood commingled, tasting salty on my tongue. Sleed whistled and said, "Rooster, you one crazy son of a bitch."

* * *

Following the graded path that paralleled Big Hunting Creek, Sleed and I returned to the parking area. There, Grossnickle dressed my wound with his first aid kit. Before returning to his nap on the bus, he said my finger would need stitches. Nothing new there—over the past seven months I had become a veritable expert in plastic surgery, obsessed with the latest advances in facial nerve damage, tear duct injuries, ear avulsions. Able to extemporize on the differences between split and full-thickness skin grafts, tissue expansions, random-pattern flaps, pedicled flaps, free-form flaps, my dream was to someday receive a face transplant, a procedure yet to be performed in the States. A few stitches on my hand were small potatoes in light of the larger project of reconstruction.

It was almost noon, we were the first to make it back from fishing, and the clear blue of the morning had given way to an overcast sky, rusty-grey clouds moving quickly overhead. Looking straight up, I could almost trick myself into thinking it was the trees in the foreground that were moving, and not the sky behind.

A cold front had stalled in the valley to the east and finally spilled over the mountains. A fine mist formed in the forest, muted rainbows and halos sparking in the gaps between foliage, blurring distant objects. Two soldier fishers, identifiable only by silhouette, emerged like specters from the wood line before passing again out of sight. Sleed and I sat on a squared log coated with creosote, the border of the parking lot. We took turns pitching bits of gravel, aiming for an empty soda can ten feet away. To make the game interesting, we had a few bucks riding on it. Sleed hit the target first.

"Got a call from the PI when you was fishing," he said. He picked up another pebble and shook it in his closed fist. "They're doing it in public."

"What?"

"The Bitch is banging that nigga in public!"

"Oh, shit."

"Yeah. Looks like he's got a thing for it. Restrooms, parked cars—my man said he got footage of them in the car outside my baby's daycare. He's sending me the video." Sleed flung the stone at the can, nailing it again.

"Why would you want to watch that?"

"You know," he said, ignoring me. "Krystal would never even suck me off. I mean, once in a blue moon—my birthday, right before we left for Iraq, shit like that. But I could tell she hated it. And then I'm gone for a year, and this nigga has her screwing in public. Unreal."

What could I possibly say to console this man? Really more of a boy, only twenty-one, and he had already been denied in so many ways—cuckolded, mutilated. What could I possibly say to dignify the situation? Nothing. I hung my head and picked at the gravel, embarrassed for him.

We pitched rocks, traded stories and small bills, until a red sports coupe with tinted windows pulled into the parking area, empty except for our bus. A decal on the coupe's rear window read "Princess." The doors opened and two girls got out. The driver looked no older than sixteen or seventeen, her passenger, a year or so younger. They were both dressed in flip-flops, brightly colored halter tops, and shorts cut so high, the bottom crease of their ass flesh was clearly visible. The girls gathered their book bags and locked the doors. Clearly, they were not here to fish.

Acknowledging our gaze, the younger one smiled and waved shyly. She had a kind face, and I waved back. Her friend refused eye contact; her face sharp, disdainful, ears pierced up and down with studs and dangling baubles. She looked like a stone-cold fox, like she didn't give a shit about anything. They both looked fine. I hadn't been with a woman in almost two years. Sleed never would again, not like that. When they reached the trailhead at the opposite end of the parking lot, the girls took the path to the left, hiking out of sight.

Sleed returned his focus to the can, tossing stone after stone. He lit a cigarette and smoked it down to the butt in a half-dozen drags. He stubbed it out. He cleared his throat, sighed deeply, took up his cane, and clambered to his feet.

"I'm gonna go take a walk to warm up," he said. "It's cold as hell out here."

"What about the game? It's my throw."

"I forfeit. Take the money." He stretched his long arms overhead and started off.

"Hold up, I'm coming with you."

"Just wait here."

"I'm coming."

"Fine. Suit yourself."

We had been together through some shit, and even though I had a bad feeling about what he was up to—or maybe because I had a bad feeling—I couldn't abandon him now.

At the trailhead, Sleed took the right-hand fork, easing my suspicions some. The birds that had called so noisily that morning were now quiet. Empty tree limbs swayed in a moderate wind. It was the type of weather you see before a big storm, a lot of rotation in the sky, the barometric pressure going haywire.

We had been walking for a few minutes when Sleed made an abrupt left off the trail. "It's a damn school day," he said, apropos of nothing.

"What?"

"I said those girls should be in school."

"What are you now, a truant officer?"

He smirked. He had this wild look in his eyes. "No. A messenger."

"Have you lost it or what? Wait. Wait a minute. I said stop! This is—"

"Look, Sergeant." He stopped. "Why don't you go back and wait."

Still I could not desert him. I thought about picking up a tree branch and clubbing him from behind, but then again, he hadn't done anything yet.

We hiked awhile longer before cresting the top of a gentle rise. Fifty meters down the other side was the left-hand path, the one the two girls had taken. Sleed began to parallel it on the far side of the rise, observing what was ahead without silhouetting himself on the ridgeline.

"What are you gonna do when you find them?"

He would not answer or even acknowledge me following him. I reasoned hopefully that perhaps his intentions were not wholly malicious; maybe he only wanted to give them a good talking to, scare them a little, tell them playing hooky all alone in the woods wasn't smart. Maybe, I thought—my imagination ranging to the sexually fantastic—maybe he'll use that legendary charm to sweet talk them into laying me for the first time in years, conjuring up, with sheer charisma, a sympathy fuck *au naturel*, a therapeutic *ménage à trois* for the national good. Maybe this is not what it seems.

But soon I returned to reality: the shale outcropping beneath my feet, a mat of leaves, the root of a tree, exposed and gnarled. Sleed tottered along in front, herky-jerky, hunched over, pursuing his prey like a man in a trance, Jake Barnes and Captain Ahab rolled into one, his focus both monomaniacal and directionless. I followed on.

A quarter mile down the trail, we spotted them sitting on a bench just off the path, taking turns dragging on a one-hitter. Big Hunting Creek ran behind them, masking the sound of our approach. They had not seen us. Sleed ducked behind a tree. He motioned for me to do the same. It felt wrong, but I took cover. Part of me wanted to see what he would do.

They passed the pipe. It must have been the younger girl's first time, because she handled it awkwardly. Her older friend drew an exaggerated breath, demonstrating what she should do, and held the lighter. The younger girl took a big hit, kept it in her lungs for a few seconds, then coughed, doubling over, hacking up a rope of spit that hung from her mouth. The one with all the piercings laughed and patted her back until she recovered. Their mouths moved but I heard no words.

Sleed stepped out like a sleepwalker from behind the tree.

"What are you doing?" I asked.

He did not answer.

He made it to within thirty feet before they saw him and sprang to their feet. The older one fumbled with the pipe, a small bag of dope, and her book bag.

"Don't worry," he said, waving an arm in a gesture of beneficence, approaching closer. "We're not gonna hurt you. I want to show you something."

The older girl glanced down the path like she was thinking about making a break for it.

"No," he said, his expression oddly serene. He moved his right hand behind his back. "Don't do that. I have a gun."

Standing behind him, I could see very well he didn't. I stepped forward.

The younger girl started to cry. "Please don't kill us," she said.

"I told you I wouldn't. But don't run." He dropped his cane and began to unzip his fly. "I need to show you something. You should see what they did to me."

He started to pull down his jeans, slowly, as if this were a striptease. The younger girl stepped back, her mouth half-open. Like diseased, molten flesh, scar tissue covered Sleed's left hip, now exposed. This was not right. This had gone too far. Before it could go any further, I rushed him and shoved him to the ground.

"Run," I said. "Get as far away as you can."

The girls took off. Sleed struggled to get up. I tackled him. We wrestled around on the ground, tussling, ending up with me on my back, him on top facing away, my legs wrapped around him, feet in his crotch, his neck in the crook of my forearm—a rear naked choke, a move taught to every private in basic. I cranked down. Sleed struggled valiantly, tensing his neck, clawing at my arm, and rocking back and forth, but I had him in a superior position, and without a solid base he didn't have the leverage to shake me from his back. His face turned red and then purple as blood drained of oxygen. His thrashing stopped and I felt him go limp. I released the choke and shoved him off. Scooting up, I grabbed his cane to use as a weapon, just in case he had any fight left in him. It seemed doubtful. He looked downright pitiful, out cold, his jeans still unzipped around his thighs. He was a mess, down there, like a chewed-up Ken doll.

His limbs jerked involuntarily as his brain came back online. He took a deep, whooping lungful of air, then, wracked by coughing, rolled over on his side and pulled up his pants. He remained there in the fetal position until he caught his breath, at which point he began to drag himself toward a hickory growing near the bench where the girls had been sitting. His prosthesis had come loose in the struggle and lay disembodied in the center of the path. I placed his cane beside it. He made it to the tree and sat with his back against it, holding onto himself carefully and delicately.

I turned and started to walk away, back to the trailhead and whatever waited.

Sleed called out after me. "Hey, Rooster. It's funny. I can feel my heart beat through the leaves."

It didn't sound like something he would say. I left him there, lying against the hardwood. Hailstones began to fall. They hit Big Hunting Creek like bullets ricocheting off depleted uranium armor.

13

ROLL CALL

David Abrams

"REMEMBER KNOBLOCH?"

"IED, right?"

"Yeah. Mosul."

"Motherfucker sure could play Texas Hold 'Em."

"Damn straight."

We were standing around after the memorial service. Seven of us, the ones who'd made it this far.

The afternoon wind kicked up and we bent our heads, tucking up under our Kevlars. Two of us realized the dust covers on our 16s were open and clicked them shut. To someone passing by, it might have looked like we were praying, huddled in a tight circle of faith and brotherhood.

Bullshit. It was just the motherfucking wind.

But yeah, God and the hereafter and all that come-unto-me crap was fresh in our minds, since we'd just wrapped up Carter's memorial service. We could hear the dog tags clicking against the receiver on Carter's downturned M16.

Twenty minutes ago, First Sergeant had bellowed out the roll call in the formal tradition of army memorial services. It was down in a corner of the FOB, this makeshift outdoor theater where the Fobbits came for their entertainment—movies and boxing matches and USO shows. Last week, there'd been a country-western singer and two *Maxim* "Girls Next Door" signing autographs right where we were sitting.

Now it was set up for the memorial service. A plywood stage, rows of plastic chairs, a three-tiered platform that looked like something you'd see at the Olympics. At the top of the pyramid—the gold-medal winner—were the 16, the dog tags, and a pair of boots. Those boots weren't Carter's—his had cooked to char in the Bradley. These were a fresh pair someone had procured from Supply.

In front of the boots was a picture—a portrait someone had printed out on a computer and taped to the back of an MRE box. The face, at least, was Carter's. He was all sunglasses and attitude, real Clint Eastwood. The dumb fuck.

The chaplain had had his say and now First Sergeant stood up there in front of us, his face all red and puffy and shit. He unfolded the company roster and held it in both hands. He had to cough a couple of times before he could shake the words loose.

"Sergeant Guerrero!"

"Here, First Sergeant!" Guerrero answered.

"Specialist Kleinman!"

"Here, First Sergeant!" Kleinman replied.

"Staff Sergeant Daniels!"

"Here, First Sergeant!" Daniels responded.

"Private First Class Carter!"

Silence.

"Private First Class Carter!"

Silence. A faint rustle as some of us shifted in our seats. The wind picked up again and rippled Carter's face.

"*Private First Class Carter!*"

Still no answer.

First Sergeant stopped there and folded the roster. For a minute nothing happened. Even though we knew it was coming, we flinched when the volley cracked the air to our left.

Then we all lined up and, one at a time, walked forward to have our moment with Carter, saying whatever we needed to say to his rifle and boots.

Now we pulled in tight together against the wind. We cupped our cigarettes and made the best of it.

"How about Goldman from over in Delta? 'Member that faggot?"

"Shit yeah. Me and him bunked together for three weeks in Kuwait."

"Oh, yeah. Forgot about that."

"Why you wanna bring up Goldman anyway?"

"He just came to mind, that's all."

"Well, next time, keep it to yourself."

"What the fuck? Sorry."

We fell silent, remembering the last time we'd seen Goldman on Route Irish. His chest plate had cracked and his DCU top had ripped open. You could see the wet jumble of Goldman's guts tumbling into the street. No one deserved to end up like that.

The wind surged in a roar, then died down like it was pondering some heavy shit, then started back up like before.

"Oh, fuck. Private Martinez?"

Someone barked a laugh. "Yeah. Shit. Little Manny the Moocher."

A few of us chuckled.

"Damn, he was slick."

"Like grease on butter."

"He get hit by a sniper or something?"

"Hell no, asshole, he was in the Humvee that day. The one that went into the canal."

"He *was* in there, wasn't he? Damn. Him and Sergeant Randolph."

"Fuckin' Martinez. 'Hey man, you gotta smoke? Gotta smoke?' Motherfucker never bought a pack of smokes in his entire shit-eating life. 'Gotta smoke?'"

"Yeah, fuckin' Martinez." Nobody mentioned his wife and kids, but those of us who smoked raised our cigarettes in salute.

"And Navarro."

"Fuck *yeah*, Navarro."

"Funny as fuck."

"Damn straight."

We thought about Navarro and his Kevlar. Huddled there, each of us imagined cupping that empty helmet in our hands, just as we had three months ago. On that day, standing beside the IED crater, we passed that Kevlar from hand to hand like a communion tray. We looked at what was inside. The paint-splash of brain, the splinters of bone, small as clipped fingernails. In the dry canal to our left, bitter smoke rose from a tire that wouldn't stop smoldering. The helmet went around. One of us lifted it to his face, announced it smelled like pussy. It sounded like something Navarro would have said.

"That Navarro," one of us said now as we smoked after Carter's service.

"Fucker always had a joke."

Somebody coughed, and it was like something hard came loose: the names started pouring out, dropping to the dirt in the center of our circle. It was like a game to see who could remember the most.

"Sanders, Washington—"

"—Hemmings, Arcala, Martinez—"

"We already said Martinez."

"Bebout, Kaufman—"

"Kaufman doesn't count."

"So, a foot and punched-out kidney don't count?"

"I'm just saying, he got medevacked. If you're gonna be consistent—"

"Fuck you."

"Yeah, why don't you shut the fuck up? Kaufman counts."

"Whatever."

"As I was saying: Bebout, *Kaufman*, White—"

"Sterrett, that clerk-n-jerk in headquarters. And what the fuck was that fucker doing outside the wire anyway?"

"And Coston from 3–7."

And on it went until finally First Sergeant called to us, his voice barking but gentle in a way we rarely heard. We looked over our shoulders. He was standing by the Humvees, waving his arm impatiently.

We stood, shouldered our rifles, sucked down one more drag from our smokes, then finger-flicked them into that motherfucking wind.

On the way back, we passed the jagged remains of Carter's Bradley parked in the sun-blasted motor pool. Nobody looked. We didn't want to keep thinking about Carter trapped in there, roasting like meat in an oven, rounds cooking off in his face. We'd already been at it all day, and still had a full shift waiting for us when we got back—not even any rack time, just pull up, load up, get the coordinates, then roll back out. We didn't have time to get distracted by Carter and his fucking dog tags slapping the side of his rifle.

Later, at the next memorial service, maybe we'd bring up his name and talk about it. Those of us who were still around.

14

AND BUGS DON'T BLEED

Matt Gallagher

"I'M SORRY TO BRING IT UP." Brett leaned across the table and placed his hand on Liz's arm. "But has he been, I mean, did he . . . "

At a coffee shop table overlooking a grey Koko Marina, Liz poured sugar into her mug. A summer wind wailed in the afternoon; palm trees and docked sailboats swayed to its will. A light rain rapped at the roof and the concrete sidewalks. Though the only customers in the shop, Liz kept her voice low and measured.

"No, no, it's okay," she said. "And no, not anything like that. I'm sorry, Brett. We should study. We need to study." She pointed to the law books piled on the table, but Brett, dressed in a checkered, button-up shirt, khaki shorts, flip-flops, and a yellow bracelet with the words "Live Strong" etched into it, shook his head.

"It's fine. That can wait. Talk to me."

She sipped her coffee and laughed. "I just don't know anymore. Last week, I woke up and saw the light on in the living room."

"Okay," he said.

"I got up to see if everything was alright. And Will was sitting there on the couch, holding a poster of that Sadr guy."

"Who?"

"He's an Iraqi terrorist. He brought it back with him from the last deployment." She was silent for a moment, then continued. "I told him to throw it away a year ago. I think it was a year ago. It freaks me out. His counselor told him keeping stuff like that wouldn't help him move on. It's all crinkled up and has Arabic scrawl on it and terrorists in the desert with guns—big guns—and a big red moon and that creepy, creepy fat man. It's terrible."

"Then what happened?"

"I told him to put it away because I thought it might trigger something. And then he turned to me and said, 'Why the long face, killer?' I grabbed the poster and ripped it up and threw it away. He wouldn't . . . he wouldn't come back to bed."

"What did he say the next morning?"

"We didn't discuss it. He doesn't like talking about his freakouts. And they really don't happen that much, especially compared to some of the other guys. You should see what their wives and girlfriends have to put up with."

"I don't even know what to tell you," Brett said, removing his hand from Liz's arm. Their skin glowed with the layer of warm sweat native to the islands. Brett looked out the far window at a cluster of thunderheads cresting the mountains. He'd normally see a series of jagged, green cliffs and ridgelines, but the clouds concealed all of this. "I'm sorry, but I'm sick of him taking his issues out on you."

A barista walked by their table, mopping the floor in slow, deliberate swirls. Neither Liz nor Brett moved their feet for the mop. The shop was well lit and clean, and the humming of an unseen air conditioner filled the silence. Liz studied the walls splashed with abstract portraits of dead Hawaiian kings and queens. Eventually the barista moved out of earshot.

"The coffee guy is definitely checking you out. He must have a tall blonde fantasy."

"Brett!"

"Hey, it's not his fault. Seriously, your shorts—I have boxers that cover more."

"Stop it! They're just normal workout shorts."

"No worries, my dear. This is Hawaii! All in the Aloha spirit." An elastic smile stretched out across his face and he gave her the shaka sign. His eyes moved up and down her body, settling on the moisture at the edge of her neck. "But a sports bra?" he continued. "The poor boy must be about sixteen. You have no idea what you're doing to his brain."

"What do you know about the Aloha spirit? You're more of a mainlander than I am. At least I lived here before law school."

"Very true," Brett said. "But to be fair, if my college girlfriend—boyfriend in your case—dropped out after 9/11 and got stationed in paradise, I'd have followed, too."

"Don't be a jerk. Let's study. I've been so worried about our Torts exam, I've been getting headaches."

"Torts?"

"Torts."

"Yes, well, I brought everything we should need. Sometimes I feel like your little errand boy."

"I know, I'm sorry. But it's been so crazy these past couple weeks."

Brett attempted to peer into Liz's shaking eyes, but she looked away, though not before he noticed the puffy bags she'd tried to obscure with a cream-colored makeup. He took a deep breath and smelled a blend of ocean water, orchids, and coffee grinds. After a few seconds, he spoke. "You sure you're okay with him leaving again?"

She looked down at the table and put her head into her hands. In response, Brett slid his plastic chair around the table, and put his arm around her shoulder, covering up a sigh with a quick sweep of his long, brown bangs.

"He do anything else?"

"Not really," she said. "But things have been, they've been . . . I guess things have been weird for a while."

"How so? Is it because you moved into his place?"

"I don't think so. That was supposed to fix things. Mainly since we got back from our trip home to Michigan. So it's not . . . it's not that. It's all the other stuff. I told him that he doesn't need to go back, because of his, well, because he's already been over there and done his part."

"Absolutely right."

"But he doesn't listen to me. He only listens to Sergeant Snow, who says they're going to finish the job this time. And Will thinks that if he stays here, he'd be abandoning the platoon."

Brett grimaced and removed his arm from her shoulder. "That's . . . gallant, I guess. But there are plenty of soldiers. Who's Sergeant Snow?"

"His squad leader. Will absolutely worships him. He went to Diyala and his tank got bombed."

"Oh."

"He won a big award for pulling out his driver before it blew up. The Silver Star."

"Oh."

"He's overly demanding and unfair, but I understand why. Or at least I think I do. I try to."

"Of course."

"I don't know what to do," she said. "Every time I try to talk to Will about this, he either ignores me or tells me he's fine and not to worry, but I just want him to talk to me."

"Well," Brett said, bringing his hands together, "you want to know what I think?"

"Of course."

"You sure? You might not like it."

"Brett."

"I think that you need to be selfish about this."

She frowned and stared at a Hawaiian queen on the wall made of red and yellow circles standing by a sea of blue circles. The queen held a spear in one hand and a dark Tiki mask in the other. A strong gust of wind blew by the shop, bending the palm trees by the windows into upside-down horseshoes. Rainwater cut across the air sideways.

"It's *okay* to be selfish about this," he continued. "It doesn't help either of you, being stuck in an unhealthy relationship."

"It's not—"

"He's self-destructive, controlling, and emotionally abusive."

"That's not fair." Her cheeks flushed as she said this. "I don't think he is, I don't think he is those things."

"That's the way it seems to me, Liz. Being a soldier is a wonderful thing, but that doesn't erase all of the other aspects of his personality. And he's about to go back to the place that contributed to making him that way. Did he even consider you or your relationship?"

"He did. We talked about it."

The smile stretched out again. "And did it change his decision?"

"No."

"No. Remember—he signed on that dotted line, not you, and now he wants to drag you into that world, too. And it's not like you're married or anything. How can he possibly expect you to stay with him for an entire year while he's away? You told me that you two broke up the last time he went to Iraq. Do you really want to go through all that again?"

"It was just for a month. And that was because . . . never mind, it doesn't matter. He's going to need me. He will need my support. I know that this time."

"That's his self-centered worldview talking. He's using you as a crutch instead of dealing with his problems. You have your own life to lead—you're young, fun, social, and there's a lot going on beyond these wars. You need to ask yourself—is this what you really want? To be a military wife for the rest of your life, wondering when or if your husband will return? And even if he does, whether he'll ever be normal again? You want to support him. I understand that, and that's very noble of you. You're a good person. But that doesn't mean you have to stay with him right now. You can always just get back together when he comes back. Until then, you can support him the same way the rest of us do."

Liz held her gaze steady, and though her eyes were wide, she didn't speak. Brett looked back without blinking.

"Well?"

"I didn't know you felt so strongly about it," she said. "And I'm not at all sure what 'support him the same way the rest of us do' means. These guys have been completely abandoned by the rest of the country."

"I don't think that's true," Brett said. "And it's not about me feeling strongly, because I don't. It's your life. I just think you should be reasonable about this."

Liz's back bristled and she tilted her head. "Most things in life aren't reasonable. I love him, Brett. I've loved him ever since I broke my ankle ice skating at the Valentine's Day formal, and he stayed with me at the hospital all night, just holding my hand and making jokes about the drugs I was going to get. I love him."

Brett unclasped his hands and smiled. "Of course you do! And that's what is most important."

"Maybe," she said. "I'm going to find him tonight at Sergeant Snow's house. He leaves Tuesday, after all. Things are going to be fine with us this time. I just need to remind him of that."

"If that's what you want to do."

Brett stared behind Liz at the clouds outside, rolling off of the mountainside. The tops of the distant cliffs were now visible from the coffee shop, bearing down from above like a mouth of green razorblades. The wind whistled sharply and the sound of rain echoed through the coffee shop. The barista watched his only customers from behind the front counter and grinned to himself.

"Stupid tropics," Brett said, yawning. "Always storming." A clap of thunder shook the windows. "See? There it goes."

* * *

"Why is that person sitting in the rain?"

"Because," Cheryl said to Sunny, "some people like the rain." The two sat under a covered patio, feeding breadcrumbs to a group of wild chickens. The night was dark and still. Grey clouds hung in the sky like ornaments, masking a dull moonrise. The area around the house was a jungle, all thick, wet leaves and sticky air. Across the two-lane road, black rock crags formed the land's first line of defense against crashing metallic waves.

"I don't like the rain, Grandma," Sunny said, as she tugged at a pair of overalls. "It's ugly and sad. I like pretty things."

Cheryl laughed. "Of course you do, sweetheart. That's why your name is Sunny!" She tickled the girl with bony fingers and continued. "But rain isn't always sad. You remember what comes after rain, don't you?"

"Rainbows!"

The noise caused Will to look over at them from the adjacent yard. He squinted at first, adjusting to the porch light. Sitting alone in a lawn chair with a bottle in his hand, he waved and called out.

"Hello!"

Slender in a white T-shirt and cargo shorts, he didn't seem to notice that his clothes were drenched. A baseball hat with a marlin on the front of it crowned a head of short, brown hair. A small, pink scar the width of a piece of silly string ran down from his left earlobe to the top of his neck. Cheryl told him to come over. Will grounded the bottle and walked through the gate in the fence that separated the two yards, joining them under the covered patio. He moved through the group of chickens without care, the birds parting around him in disturbed squawks, though most quickly returned to their previous positions.

"Evening."

"You are soaked to the bone!" Cheryl said. "That fire water may keep you warm, but it won't keep you from getting sick."

Will smiled. "I don't mind the rain here."

"Are you crazy? Grandma says that crazy people live next door. Is that why you don't feel the rain?"

"Sunny!" Cheryl said, while Will laughed again.

"Your name is Sunny?" he asked.

"Yeah. And this is my grandma, Grandma."

"You may call me Cheryl, if you'd like."

Will studied the old woman's pointed nose and sunken eye sockets. Sunny was also thin but all limbs, like a colt. Her skin glinted with the deep brown of an Islander, contrasting with the milky complexion of both adults. The girl's overalls were bright orange and caked with mud at the knees and hips, matching her hands.

"Pleased to meet you both. My name is Will." He paused. "Kind of a boring name, when you compare it to Sunny."

"Do you want another name?" Sunny asked.

"Sure. What do you have in mind?"

Cheryl whispered something to Sunny, whose eyes widened in agreement.

"You have a new name, now," Sunny said. "You are Jade. 'Cause you have green eyes."

"Jade? I like it, although I'll admit to hoping for something a bit more . . . disreputable."

"You're silly," Sunny said.

"Well that's a good thing, Sunny," he said. "Because you seem to be far too serious of a girl for . . . eleven, twelve?"

"I'm eight!"

"Eight years old, and already you can recognize crazy people? Impressive. I didn't learn how to do that until I was at least ten."

"I don't think you're crazy," Sunny said. "How old are you?"

"I'm twenty-three. Which is pretty old."

A loud crash echoed across the yard from the house next door. This was followed by shouting, which was in turn followed by glass shattering. More shouting followed.

"My friends. My platoon."

"Ah," Cheryl said.

"I've lived here my whole life, and they always break things," Sunny said. "I don't like them, and I told the ugly man that lives there that I don't like them. He has bad breath! Why do your friends always break things?"

Will looked at her and frowned. "I don't know," he said. "I guess because that's why we're here. To break things."

"Do you live up here, too, Jade?"

"I don't. I live in Waikiki. I like it up here, though. It's calming. I wish I'd moved up here when I had the chance."

"Are you going to Iraq too, then?" Cheryl asked. Will nodded. "I'm sorry to hear that."

"Don't be," he said. "I don't mind. I've been there before, so it should be easier this time."

"And what do you do in the military?" Cheryl asked.

"I'm a scout."

"Is that a good thing to be in war?"

Will thought for a few seconds and then said, "I'm proud of it."

Cheryl shook her head and closed her eyes. "You're not even old enough to shave."

"Ehh, I won't be able to grow a beard at fifty. It doesn't matter."

"Want to see something?" Sunny asked Will.

"It depends entirely on what you want me to see," he said.

"Follow me."

"Wilco."

"Huh? What's a wilco?"

"Oh, sorry. It means will comply. Which means, okay, I'll follow you."

Sunny grabbed Will's hand and took him into the rain and to the backyard. She led him to a silky oak tree in the back corner, through a maze of plants and bushes, the dull moon providing just enough light to guide them there. Sunny knelt onto the ground, tucking her legs underneath her knees. She pointed to a spot in the dirt and then rubbed it with her hands, getting a fresh batch of mud on her palms.

"That's where Lady Gills lives now."

"Lady Gills?"

"My goldfish. She used to live in the house, but now she's in Heaven."

"Oh. I'm sorry," Will said.

"Grandma says that Lady Gills is happier now," Sunny said. "But I'm not."

"You should get another goldfish, maybe."

"We did. But it's not the same. Lady Gills Number Two isn't as much fun as Lady Gills was."

Will stared at the spot in the dirt. "They never are."

"I want a pet iguana next! But Grandma says iguanas aren't allowed in Hawaii, so I want a gecko or a chameleon instead."

"You've lost me now. I hate lizards. All of them."

Sunny stood up and pulled at her hair, getting wet mud in both of her thick, black braids.

"Do you like my pigtails?"

"Yes, I like them very much."

"Do you like my overalls?"

"I do. They're very colorful."

"You just told Grandma that you're going to go to war."

"I did."

"War is the place where you kill people," Sunny said. "I know about it."

"Yes. Bad people, though. I'm just going to kill the bad people."

"I've never killed anything. One time, though, I got super mad at Jamie Takemoto because he kicked my sand castle, and I told him I could kill him if I wanted to, and I made him cry. Have you?"

"Have I ever what? Gotten my sand castle kicked? Of course."

"No, Jade. Have you ever gotten so mad you killed something?"

"Do insects count? Like spiders and stuff?"

"No," Sunny said. "It only counts if they bleed. And bugs don't bleed."

'Well . . . maybe," Will said, looking at the oak trunk. "Or no. No, I've probably never killed anything."

Will followed Sunny back to the porch, where Cheryl watched them. The chickens made way for their return. Sunny sat back down, cross-legged on the floor, while Will remained standing.

"Sunny, you've been playing in the mud again," Cheryl said.

"No I haven't, Grandma."

"Don't lie to me, young lady."

Sunny rolled her eyes and rested her chin on her hands, grunting in the process. Her grandma shook her head and turned her attention to Will.

"Are you leaving anyone special behind?" she asked.

"Yes," he said. "Well. Kind of."

The rain had eased to a drizzle. Most of the wild chickens wandered off in search of more food. A few remained, and a red rooster with a full black tail strutted over to Sunny. She picked it up, put it in her lap, and stroked its feathers.

"This is my favorite thing in the whole world," she said. "His name is Bob."

"Bob?" Will asked. "That's quite a name for a chicken. Well, Mister Bob"—he pressed the rooster's claw into his hand and shook it—"it's a pleasure to meet you."

Sunny laughed. "He's not a chicken, Jade. He's a rooster. And he's the prettiest, most funnest rooster on the entire North Shore. Grandma said so."

Cheryl nodded.

"And even though Grandma named him, he's all *mine*." She emphasized this by squeezing the rooster close to her chest. The rooster flapped its wings in protest, and Sunny sat it down on the floor.

"I'm bored," she said, yawning.

Cheryl looked into the house where a clock hung on the wall. "It's nearly nine o'clock! It's past your bedtime, Sunny."

Sunny yawned again.

"I'm fine!" she said. "I want to stay up with you and Jade and talk grown-up talk."

"You go brush your teeth and crawl into bed. And wash your hands. I'll be in soon."

"No!"

Cheryl's face snapped toward her granddaughter so swiftly the wrinkles and bags under her eyes quivered. "If you're not in bed and asleep in five minutes, we're going to spend all day tomorrow doing math. Which means no TV and no playtime outside with Bob. And definitely no iguana or gecko, ever."

Sunny's eyebrows shot up, and her mouth dangled open. She stood up and shook hands with Will.

"Okay. Good night, Grandma. Good night, Jade."

"Night," Will said.

Once Sunny was inside, Cheryl turned to Will, who was looking out at the sea. Wave after wave of wild blue crashed into the crags with increasing recklessness, allowing some of the seawater to spill onto the shore. For the first time all evening, the smell of storm filled the air.

"Where are her parents?" he asked.

"On the Big Island for the week. A much deserved vacation."

Will smiled. "Good for them."

She started to say something but instead waited for him to continue. He didn't, and a strained quiet seized the porch. They listened to the night song of crickets and the rumblings of waves. A burst of summer wind blew through the yard, followed by a distant, lone thunderclap. A few minutes later, Cheryl stood up and cleared her throat.

"Well, Will, I wish you the best of luck, and know we'll keep you in our thoughts and prayers. Would you mind trying to keep it down tonight? We've got a little girl sleeping over here."

"Of course. And thank you. Have a good night, ma'am."

Cheryl walked inside. Will went to his chair, picked up the bottle, and rejoined the platoon.

* * *

Will sat on a couch on the front patio. He watched the sun creep over a slow, steady ocean surf. A bottle rested by his feet, and he held a lukewarm can of beer. His eyes were coral red, and he reeked of cigar smoke. Now shirtless, he rubbed the pair of dull-gold, crossed sabers tattooed onto his right shoulder.

A small smile emerged on his face. "What the fuck happened last night?" he said. "Oh, yes. Well. That's the end of that. Finally." He laughed to himself. "I bet she regrets trying to get me to leave the party." He bit his bottom lip and tapped his forehead.

The smile faded away. "I wish she hadn't cried like that. Would've made things easier."

Time passed and the sun rose.

Turning his eyes toward the sky, Will stared at an empty blue. "In case You care," he says, "I'm at peace."

A group of wild chickens wandered up the driveway.

"Why, hello there. How is the prettiest, most funnest rooster on the entire North Shore feeling this morning?"

Will stood up and grabbed the rooster with the black tail. The other chickens dashed away.

The rooster flapped its wings in protest and attempted to bite and scratch him, but he held it tight to his chest. Walking around to the back of the house, he clutched the rooster by its neck and repeatedly smashed it against the cement pavement until it ceased to move or squawk. He walked around to the front of the house and tossed the rooster into a cooler. He cleaned his hands on the grass, and sat back down on the couch.

"There it is," he said. "There it is."

15

RED STEEL INDIA

Roy Scranton

WE WOKE UP KUNKLE AND GERALDO: "Get up, fuckers. You're relieved."

"Where's Sergeant Barton?" Kunkle asked, blinking.

"He's off. Sergeant Reynolds is SOG."

Reading took off his Kevlar and set it on the Jersey barrier. His buzzcut red hair glowed a sickly brass in the fluorescent light, like a field of bruised pennies.

"Where Sergeant Reynolds at?" Geraldo said.

"He's right behind us," I said.

"Aight. We out," Geraldo took his rifle and stepped off down the road. Kunkle followed and they met SSG Reynolds at the clearing barrel, where he watched them unload and clear their weapons.

When there was a pause in the radio traffic, I picked up the walkie-talkie: "Red Steel Main, this is Red Steel India. Radio Check over."

"RED STEEL INDIA THIS IS RED STEEL MAIN ROGER OUT."

SSG Reynolds came up, glaring at us with his bug eyes. "I want you to have your Kevlar on at all times, Reading."

Reading ignored him.

"Now look, you need to make sure you clean up this AO. There's cigarette butts in the dirt back there. This is a high-visibility area, and the Sergeant Major's gonna come through. So clean it up. And get inside the guard shack, too."

"Hooah," I said.

"Now what do you do when you open the gate?"

"One of us goes up and the other one covers him."

"Right. Now, if you're gonna open the gate, I want both of you up there, one to handle the door and one to watch outside. Somebody could shoot an RPG right through there. That's what I'd do, if I was them. I'd come by in one of those pickups and send somebody to knock on the door, and when you opened the gate, I'd shoot an RPG right through. Bam! Then what?"

"Nobody's gonna shoot an RPG through the gate, Sergeant."

"You gotta think tactically. Tactically. Now, what do you do if somebody comes over the wall?"

"Shoot 'em!" Reading barked.

"Right, and then you call it up higher."

"Nobody's coming over the wall. It's like fifty feet high."

"That's what you think. That kind of complacency is what gets soldiers killed."

"Roger, Sergeant."

"And when ICDC come through, I want you to check each one. Don't let the ICDC do it. They could have bombs hidden anywhere."

"No way," Reading said. "Hajjis fucking stink."

"Roger, Sergeant," I said. "We'll take care of it."

"You know these ICDC," he said. "They've taken an oath and everything, but they still could be Fedayeen or al-Qaeda or who knows what. Just because they're on our side doesn't mean you can trust 'em. One ICDC with a hand grenade could jack up your whole day. What would happen if they got into the chow hall? You don't wanna be responsible for that. Check and double check."

"Shit," Reading said, "I wanna blow up the chow hall."

"Roger, Sergeant Reynolds. We'll search each one ourselves."

"Okay. You guys already get breakfast and everything?"

"Roger."

"Make sure you do your radio checks."

"Just did."

"Okay. I'll be back in a couple hours, and I expect this AO to be straight."

"Roger."

"And Reading, keep your Kevlar on. Carry on, men."

We watched SSG Reynolds walk away.

Reading giggled. "In the case of an all-out assault, I'm gonna shit myself and throw it at 'em. Take that, hajji! Shit-bomb!"

*   *   *

It began with a knock at the gate, prom-prom-prom. The sliding rusted-metal door, thirty feet wide and twenty feet tall, trembled from the pounding.

"F'tal bob," I said.

Reading snickered.

The two ICDC looked at him.

"F'tal bob, motherfucker!" I shouted, pointing at the gate, then pointing at the younger of the two hajjis.

The light was a clear yellow-gray, the sun a white smear still low in the sky.

The younger hajji got up and picked up his AK and started walking out toward the gate.

"See who it is," I said.

"You," Reading said back, not looking up from his Gameboy. "I'm in the middle of a level."

"Fuck your level. Go see who it is."

"Why you such a bitch, Wilson?"

"Cause I hate freedom, motherfucker. Go see who it is."

"Whatever," Reading said, pausing his game and setting it on his chair. "But don't touch my game."

"I'm gonna kill your fucking Metroid, what I'm gonna do."

Reading flipped me off and walked around the barrier, putting his Kevlar on as he went.

"Hey, John Wayne. Forget something?"

Reading looked back at me, then scowled and shook his head. He came back for his rifle, picked it up, and went back toward the gate. The ICDC had unlatched the gate and was throwing his weight against it, sliding it slowly open with a rumble and a creak. Reading held his weapon at the ready.

A hajji in civilian clothes stood outside the gate with a gym bag. Thin and scraggly, with messy black hair and a large mustache, he wore a checkered work shirt, track pants, and sandals.

"ID," Reading said.

He pulled out his Iraqi Civil Defense Corps badge and showed it. Reading checked the badge against the man's face and nodded, directing him inside.

"Come here," I shouted, waving him forward. I stood, picked up my rifle, and slung it at the ready. I nodded to the older ICDC sitting smoking against the shack wall. "Check his bag," I said.

He lurched up and went around the Jersey barrier, and when the hajji came up he took his bag and poked through it.

"Pat him down," I told the older ICDC. I looked at the one in civilian clothes and spread my arms and legs. "Search, search," I said.

The one in civilian clothes mimicked me and the older one patted him down. I caught a whiff of old hajji sweat.

"Turn around," I said to him, swirling my finger.

He stared at me.

"Turn around," I shouted, swirling my finger again.

He turned to face the gate. The older ICDC patted him down, then looked at me.

I swatted at the Iraqi's ass and said, "Check here, yeah." I cupped my groin. "Check his package."

He shook his head and grimaced, but I told him to do it, so he stuck his hand between the other man's legs and batted it around.

"Mota dudeki," I said. The hajji in civilian clothes laughed.

The guard stepped back, scowling, and tapped the man on the shoulder, who turned back around grinning.

"Go on," I said, pointing down the road to the ICDC barracks. Meanwhile, more hajjis had showed up for their shift, and Reading checked their IDs and lined them up. I gestured the next one forward. First one by one, then in twos and threes, then one big gaggle, and at last the last stragglers. All of them carried their uniforms and boots in cheap gym bags, all of them wore castoff, dirty clothes, most had mustaches. Two or three had knives in their bags that I looked at then gave back. One carried a pistol that he handed over to me, which I cleared and put in an old MRE box by my chair.

"Y'all stink," Reading muttered to the last few through the gate.

The sun was up now, the morning chill burnt off.

Soon two new ICDC in ill-fitting fatigues and old boots came to relieve the two at the gate. The old shift handed over their AKs and second-hand flak vests and the new shift took up positions in the cheap white plastic chairs.

One was middle-aged and walked with a limp. He had a mustache. The other one was younger, barely seventeen, no mustache. Both lit cigarettes.

There was another bang at the door and I told Reading and the young ICDC to go answer it. Walid, our Iraqi rent-a-cop from Facility Protection Services, stood at the gate in his blue shirt and slacks. He was a small and skinny man, with a shrunken chest and a thin mustache. The skin of his face stretched tight over his skull, his cheekbones sticking out like little ziggurats.

"Walid!" Reading shouted.

"Sadiki," Walid said back.

All three came in and Walid took out his pistol and cleared it.

"Wally dudeki," I said.

The ICDC grinned.

"You mota mota good," Walid said to me.

"You mota dudeki, good good," I said, miming a blowjob with the barrel of my rifle.

Walid grinned and went inside the shack and dropped off his bag. Then he walked down to the ICDC shack, drew an AK, and came back to the guard point. He sat next to the ICDC and lit a cigarette.

"Well that's done," I said.

"Three more hours," Reading said.

He picked up his Gameboy. I took off my Kevlar and dug through my backpack. I pulled out a *Maxim* and an *FHM* and a *Harper's*, and the ICDC leaned toward me, staring. I gave them the *Maxim* and kept the other two for myself.

* * *

It went like this: the first day you report for guard mount at 0750, then you're on duty in the sun till 1400. Then you clear your weapon and walk back to the barracks and sleep until 0100. You get up in the dark, get ready, and make it to guard mount at 0150, pull duty until 0800. The sun's come up. Then you go eat breakfast, jerk off, and sleep until 1300. Guard mount 1350, on duty till 2000, clear your weapon, walk back to the barracks in the dark, think of some other life you had once, sleep, get up at 0700, back to guard mount at 0750, and the cycle repeats. Light, dark, dark, light, night day whatever.

* * *

Reading played *Metroid* in the doorway. I sprawled on the cot inside the shack, dozing in and out of consciousness. The two ICDC sat outside in the night, smoking and looking at bodyspray ads in *FHM*.

"Shit man," Reading said.

I ignored him.

"Shit, I'm so bored, I'm bored of *Metroid*."

I lay still, pleading with God to make him be silent.

"I know you're awake, man. When you think we'll get off this shit?"

"Let me sleep, fucker."

"All you fucking do is sleep."

"That's because I don't drink all those fucking Red Bulls."

"Shit keeps me alert. I'm a killing machine!"

"You're a fucking talking machine."

"Shit! Shit man. When you think we'll get off this?"

"Never."

"We gotta get off sometime."

"No. Never. The unit's gonna redeploy to Germany and they're gonna leave us here to guard the ICDC gate. We're professionals. We're mission essential. We're the tip of the goddamn spear."

"I wanna go out on patrols like the other guys."

"So tell Lieutenant Perez you wanna go out on patrol."

"He's pissed at me 'cause I shot up that house."

"You shot the shit outta that house."

"There was a dude with an AK up there."

"Yeah, he was up there fucking your mom."

"Shit. Whatever. He was up there."

"That's why you got taken off the SAW?"

"Yeah."

"Dumbass."

"What'd *you* do to piss him off?"

"I don't fucking know, man. I read a book one time. I just fucking do what I'm told."

"Well, you musta done something."

"Maybe he wants me to watch your stupid ass, make sure you don't shoot up the gate."

"Shit, whatever."

The radio popped: "RED STEEL MAIN THIS IS RED STEEL FIFTEEN. BE ADVISED WE GOT A VEHICLE STOPPED ACROSS THE ROAD."

"ROGER THAT, RED STEEL FIFTEEN."

"That's our tower."

"Yeah."

"RED STEEL FIFTEEN THIS IS RED STEEL SEVEN. MONITOR THE VEHICLE. IF IT STAYS LONGER THAN FIVE MINUTES CALL US BACK."

"ROGER, RED STEEL SEVEN. STANDBY."

I sat up and grabbed my Kevlar. Reading paused his game. We looked at each other, then reached for our rifles.

"RED STEEL SEVEN THIS IS RED STEEL FIFTEEN. THE VEHICLE HAS LEFT."

"ROGER RED STEEL FIFTEEN. RED STEEL SEVEN OUT."

I dropped my Kevlar and lay back down. Reading dug through his backpack and pulled out a Red Bull.

"Hajjis coming," he said. "Ali and Ahmed."

"Ali Dudeki?"

"Yeah."

"Fuck."

Ali was tall for an Iraqi, with a stubborn, dopey face and mischievous eyes. He liked to grab our nuts, though ever since Kunkle hog-tied him with zip-strips and left him like that for an afternoon, he was less inclined. Ahmed was shorter, a hunchback,

and had some kind of rank with the ICDC—he was always polic-
ing the guards, berating them, checking their AKs. With us he
played the clown, shouting the handful of obscenities he knew in
English over and over. Ali seemed to be Ahmed's sidekick; it was
clear the hunchback ran things.

"Sadiki! Sabbah h'annur!" Ali shouted.

"Ali Dudeki," Reading croaked, not looking up from his
game.

"Fuck shit, shut up!" Ahmed barked, slapping Ali on the back
of his head. "Yeeeeeah," he crooned, twisting back over his hump.

"Ahmed, sadiki," I said, sitting up. "Chaku maku?"

"Very good, very good, yeeeeah! No problem!"

"Sadiki," Ali said, lifting his eyebrows and pointing at my
bag, "you bring ne ficky ficky?"

"No, Ali. No ficky ficky."

"Tomorrow and tomorrow, Sadiki? Any o'clock? You bring
ne ficky ficky?"

"Maybe if you're good."

Ali tiptoed over to Reading and smiled back at me sneakily.
Reading, absorbed in his game, seemed not to notice the big man
as he reached out slowly for his nuts. Then, in a swift blur,
Reading dropped his Gameboy, grabbed Ali's hand, and lunged
up, pulling his arm around his head and lifting him into the air,
then dropped him down on the concrete. Reading fell on the big
hajji, pinning him with his knees, slapping his face.

"Shit fuck, cunt shit ass, shit!" Ahmed shouted in excitement.

"You mota mota good, huh?" Reading asked Ali, slapping
him, "You mota me, huh? Mota mota? Ali Dudeki? Ali Menuch?"

Ali grinned and tried to cover his face and buck Reading off,
but Reading had him wrapped up. "Now you're getting zip-
zipped," Reading said.

"No, no," Ali said, cringing and shaking his head. "No zip-
zip. Sadiki no zip-zip."

"Then knock it the fuck off!"

"No zip-zip. Ali no zip-zip."

"All right, fucker," Reading said, standing and helping Ali to his feet. "No zip-zip—this time!"

"Sadiki," Ali said to him, very seriously.

"What?" Reading asked.

"Tomorrow and tomorrow, you bring ne ficky ficky? Any o'clock?"

"No, you fucking faggot."

"Tomorrow you, you, meshi meshi, go home, ficky ficky?" Ali pointed at Reading, then at himself, then at the gate.

"What? . . ."

Ali made moon-eyes at Reading. "You, you, meshi meshi? Mota? Mota?"

"I think he wants you to go home with him," I said.

"No fucking mota, dudeki!"

"Yeeeeeah!" Ahmed crooned. "Shit! Fuck! Shut-up!"

Then Ahmed the hunchback went outside and started talking to the ICDC. Ali sat on the edge of my cot but I kicked him in the side and he walked off, staring at Reading, who resumed his game. After a minute, Ahmed called Ali away.

"Fucking fag," Reading said.

*   *   *

Explosions in the night. We tumble out of bed and throw on our armor and wait for more mortars. Silence. Half an hour later someone comes and tells us stand down. The next day there's a scar of blasted earth gouged out behind the guard shack.

Two EOD sergeants and a First Sergeant from DIVARTY come down and do crater analysis, stepping in and out of the hole, divining esoteric data.

*   *   *

The radio squawked: "MEEEOW!"

"What the fuck?"

"MEEEOW."

"It's the fuckers in the towers."

"MEEOW."

"THIS IS RED STEEL SEVEN. WHOEVER'S DOING THAT, YOU BETTER KNOCK IT OFF."

"MEEOW."

"Fucking retards."

"LIMIT YOUR RADIO TRAFFIC TO ESSENTIAL MESSAGES. I'M SERIOUS. RED STEEL SEVEN OUT."

"OR I'LL FUCK YOU IN YOUR EYEBALLS. FUCK-A-DOO!"

"MEEOW."

"THIS IS RED STEEL SEVEN KNOCK THAT SHIT OFF. RIGHT NOW."

* * *

Clouds hung low over the mucky earth, turning everything gray. Shots had been fired at the guard tower in a drive-by, so everyone was on alert. SSG Reynolds had warned us Sergeant Major might be coming through. Reading worked his thumbs on the Gameboy.

"What fucking day is it?"

"Today?"

"No yesterday, motherfucker."

"Yesterday was the day before."

"What day today?"

"Fucking shit day."

"Tuesday?"

"Whatever."

Two ICDC guards sat smoking, flipping through my copy of the *Vanity Fair* issue with the big Michael Jackson exposé. One of the ICDC was younger, chubby, trying to grow a mustache and failing, the other was slightly older, his face pocked with acne scars. I watched them look at the fashion shots, the pictures of Neverland Ranch, the ads for J. Lo perfume and Philip Patek watches.

"You like America?" I asked them.

"Ameriki?" the younger one said.

"Yeah. America good?"

"Yes, Ameriki good," he beamed.

"Michael Jackson good?"

"Yes yes, Michael Jackson. *Ee-hee*. Very good."

"You like Bush? Bush good?"

"Boosh good, yes."

"How 'bout Saddam? You like Saddam?"

"Saddam no good. Saddam Ali Baba," the older one said, stamping his foot and spitting.

"You shi'a?"

"Sun'na."

"Ayatollah Sistani good?"

He shrugged.

"Moqtada al-Sadr good?"

"Al-Sadr very good," the young one said. The older one shrugged.

"Shi'a?" I pointed at the young one.

"Nam. Shi'a," he pointed at himself.

"Bush good, no Saddam?"

"Saddam no good."

"Bush no good," I said. "Bush Ali Baba."

"No!" the older one said, aghast.

"Saddam, Bush, same-same," I said. "Ali Baba, Ali Baba."

"No, Boosh good," the young one said.

I shrugged. "Ali Baba."

The older one pointed at me. "You Christ-ian?"

"La. No god."

He looked cross: "Yes, God."

"La."

He shook his head. "No good."

I shrugged.

There was a bang at the door. I pointed at the young one and pointed at the door, then got up and grabbed my rifle and followed him to it. "F'tal bob," I said, and he unlatched the gate and put his shoulder to and slid it open.

A middle-aged hajji stood outside in a dishdasha. A couple more stood back behind him.

"Salaam a-leykum," I said.

"Leykum-a-salaam," he said back, bowing slightly.

"What's up?"

He started talking Arabic, but then he said, "Bomb, bomb, koom-ballah. Ali baba." He gestured back for one of his friends to come up.

"We have information," the guy said. "Bomb and bad yes."

"Okay, hold on." I turned back to Reading. "Fucker," I shouted. He looked up.

"What?"

"Get on the radio and see if you can get a translator."

"For what?"

"This guy says he has information."

"About what?"

"About your mom. Fucking call somebody."

Reading picked up the walkie-talkie and called SSG Reynolds. They talked back and forth for a minute, then Reading shouted, "Sergeant Reynolds gonna go see if he can get one."

"Call up Red Steel Main and see what they say."

"What I tell 'em?"

"Tell them we have an Iraqi here who says he has information on a bomb."

"He got a bomb?"

"He has *information* on a bomb."

"Information."

"Yeah."

"So what?"

"So call Red Steel Main."

He picked up the other walkie-talkie and called Red Steel Main. He talked to them for a few minutes, then shouted at me, "They said he gotta go to Foxtrot Gate."

"That's the one on the south side, right?"

"Fuck if I know."

Then SSG Reynolds called Reading back, so I waited, and when they were done Reading shouted, "He said he can't find a translator, and I told him Red Steel Main said send him to Foxtrot Gate and he said that's fine."

I shrugged and turned back to the hajjis.

"You go around, go to Foxtrot gate," I gestured around, pointing toward the south edge of the FOB.

"We have in-formation," the one said again.

"Yeah, I know. You have to go around."

"Go round?"

"Yeah, go to Foxtrot gate. The other bob."

"You help us? Ali Baba?"

"No, go around. You gotta go to the other gate."

"We have in-formation. Koom-ballah."

"Yeah, I understand. Look, you gotta go around. Salaam," I said, grabbing the gate and yanking on it. "Sit'l bob," I shouted at the ICDC.

The hajjis started shouting in Arabic, but I closed the gate and latched it and we went back and sat down.

* * *

"What's that?"

"What's what?"

"That noise. Like grunting."

I listened. It sounded like it was coming from the tower.

"What the fuck?"

"They fucking up there?"

"Dude, I hope one's female."

"Turn the hose on 'em."

"Shine the flashlight."

I shined my flashlight up at the guard tower. We couldn't see anything. The grunting continued and I turned off the light. A few minutes later the grunting stopped, and then about twenty minutes after that a soldier came down and used the Porta John. Under the Kevlar and armor and shapeless DCUs, you could almost tell she was female.

"I'm gonna say something," Reading said.

"What you gonna say?"

"I don't know. Lemme think."

"Ask her how it feels to be on the tip of the spear."

"That's fucked up."

"See if she cleaned her weapon."

"Oh yeah."

"Ask if she did a proper PMCS."

The soldier came out of the Porta John.

"How's it going?" Reading said.

She ignored him and headed back to the tower.

"Let us know if you need anything," he called after.

"Fuck off," she shouted, not looking back.

*　　*　　*

We got off shift. Daytime, nighttime. I slept about five hours. When I got up, I worked out, then cleaned my rifle and watched *Malcolm in the Middle*. Reading slept.

We lost track of the other guys, the daily patrols, what the fuck was happening. We started talking all the time in pidgin

English. The big news was that one patrol got attacked by a retarded kid throwing rocks. He threw a rock and hit Jasper in the
face, knocking out one of his teeth. The patrol stopped and
Lieutenant Perez y Luca and Roberts covered the kid.

The kid picked up another rock.

"Put the rock down," Roberts shouted, but the kid lifted it up
like he was going to throw, so Roberts shot him in the chest.

Healds was with them, so he patched the kid up and they
drove him to the hospital in the Green Zone.

A week or so later they got me and Reading up in the middle
of the day, when we were trying to sleep, and made us go down to
formation. They had a little ceremony and awarded Roberts a
Bronze Star for valor. Captain Yarrow talked about what a great
job he'd done defending the patrol.

"The only thing Roberts did wrong was forget his training,"
he said. "We trained and trained, *two* rounds center mass! Maybe
next time you'll get it right!"

We all chuckled. Roberts stared straight ahead.

*　*　*

A couple days later I ran into him outside.

"Chaku maku," I said. "Congratulations."

"For what it's worth," he said.

I shrugged. "You did what you had to."

"Sure."

"Look, I'm sure you did the right thing. Least you got some
action."

He shook his head. "Yeah. Whatever."

"Any word on when we're leaving?" I asked.

"Man, they don't even pretend to tell us dates anymore."

*　*　*

Reading sat watching *Friends*. I read Chomsky's *For Reasons of State*. Headlights flashed at us from down the road and I shouted at Reading to put his DVD player away. I put on my Kevlar and stood and grabbed my rifle. A big black SUV rolled up and a Sergeant got out.

"At ease," he said. "You on guard here?"

"Roger."

"Look there's a suspected VBIED attack tonight. We've got jammers in here, but you've gotta shut your radios off while they work."

"Uh, alright. Let me call up higher and let them know."

I called up Red Steel and SSG Barton and let them know we were gonna be out of radio contact. Red Steel verified that the jammers had priority. Then I shut the radios off and the Sergeant said thanks and climbed back in his truck.

Reading went back to *Friends*. I went back to my book. They stayed there for about two hours, then the Sergeant opened his window and told us we could turn our radios back on. After that they left.

Ali Dudeki came by and asked us to bring him ficky ficky magazine. I offered him the Michael Jackson *Vanity Fair* but he didn't want it.

"You bring ne ficky ficky tomorrow, any o'clock?" he asked.

"Tomorrow and tomorrow?"

"No ficky," I told him. "Tomorrow and tomorrow and tomorrow."

CONTRIBUTORS

David Abrams is the author of *Fobbit* (Grove/Atlantic). His short stories have appeared in *Esquire, Narrative, The Literarian, Connecticut Review, The Greensboro Review, The Missouri Review,* and other literary quarterlies. Abrams retired in 2008 after a twenty-year career in the active-duty Army as a journalist. In 2005, he deployed to Baghdad with the 3rd Infantry Division in support of Operation Iraqi Freedom.

Colby Buzzell served as an Army infantryman in Iraq from 2003 to 2004. Assigned to a Stryker Brigade Combat Team, Buzzell blogged from the front lines of Iraq as a replacement for his habitual journaling back in the states. He is the author of *My War: Killing Time in Iraq* and *Lost in America: A Dead-End Journey.*

Siobhan Fallon is an army spouse whose debut collection of stories, *You Know When the Men Are Gone,* was listed as a Best Book of 2011 by the *San Francisco Chronicle* and Janet Maslin of the *New York Times.* Fallon's stories and essays have appeared in *Salamander, Women's Day, Good Housekeeping, New Letters, Publishers' Weekly,* among others, and she writes a fiction series for *Military Spouse Magazine.* She earned her MFA at the New School in New York City and lives in Falls Church, Virginia, where her husband is still active duty. More can be found at her website www.siobhanfallon.com.

Matt Gallagher is Senior Fellow at the nonprofit Iraq and Afghanistan Veterans of America and the author of the war memoir *Kaboom*, published in 2010 by Da Capo Press. A former Army captain who served fifteen months in Iraq, he is currently an MFA candidate at Columbia University.

Ted Janis graduated from Wake Forest University and was commissioned as an infantry officer in the United States Army. He served in the 101st Airborne Division and 75th Ranger Regiment, deploying twice to both Iraq and Afghanistan. "Raid" is his publishing debut. He currently lives in New York City and studies international affairs at Columbia University.

Mariette Kalinowski served in the United States Marine Corps, deploying to Iraq twice, in 2005 and 2008, and discharging as a sergeant. Her experience as a heavy machine gunner on convoys led her to focus on women's perspectives of combat and war, since women's involvement in the wars is too often dismissed. She is an advocate for women veterans and participated in the documentary *Service: The Film*. She currently studies in the Hunter College Master of Fine Arts program and is working on her first novel.

Phil Klay is a Marine Corps veteran of Operation Iraqi Freedom and a graduate of the MFA program at Hunter College. He has been published by the *New York Times*, the *New York Daily News*, and *Granta*, and is completing a short story collection to be published by Penguin Press.

Gavin Ford Kovite was an infantry platoon leader in Baghdad from 2004 to 2005. After his deployment, he attended NYU School of Law and has since returned to active duty as an Army lawyer. His work has been published in *Flatman Crooked* and in *Nine Lines*, the journal of the NYU Veterans Writing Workshop.

Perry O'Brien is an Army veteran of Afghanistan and a conscientious objector. He is currently a labor organizer and an MFA student at New York University. His work has appeared in *New Letters* and *New Labor Forum*, and he is the co-author of *After Gandhi: 100 Years of Nonviolent Resistance*.

Roy Scranton's poetry, fiction, and essays have appeared in *Boston Review*, *The Massachusetts Review*, *Denver Quarterly*, *LIT*, *New Letters*, the *New York Times*, and elsewhere. He earned an MA from the New School for Social Research and is currently a PhD candidate in English at Princeton University. He was an artilleryman in the US Army from 2002 to 2006, and served in Iraq from 2003 to 2004 (1st AD). "Red Steel India" is from his novel *War Porn*.

Jacob Siegel is an Army veteran who served in Iraq and Afghanistan. He is from Brooklyn. Mr. Siegel's work has been published in *New York Press*, *New Partisan*, and *The Arch*. Currently he is writing a book that he describes as a pulp detective novel set inside an epic detective novel. He would rather not say anything more about it but if agents or wealthy patrons are interested the working title is *Lucifer's Nightgown*.

Roman Skaskiw's work has appeared in the *New York Times*, *The Atlantic*, *Stanford Magazine*, *Front Porch Journal*, on GoNomad.com, the Mises Institute website, and elsewhere. He is a graduate of the Iowa Writers' Workshop. His six years in the US Army included completion of Ranger School and Jumpmaster School, two combat tours with the 82nd Airborne Division, and one with the Kunar Province Provincial Reconstruction Team.

Andrew Slater served in the US Army as an infantry and Special Forces officer from 2000 to 2010. He deployed to Afghanistan (2002–2003) and Iraq (2004) as an infantry platoon leader with the 82nd Airborne Division, followed by two deployments to Iraq (2006–2007) and one to Afghanistan (2009) with 5th Special Forces Group. He received a Master of Fine Arts in writing from Columbia University and currently teaches high-school English in Erbil, Iraq.

Brian Turner (author of *Here, Bullet* and *Phantom Noise*) served as an infantry sergeant in Iraq (2nd Infantry Division) and in Bosnia (3rd Mountain Division). He received a USA Hillcrest Fellowship in Literature, an NEA Literature Fellowship in Poetry, the Amy Lowell Traveling Fellowship, the Poets' Prize, and a Fellowship from the Lannan Foundation. His work has appeared on National Public Radio, the BBC, *NewsHour with Jim Lehrer*, and *Weekend America*, among others.

Brian Van Reet was born in Houston, Texas. In November 2001, he dropped out of the University of Virginia and enlisted in the Army. He served as a tank gunner with the 1st Cavalry Division and was awarded a Bronze Star with "V" Device for combat actions in Baghdad. His fiction has received special mention in the Pushcart Prize anthology, won the Gulf Coast Prize, and has appeared in journals including *The Southern Review*, *Shenandoah*, *Brooklyn Review*, and *Evergreen Review*. He lives in Austin where he holds a James A. Michener Fellowship.

CREDITS